# MUNDY'S LAW

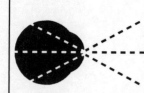

This Large Print Book carries the
Seal of Approval of N.A.V.H.

# MUNDY'S LAW

## THE LEGEND OF JOE MUNDY

## MONTY McCORD

**THORNDIKE PRESS**
*A part of Gale, Cengage Learning*

GALE
CENGAGE Learning·

Detroit • New York • San Francisco • New Haven, Conn • Waterville, Maine • London

## GALE
CENGAGE Learning®

Copyright © 2013 by Monty McCord.
Thorndike Press, a part of Gale, Cengage Learning.

Thorndike Press® Large Print Western.
The text of this Large Print edition is unabridged.
Other aspects of the book may vary from the original edition.
Set in 16 pt. Plantin.

**LIBRARY OF CONGRESS CATALOGING-IN-PUBLICATION DATA**

McCord, Monty.
   Mundy's law : the legend of Joe Mundy / by Monty McCord. — Large print edition.
     pages ; cm. — (Thorndike Press large print western)
    ISBN 978-1-4104-6486-6 (hardcover) — ISBN 1-4104-6486-5 (hardcover)
   1. Law enforcement—Fiction. 2. Large type books. I. Title.
PS3613.C38227M86 2013b
813'.6—dc23                         2013033199

Published in 2013 by arrangement with Monty McCord

Printed in the United States of America
1 2 3 4 5 6 7 17 16 15 14 13

*For Ann . . . always.*

# CHAPTER ONE

Joe Mundy heard the shots, three, spaced evenly apart, on the crowded streets of Baxter Springs, Kansas. He headed for Ninth Street, where the shots had been fired. As he rounded the corner of Cleveland Avenue onto Ninth, a fourth shot shattered an upstairs window at the Hancock Hotel. A woman screamed. People ran into nearby buildings and alleys to escape flying bullets. An older man dressed in a fine suit tripped on the boardwalk in front of the millinery and scrambled on his hands and knees through the door.

The gunshots spoiled an otherwise pleasant Saturday afternoon in the town of eight hundred people. Folks were in town buying supplies and visiting friends. Texas cattle herds came to Baxter Springs after the Civil War and a stockyards association was formed for trading in cattle. Some of the Texas cattlemen found homes in the area rich in pasture and woodland. Some found trouble as well.

Joe found the source of the shooting in the form of three men, each carrying a whiskey bottle. One had the bottle in his left hand, a shiny handgun in the other. As Joe approached the three men, the gun handler wisely holstered the pistol.

Joe took a slow breath as he recognized Hobe Ranswood, the largest rancher in southeast Kansas; his son, Arliss; and Hobe's foreman, Bill Meyerhoffer. Arliss was the shooter. The level of Ranswood's success in the ranching business was directly proportionate to his attitude of superiority. This wasn't the first time he'd caused trouble in town, but Marshal Oster usually took care of it. Joe figured the rancher was basically a good man with a skewed attitude.

"Mister Ranswood, what are ya' celebratin'?" Joe asked.

"Well, if it isn't Deputy Marshal Mundy. Son, show your 'spect. Say hello to Deputy Mundy, the town's knight in shining armor."

"Hellooo . . . Deputy Joe," Arliss said slowly and chuckled, proud of his rhyme. He swayed gently back and forth. His face was flushed, and he was sweating.

Joe looked the kid over. He was wearing a stiff new gun belt and an embossed Mexican loop holster, which housed a nickel-plated Colt single-action revolver with black grips. Arliss was just a titch cross-eyed, so slight that it took a few meetings with him before a person noticed it. The whiskey seemed to worsen the affliction.

Ranswood took a draw on his bottle and said, "Joe, my boy Arliss here is fifteen years old today. He's a man now, and we're celebrating, so don't give me any of that town law bullshit."

"He's big for his age, Mister Ranswood. Congratulations, Arliss," Joe said.

Arliss smirked at Joe and tipped his bottle again. Joe didn't like the look that Arliss was too young and stupid to be offering. His holster hung precariously in front of his manhood.

Town folks began to gather across the street now that the shooting had stopped. Joe could hear their whispers. A gust raised a small cloud of dust that filled the air with the smell of fresh manure. A town employee was assigned to keep the waste picked up, but Joe hadn't seen him today.

"Mister Ranswood, it's three o'clock in the afternoon, a little early to be celebratin' so large, isn't it?"

"Joe, I reckon I can celebrate any goddamn time I want. Ain't that right, Bill?"

Ranswood said and roared with laughter. Bill nodded and laughed as well, but not as much. Joe noticed they, too, were armed. Bill's pistol was clearly visible, but Ranswood's was under his brown sack coat.

"Why don't you trot on along and find something else to do?"

"I sure will, Mister Ranswood, but first I need your guns. Then you can celebrate without a hold," Joe said. "Pick 'em up at the marshal's office when you head out."

"Nobody takes our guns, Joe . . . you oughta know that," Ranswood said and took another drink. The fact that Bill hadn't taken a drink since he had confronted them wasn't lost on Joe. Ranswood's eyes surveyed Joe.

"Hand 'em over . . . now," Joe declared, his smile gone. The manure smell crossed his nose again, maybe a not-so-veiled indication of where the conversation was heading.

The jocularity ceased. Uneasy moments ticked by, and nearby whispering ceased. Any moisture in Joe's mouth evaporated. Joe had often wondered about his first gun fight, how he would fare, but hadn't thought about it today. A day that began with breakfast at the hotel with Alice. Most of this bright, sunny October day had been spent walking the streets of Baxter Springs thinking of her. He wondered what the future would bring. He couldn't picture a little cottage with a white picket fence and an old sheep dog on the porch, but didn't mind the idea of her being regular company.

"Hell!" Ranswood said.

Joe didn't know what that was supposed to mean, and wasn't exactly sure how to respond except to demand their guns again. "It's not a request, Mister Ranswood."

The silly grin on Arliss's face disappeared. He froze icicle still, holding the whiskey bottle in his left hand. The three men stared at Joe. His stomach tightened. He heard a mule bray down at the livery and a frantic whisper by someone in front of the dry goods.

"Shit, let's go," Ranswood said and started to turn away, as did Bill. Arliss didn't move, his unblinking eyes locked onto Joe. Marshal Oster told Joe to watch their hands, "Can't hurt ya' with a look," he'd say. He was right.

Arliss's right hand swung to the shiny pistol. An eternity later, Joe's own gun exploded, knocking Arliss down. He heard a woman scream from across the street. Joe's Colt had a barrel of just under five inches and had cleared leather smoothly. Ranswood and Bill stopped and turned, as in a slow-motion dance. And it seemed Joe

11

could only move in slow motion as well. Bill went for his gun first, and Joe shot him only inches south of his Adam's apple. Old man Ranswood looked startled but had his cavalry Colt pointed at Joe before shots were traded. Ranswood's made an ugly gouge through Joe's left hip turning him slightly sideways — Joe's hitting its mark almost dead center of the rancher's chest. It was over before he was scared. Joe's first rational thought was that he would have missed, or only winged Ranswood, had not the rancher's shot turned him off balance. Ranswood would have killed him sure.

Joe stood there looking down at the three men on the ground. Arliss shivered and wet his new gray trousers. His new white shirt was splattered red. The shiny, half-cocked Colt lay in the dirt beside him. He sighed and stopped moving. His half-open eyes glazed over. Joe felt anger building inside him. *Why would the stupid kid do that? For what good reason would he try to pull on me? Was it the arrogant attitude he was raised with and the whiskey?* It bothered Joe knowing that he had not been fast pulling his own gun. Marshal Oster had often told him, "Don't do no damned good bein' quick if you don't hit nothin'." And that was true, but, *if I'd taken any longer, accuracy wouldn't*

12

*a' mattered much.*

Frank Lyman heard the pounding of hooves and looked up from the bridle he was re-stitching. He had been ruminating about how hard that new kid was on tack and how tired he was covering for him. But no more. The next time Hobe hired a green kid, he'd inform Bill that he wouldn't be responsible for him. He wished that's what he'd tell him anyway. That's about where Lyman's thoughts were gathered up when he heard the horses at a dead run pulling the buckboard.

"That tears it!" Lyman declared to no one special and threw the bridle at the stump that he had been sitting on. He grabbed at one of the horses as the Negro cook pulled back on the reins, bringing the buckboard to a stop. The following dust cloud enveloped them.

"What in hell you doin', Dalmar? Christ's sake, you tryin' to kill these horses?"

"They dead, Mister Lemon, they all dead!" Dalmar screamed.

"Who's dead? Dalmar, slow down!"

"They dead in the street. Boss, all dem, dead as hell, dead as fence post, Mister Lemon!"

Lyman took hold of the Negro by his vest,

13

yanked him off the wagon, and pulled his face close. Lute Kinney stepped from the Rocking R bunkhouse with his ever-present pair of Smith & Wessons.

"Dalmar, listen to me. Speak slowly as you can, and tell me what the hell you're talkin' about," Lyman ordered.

Tears came to Dalmar's eyes. "Boss is dead. Mister Meysofer is dead, and the po' boy is dead. They all dead in the street in town." More hands from the bunkhouse gathered around Lyman and Dalmar.

"Dalmar, you mean Mister Ranswood, Bill, and Arliss?"

"Yes sir, Mister Lemon. All dem, dead. Dead as hell!"

"Are you sure? You been drinkin', Dalmar?" He sniffed the old man's breath.

"No sir. Not a drop, I swears."

"How'd they get dead, Dalmar? What happened?"

Lute Kinney stood near Lyman, listening along with the cowhands. His face showed no emotion one way or the other. It never did. Kinney's dark eyes were piercing and made most folks uncomfortable when meeting them. One eye socket looked larger than the other, and no one knew if he was born that way or it was the result of an injury. The man never looked sad, angry, or surprised, and most certainly never happy. It was as if he was born without the muscles in his face that made those expressions possible. Some said that a contempt for life itself would be how they would describe him.

"They was drinkin' and celebratin' Arliss's birthday. They was drinkin' an' having a good time while I was loadin' supplies on the buckboard. I heard shots and peeked out from Dever's store, and I guess it was Arliss shootin' off his new pistol that Boss bought 'im," Dalmar said, and stopped.

"Go on, Dalmar, then what happened?" one of the hands joined in.

"The shots, I s'pose that what brung Marshal Mundy. I went back into Dever's and was stackin' some cloth Missus Ranswood ordered when I hears more shots. Us in the store, we peeked out again, and that's when we saw Marshal Mundy standin' over Boss, and Mister Meysofer and po' Arliss," Dalmar looked down and wept.

They were all silent, except for Dalmar.

Lute Kinney broke the silence. "Mundy couldn't a' shot all three. You stinkin' cur, who else was there?" Even though his voice was coarse and seemed forced, Kinney's mouth barely moved when he spoke.

"Kinney, hold up there. I've known Dal-

15

mar for most of ten years, and he don't lie," Lyman said. "He drinks some, but he don't never lie."

Dalmar looked up and met Lyman's eyes. "I tol' what I saw, Mister Lemon, just as I said."

"Jee-sus," one of the hands mumbled.

"Where you goin', Kinney?" Lyman asked. Kinney stopped just inside the barn door. "I'm goin' in to kill Mundy." He said it as if he was breaking for lunch.

"When Bill ain't here, I'm in charge. You know that. Stay put for now. Hobe, ah, Mister Ranswood expects you to make another visit to the Greens on the Neosho. Nothin's changed there. You're still on the payroll here, and you can't be goin' into town causin' trouble." Lyman turned back to face the Negro. "First thing is, Dalmar and I have to go up to the house and tell Missus Ranswood."

Kinney gave Lyman a cold stare. "Okay, Mister Boss." He spat a black mass of tobacco on the ground and walked slowly back to the bunkhouse. Some of the hands called him purely ornamental, not to his face, of course, as Kinney didn't actually do any ranch work. Only the most naïve of the crew didn't know his exact purpose for drawing pay.

16

"Chip, you ride into town and find out what you can, then git right back here to me."

"Okay, boss." The young hand grabbed his saddle horn and swung into the saddle without using the stirrup. He spurred the mare and galloped toward town.

"Well, Dalmar, let's go on up to the house now," Lyman said. He would rather have a tooth pulled without whiskey if given a choice, but they must tell Elizabeth Ranswood that her husband and son were dead, before she heard it from someone else.

"Gawdamn, Joe!" Marshal Oster declared when he came through the door. The marshal had sent Joe back to the office to wait for him while he made arrangements to have the undertaker pick up the bodies.

Joe sat quietly in a chair across from the marshal's desk. He watched his boss as he continued to blow off steam. Oster was a tall, large-boned man, fifty years old with a growing potbelly. He barely missed the top of the door frame with his hat on. His bushy walrus mustache had so far escaped the shift to gray that most of his hair had already completed.

Although many people witnessed the shooting, only two gave Oster a statement as to what they saw. "Gawdamn," he repeated, shaking his head slowly back and forth, as if trying to comprehend the magnitude of the incident. He laid three gun belts and pistols on his desk and collapsed into his swivel chair. He dipped a pen into an ink bottle and scratched down the names of those witnesses and what they'd told him. When he finished writing, he dropped the pen and pulled the hat off that he just realized he still wore.

"Gawdamn," he said again in a low tone. "There's gonna be hell to pay in this town now. Hard tellin' what's gonna happen," he said with a sigh.

"Do you want me to tell you what happened, Charlie?" Joe asked, slowly moving his eyes from the shiny Colt on the desk to Oster.

"Well, hell, yes. I'll write it down too, so Cyrus can read it."

Joe explained every detail he could remember as Oster scratched it down on paper. Over the past three years that Joe had worked for Charlie Oster, he'd gained a respect for the lawman that he held for few others. They had finished and were sitting silently when County Attorney Cyrus Carter walked in, followed by Judge Benjamin Drake.

Ignoring Joe, Cyrus erupted. "What the hell happened out there, Charlie? Why did Mundy have to shoot them *all* down for Christ's sake? Isn't he supposed to arrest them, bring them into court?"

"Now hold on just a damned minute, Cyrus. That kid pulled on Joe, set on killin' him. It was self-defense, clear cut!" Oster said.

"Well then what? While he had his gun out, he thought he might as well shoot the others, too?" Carter said. He turned back and glanced at Joe, who ignored him, staring straight ahead.

"Now that's horseshit, and you know it," Oster said, standing up, forcing Carter to move his gaze upward at an uncomfortable angle. "Joe's been the best deputy I've had in a while. He had to shoot the kid or die, then it was like dominoes after that. Joe had no choice, and it's a damned miracle that he wasn't killed. That Bill Meyerhoffer was a pretty fair hand with a pistol . . . for a ranch foreman."

"I was told there was a crowd. Did they all agree with your story?" Carter asked.

"It ain't *my* story, Cyrus, gawdamnit! That's what happened. Two of them folks tol' me that's just the way it happened, just as Joe said."

19

Marshal Oster handed his notes over to Carter and Judge Drake. The two men stood there for several minutes studying the paper, until Cyrus dropped it on Oster's desk. "There's no sense in wasting a lot of time and taxpayer's money, Judge. No jury would convict Deputy Mundy of anything."

"I suppose you're right, but we should go through the motions to show folks we're not sweeping it under the rug," Drake said. "We'll have the inquest at nine o'clock Monday morning. Deputy Mundy, you will then give your statement for the record, and Marshal Oster, you can present witnesses. Shouldn't take long." Carter looked down, shaking his head. "Do you have a problem with that, Mister Prosecutor?"

"Huh? Oh, no, Your Honor. I'm praying the Rocking R doesn't burn the town to the ground when they find out."

"They already know," Joe stated in a matter-of-fact tone. The two men turned and faced him.

"How?" Carter said.

"Their Negro cook lit out of town in a buckboard right after the fight."

The two looked at each other. They glanced at Joe and, for the first time, noticed that blood covered his coat tail and left thigh. They turned and walked out of the marshal's office.

Elizabeth Ranswood was a handsome woman of forty-three years. She sat erect on a velvet-upholstered armless chair and waited for Lyman to speak. Her red hair was piled and pinned on top of her head, her blue taffeta dress immaculate. Dalmar stood near the divan that Lyman was seated on. The frightened Negro looked at the floor and kneaded the hat in his hands. Tears ran down his cheeks, and he appeared ready to run away.

"May I get you something, Mister Lyman?" Mrs. Ranswood asked. The maid stood nearby awaiting orders.

"Uh, no, ma'am. Thank you." He sat nervously, momentarily awestruck by the rich woodwork and fancy furniture that filled the parlor of Hobe Ranswood's home.

"Well, Mister Lyman, what is it that's so important?" She eyed Dalmar, then held her gaze on Lyman.

"Uh, Missus Ranswood, uh, well, Dalmar here, well you see, Dalmar went with Hobe, I mean Mister Ranswood, Bill, and Arliss to town."

"I'm aware of that, Mister Lyman. I asked him to pick up some things for me," she said, glancing at Dalmar again.

21

"Yeah, uh, it's just that . . . Well, what I mean to say is, Dalmar just got back and brought along with him some bad news. Some fearful bad news." Lyman swallowed hard. He could hear a clock ticking that he hadn't noticed before. "They was celebratin' in town there, and uh, Arliss got this new pistol, and he was shooting it off, and the marshal showed up, and . . . well . . . there was a shooting . . ."

"Oh my God! I told him not to buy Arliss that gun, I told him! Is Arliss all right? Well, is he, Frank?" Missus Ranswood's calm demeanor had elevated to a raging storm.

"Well, no, but that's not all."

"Tell me, damn it, is he hurt?"

"The truth is, ma'am, they're all dead." Lyman was shocked at his bluntness, but she'd pushed him so, he had to get it out. "Arliss may have tried shooting Deputy Mundy, and he shot him . . . along with Hobe and Bill."

She sat statue silent. Her eyes stared deeply into Lyman's, looking for some reasonable explanation. "Why would you say something like that . . . to me?" she said, her frosty voice holding back emotion.

"I'm sorry, ma'am, but that's the truth. Dalmar here saw it with his own two eyes. Ain't that right, Dalmar?"

The cook nodded furiously, tears streaming down his face.

"Speak up, Dalmar, tell Missus Ranswood
it's so," Lyman said. Dalmar looked at Lyman, and then toward Mrs. Ranswood's
feet.

"Dat's right, missus, just as Mister Lemon
said, they all dead, all three."

"I'm right sorry, Missus Ranswood, I am.
I sent Chip into town to find out what happened. I told him to git right back as soon
as he could. You just tell me what you want
done about it . . . when you feel like it, that
is." Lyman could see that she had stopped
listening.

# CHAPTER TWO

Joe noticed the stranger behind him as he rode along the Neosho River between Yates Center and Council Grove. He'd stayed well back, too far to identify. Joe had changed his course a little, and the rider followed it. He stopped the bay and extended his spyglass. The rider wore chaps and a light-toned hat, with the brim front turned upward, and rode a buckskin with black points. A meeting would be necessary soon to prevent an ambush if that was the stranger's intent.

As the bay plodded along, Joe's thoughts drifted back to his last days in Baxter Springs. The inquest was an uneasy affair. The two witnesses appeared, but one of them seemed confused. The proper chain of events was eventually brought to light as if some ancient mystery had been solved. Sitting in the witness chair and facing Elizabeth Ranswood was unpleasant. Her eyes were red, but she didn't cry during the proceedings. Next to her was Frank Lyman and, in the back row, sat another familiar face from the Rocking R. Lute Kinney seemed dead behind the cold dark eyes. He sat motionless during the inquest, and when it ended and the spectators filed out, he was still seated. He made a point to meet Joe's stare before he stood, put on his hat, and walked out. He had worn his pistols into the courtroom in spite of Judge Drake's orders.

Later, when Marshal Oster left Mayor White's office, he summoned Joe. The mayor had decided that it was best for the town to thank Joe for his service and wish him well. The mayor felt this action would possibly preclude an attack on the town by the Rocking R cowboys, and most particularly, Lute Kinney. Marshal Oster thought Kinney was wanted somewhere but could find no posters on him.

"Gawdamn, Joe. I hate this. That idiot White, why, he don't know shit from sugar. It ain't just anybody can do this job. And I need the help of somebody who *can* do the job. That's you. When these herds come in, and them damned cowboys start raisin' hell, well, you know the tussles we have. What's that peckerhead 'spect me to do? Well, Joe,

25

he ordered me to cut you loose. Gawdamn, Joe, I'm sorry."

Joe liked Oster and regretted seeing him in such a thorny position. Joe set his badge on Oster's desk and, before leaving the office, pulled Hobe's pistol out of its holster and looked it over. It was the same gun as his, a Colt single-action .45, but with the longer seven-and-a-half-inch barrel and, of course, the "U.S." stamped on the frame. He wondered how Hobe happened onto it, being's it was government property. The gun, in the owner's hand, had almost killed Joe. He slipped it into his pants on the left side, cross-draw style, and nodded at Charlie. The big marshal seemed to find it difficult to shake Joe's hand and meet his eyes.

Joe smiled at that. The marshal of Baxter Springs had a soft spot few people ever witnessed. His respect for Joe was evident and his disgust with Mayor White obvious. He told Joe that a friend up in Nebraska had said that the town of Willow Springs was looking for a new marshal. Since Joe's schedule was open now, he decided to return to his home state and check out the town of Willow Springs. *Joe Mundy, City Marshal.* He liked the way that sounded. About time he had his own town.

Doc Whelan had fixed up the painful

wound in his hip after the gunfight. When Joe stopped by to have it checked before riding out, he was surprised that the doctor was sorry to see him go as well.

Joe spent a night at Yates Center and then at Council Grove. During the last stay, the town doctor had redressed Joe's hip wound, which had started to bleed again. He pulled out before sunrise and spent a long day in the saddle. The bay was spent when he rode into Mahaska as the sun dropped out of sight. The temperature had dropped as well. A ways back he'd stopped and pulled on the black overcoat, using the stop as a chance to take a good look behind him. The rider was still following, but at a closer distance. *Time to meet this fella.*

The town of Mahaska was barely noticeable, with only a few buildings and houses. It was located about a mile south of the Nebraska line. Light from oil lamps flowed out of the only saloon into the street, so Joe tied the bay to a rail in front. The door rattled as he opened it and as he closed it. Besides the bartender, there were two men, probably farmers, sitting at a table next to a heating stove. The familiar odor of stale beer and tobacco was not unpleasant to him.

"Evenin'," Joe said.

The bartender eyed him and did not respond to Joe's greeting. He was a chubby character with naturally narrow eyes. When Joe pulled off the overcoat, the bartender eyed the holstered pistol on his right hip but didn't see the cavalry Colt on his left.

His jowls bounced when he spoke. "What can I get you?"

"Whiskey, and a meal if there's one to be had," Joe said.

The bartender pulled a cork from a brown bottle and poured a shot. "I can round up a plate of beans and ham steak."

"Sounds good."

"That'll be six bits altogether," the bartender said, no smile in sight. An almost undetectable quiver escaped from his lower lip.

"I'd like it at that table in the front corner," Joe said and dropped the coins on the bar.

Joe laid his coat over a chair and sat down with his back to the wall. From there he had a clear view through a front window and could see anyone coming into the saloon. The lamp light didn't quite fill the corner where he sat, which was fine with him. The pain of his hip wound had worsened with the constant movement in the saddle. It was most painful when mounting the bay and when sitting down in a chair, but once he was seated the pain eased up a bit.

The first sip of whiskey burned pleasantly as it ran down his throat. The other two customers ceased staring at Joe as soon as he looked their way. A few minutes later, the bartender reappeared and brought his dinner on a tin plate, then resumed his original position behind the bar and continued to polish glasses, occasionally glancing at Joe. The only sound was the muffled crackling of the stove and a low conversation from the other two men.

Joe was sawing away at his third bite of ham when he noticed a rider atop a buckskin through the window. The rider stopped behind the bay and then continued to the other rail, dismounted, and tied up. Joe switched the fork to his left hand, slowly pulled his Colt, and held it under the table edge. He scraped up a fork full of beans as he pulled the hammer back. The four clicks echoed through the room, and the two farmers glanced over. Several moments went by before one of the front doors opened and the mystery rider walked in.

Jingle-bobs tinkled against the man's spurs, which added a little more sound to the quiet saloon. Joe had suspected that he might be one of the Rocking R cowboys, and he was right. The lamp inside the door lit up Russ Pickard, a hard-working cowhand and a close friend to Bill Meyerhoffer. The wide tan hat with its brim turned up gently in front and the dirty tan chaps were the same ones Joe had been watching behind him since leaving Yates Center.

Joe didn't dislike Pickard and remembered that he rarely got drunk and caused trouble. Pickard was a top-notch working cowhand and roper; Joe believed Pickard could ride a cyclone until it petered out. Pickard was tall and lean, maybe an inch taller than Joe. His dark hair was closely cropped and had an unmistakable red tint in the sun. The mustache was neatly trimmed and was the only facial hair, other than the stubble from a couple days without a shave. There could be little doubt as to why he had been following Joe, however.

Pickard glanced around the saloon and almost missed Joe while his eyes adjusted. "Russ," Joe said. Pickard hesitated and squinted. When he recognized Joe, he pushed back his slicker and overcoat, exposing his pistol.

"Wouldn't be a good idea," Joe said. The cowhand looked Joe over, assessing the situation. Joe rested his left hand on the table next to his plate and watched Pickard's hand.

"Come on over and sit down, I'm buying."

Pickard didn't move. He didn't blink his eyes, and Joe knew he was thinking about his chances of taking him in his sitting position. Thoughts raced through Pickard's mind, and Joe could read them on his face. Pickard forced his lips into a thin straight line. Long seconds ticked away.

"I won't ask you again." A long half minute passed before Russ moved. He slowly raised his hands together in front of him and pulled at each finger of his leather gloves. He casually walked over to the table, spurs reporting each step. Joe motioned to the chair across the table from him. Several more seconds went by before Pickard sat down.

"Bartender," Joe said, giving the man a wave with his left hand.

Nothing more was said as they waited for the drink. Pickard stared while Joe loaded his fork with beans. A bottle and another glass were left by the bartender, who then returned to his refuge behind the bar. The furtive glance under the bar, probably at a shotgun, stopped Joe in midbite. When the bartender saw him looking his way, he was quick to pick up another glass to wipe.

Joe waited for Pickard to down his whiskey before he brought the Colt out from under the table, then uncocked and holstered it.

Pickard's eyes widened. "You wouldn't a' gave me a damned chance."

"This ain't checkers," Joe said. "Why you followin' me, Russ?"

"Why do you think?"

"Conversing would be a whole lot easier if we left out the guessin' games," Joe said, and continued eating.

"You murdered my best friend."

"You seem to be misdirected in your information, Russ. Plenty of time for shootin', might as well enjoy a drink and some dinner first," Joe said. Pickard's face got red. For a moment, Joe thought he might pull his gun after all.

"What were you told about it?"

Pickard seemed to be pushed off balance by Joe's continued talking. That wouldn't have bothered a gun hand.

"Mister Ranswood, Bill, and the kid were in town celebratin' the kid's birthday. You know that," Pickard said in a restrained tone.

"I do."

"Way I heard it, you asked for their guns on account of Arliss shootin' off his new iron, and before they could think about it, you killed 'em."

"Close, but the story you heard is lackin' some important parts," Joe said. He finished his meal and pushed the plate away, then refilled their glasses.

"Everybody in town says you could've took 'em to jail instead of shootin' 'em."

Joe sipped from his glass. "Did you talk to any of the people who saw it? Or to Charlie Oster, or to the two folks who offered themselves up as witnesses?"

"Why the hell should I? Everybody's saying the same thing," Pickard said.

"Well," Joe said, wiping the whiskey from each side of his mustache with his fingers. "Way I see it, a man tracks another man down, intent on killin' him, he ought to have the straight story first, before he dies tryin' it." Joe spoke slowly toward the end of his statement so Russ wouldn't miss the emphasis.

"Fact is, I did ask for their guns, more than once. They all three had plenty to drink. Course it was hittin' Arliss harder than Bill and Hobe."

"Mister Ranswood," Pickard corrected. Joe ignored him.

"Arliss pulled on me, just like you were fixin' to a little bit ago, so I killed him. The other two pulled to defend Arliss, I s'pose, Bill first, then Hobe. No time for talking then, like we do now. Not much else to it."

"Just as simple as that?" Pickard said.

"Like I said, not much else to it."

Pickard picked up his glass again, downed the whiskey, and poured another.

The other two customers had looked increasingly uncomfortable as they listened to the conversation between Joe and Pickard. Now they got up and walked out of the saloon, careful to look at nothing.

"Go on back to the Rocking R, Russ. You're no killer. You're a cowhand and a damned fine one at that."

"Can't," Pickard said.

"Why not?"

"I told Lyman I wasn't waiting for Missus Ranswood to decide what she wanted done about you. Lyman said if I left, I was fired. And not to come back," Pickard said.

"How'd you know what direction I was headed?" Joe asked.

"Chip heard Mayor White tell someone in the saloon that the marshal tipped you to a job in Willow Springs, up in Nebraska. I figured you'd follow the river up to Council Grove, so I caught up with you on the way."

"Why don't you ride on up there with me? Bound to be some ranches could use your experience," Joe said.

Pickard studied Joe for a moment. "I ain't gonna kill you, but I can't ride with you, neither."

"Sorry to hear that, Russ."

"Think I'll head up to Ogallala. Lots goin' on there, I hear," Pickard said. He stood and looked down at Joe. He pulled a coin from a vest pocket and dropped it on the table. "Can't have you payin' for my drinks, neither."

Joe gave a nod, and Pickard left. Joe felt he could trust his word. The man was a cowboy, not a gunman. He watched through the window as Pickard mounted the buckskin and trotted west down the deserted street.

# CHAPTER THREE

The blowing snow stung, forcing his eyes closed. The recollections of that last sunny afternoon in Baxter Springs evaporated from his mind and were replaced by the numbing cold of a winter storm. Joe had caught a few hours sleep in Hastings but got up late in the little hotel in Loup City. Trying to make Willow Springs before nightfall was possible but, as it turned out, not the best decision he ever made. A Nebraska blizzard roared to life quicker than he expected. Joe's horse was a trooper, but his steps slowed in the rising drifts. No longer sure which direction they were traveling, Joe had to find shelter soon. He pulled his hat down tighter. The bandana, tied around his face bandit-style, and another, tied around his head to cover his ears, kept the cold out for the first few hours, but later, not so much. As time went on, he didn't feel the cold anymore and knew that was not a good sign. All he could do was trust the bay to find shelter.

An hour and a half later, the horse stopped. Joe struggled to clear his eyes of ice so he could open them. Peering through one eye, he made out a faint light flickering in what he thought was a window. Muscles were slow to respond as he raised his leg over the high cantle and slid down out of the saddle. He held onto it for several minutes before attempting to walk, making it only three short steps before he tripped and fell against a door. He felt hands on him and knew he was being dragged inside.

"No! My horse, get my horse!"

"Don't worry, we'll get 'im in da shed," a voice assured him. It sounded like a friendly voice, but Joe couldn't do much about it if it wasn't.

Joe wasn't sure how much time had gone by when the door opened and snow blew in. "Holy God, it is nasty storm we got into dis time," the man said. He knelt down on the floor next to Joe

"How you feelin', stranger?" The wondrous heat from the nearby stove was gradually thawing Joe. He could open both eyes and looked around the room. It was a small dirt house, the walls made of blocks of sod cut from the countryside. More sod covered the skinny logs across the top to form the roof. The floor Joe lay on was hard-packed smooth. The little house had a white frame window next to the door. It was comfortably warm inside, and Joe was thankful to be out of the storm.

"I'm Lars Forsonn," the man said and stuck out his large, callused hand. Joe pulled his right glove off and took it.

"I'm Joe Mundy. Call me Joe."

"It a good t'ing you found us, Joe. Don't t'ink you'd lasted much longer out dere in da cold like dat."

"I'm obliged for your help, Mister Forsonn." As Joe's vision cleared, he noticed two children snuggled together in a narrow bed, looking at him.

" 'Ese here are Nada and Jorund. Say hello to Mister Mundy." They did. "You two get back to sleep now and stop dat starin'." Lars scolded them. The faces vanished. A woman with a tired face and golden hair scraped tightly into a bun on the back of her head approached Joe and handed him a bowl. A short smile and a nod was her greeting. Joe pulled his hat and bandana off and nodded to her. She appeared to be much younger than Lars. "Dis is my wife, Hadda."

"Nice to meet you, ma'am, and thank you

for the soup," Joe said. She nodded back again.

"You eat dat soup down. It oughta be darned good by now. Hadda made it last week and adds back to it nearly everyday since!" Lars explained with a big grin.

"Thank you, but I gotta see to my horse first," Joe said.

"Already done dat. Put him in da shed with dis gentleman's horse and our mules. Little crowded with da four of dem, but dey will warm dat way. Brushed off da snow best I could, and threw an old Indian blanket over 'im. He's got food and water dere if he wants it." Lars read the concern on Joe's face.

Joe hadn't noticed the other man. He turned around and looked up at a figure wrapped in a blanket sitting in a fancy old rocking chair. The man was asleep.

"Thank you, Mister Forsonn," Joe said and started eating. The soup was mostly broth with very few extras. Joe wasn't sure what Hadda had been adding to the soup, but it was hardly noticeable. At least it was hot. By the looks of this family, no doubt farmers, they were having a hard time of it. The children's eyes were set in deep holes, and their faces showed every outline of their skulls. Lars and Hadda looked worse.

"By golly, dis is a busy night for travelers. We've no visitors for a while, and 'den, by golly, 'ere you all stop by," Lars said. He sat down on a straight-backed chair, the only other chair, and lit his pipe.

The bright sun woke Joe to the sound of pots rattling. Even though on the floor, he was so comfortable he didn't want to move. His heavy black overcoat was dry, and he was warm again. His head rested on a small blanket that had been rolled up to serve as a pillow. Lars must have left it for him. Before he could inspect things further, the door opened, and Lars came in wearing a heavy red plaid mackinaw and a black cloth cap. The other man followed him in.

"Good morning dere, Joe," Lars said, "dis' man is Byron Siegler. He owns da general store in town."

Joe struggled to stand up. "Morning, Mister Forsonn, Mister Siegler." Siegler shook his hand.

"Heard you come in last night, Mister Mundy, but figured we could meet this morning," Siegler said. "You got caught in that storm too, eh?" Joe guessed the man was in his fifties. Closely trimmed white hair and mustache topped off a round face and stocky build. He wore a nice dark brown suit and muddy shoes.

"It seemed to come up pretty fast," Joe said.

"You fellas, come sit down. Da table is little small, but dere's room for everyone."

Hadda poured three tin cups full of very weak coffee and went back to the stove. She returned to the table carrying three bowls with steaming hot porridge and one piece of bread for each. She made another trip with three more bowls and seated the two children. Joe guessed they were between six and eight years old, the boy older. He winked at them, and they grinned back at him. Joe stood up when Hadda sat down. She smiled quickly at him.

"Hadda don't know much of da English, but we work on it," Lars said. He then said something to her in what Joe thought might be Swedish. She smiled at her husband.

"Would you tell Hadda for me, that this meal is very nice, and thank you, to you both," Joe said. Siegler agreed. Lars relayed the message, and she glanced at the two men and nodded with another quick smile.

"If you don't mind me asking, Mister Mundy, where were you headed when you got caught in the storm?" Siegler asked.

"Came up from Loup City, thought I'd make Willow Springs before nightfall."

41

"You musta' went off course a bit, but good t'ing you did where you did," Lars said with a huge grin.

"I guess so," Joe said and sipped the coffee. "My horse gets the credit, though."

"Family in Willow Springs, Mister Mundy?" Siegler asked.

"Heard they was hiring a new marshal," Joe said. "Thought I'd take a look."

Siegler stopped eating and looked at Joe. "You a lawman, Mister Mundy?"

"Have been." Joe eyed him, wondering why the sudden interest.

"The reason I ask is that our little town is looking for a new city marshal, not far from here," Siegler said. "And, I heard Willow hired a new man a month ago."

This time Joe stopped eating and looked at him. "They did?"

Siegler nodded. "I'll be heading back to Taylorsville today. Care to ride along and see the town?"

"May as well."

"May I ask where you worked, Mister Mundy?"

Joe looked at Siegler and wondered if the news of the shooting in Kansas had floated this far north. He wiped the coffee from his mustache, one way, then the other, before answering.

"Baxter Springs, down in Kansas. I was under Marshal Oster. 'Fore that spent two years as a federal deputy under Marshal Bill Daily up at Omaha."

"Well, that's fine, just fine," Siegler said.

"Glad you approve," Joe said. His reply was matter-of-fact.

"I just meant that I can introduce you. I'm on the town board, and I can tell them that you're experienced."

"Appreciate it if you would."

The bay was lively and seemed anxious to hit the trail again when Joe led him from Forsonn's shed. The shed was actually a sod addition to the house with a slanting roof and a wood door. Meant for the two mules, it was crowded with four animals. It also had three wood and wire cages inside that housed chickens. The house with addition was built into the side of a small hill, with a windmill close by. A short fenced corral, also partly dug into the hill, housed two pigs. It looked different now, being's all he saw the previous night was a faint light in the window. Off the other side of the house Joe guessed the area protected by a low barrier of sod was used for a vegetable garden.

Before Joe and Siegler rode out, Joe waved at the children watching them from the window and gave Lars two silver dollars. "I still owe you, Mister Forsonn, for everything you and your family done for me." Lars tried not to accept it, but Joe insisted.

# CHAPTER FOUR

By noon Joe and Siegler stopped their horses on a rise that overlooked the town, still a half mile away. Joe could make out two rows of buildings facing each other. From the only cross street, a few more buildings were being built. They were all varying shades of weathered gray and raw unpainted lumber, with several other structures scattered about behind them. *Ain't much of a town.* To the north of the livery were two large corrals. He didn't suppose there could be more than two hundred people living there.

"Joe, I know it doesn't look like much right now, being a new town, but it's growing every day. This is a prime area, in these sandy hills. Beautiful ranch country, and in fact, a lot of folks farm this area behind us, and they say the Indian problem is being taken care of."

Joe's thoughts drifted back through the

45

year. Part of the James gang had robbed a bank in Baxter Springs and the town had hired an extra deputy. Almost five months ago, a command of U.S. Cavalry from Fort Lincoln in Dakota was wiped out in Montana by the Sioux. Just over a month later, former Abilene marshal Bill Hickok was murdered in Deadwood Gulch. A while after that, Joe had killed three men on the streets of Baxter Springs. *Hell of a year.*

All Joe could see today through squinted eyes was the bright sun glaring across the snow. Nebraska could blow up the storms from hell eternal and, in less than twelve hours, produce a bright blue sky and sunshine. He didn't see much possibility here. But, if Willow Springs had already hired a marshal, he didn't have any other plans at present. He might as well take a look.

Taylorsville's main street ran more or less east to west and was about two blocks long. Joe could see the Loup River north of town. A narrow two-story hotel, apparently the town's centerpiece, was at the intersection. Diagonally across the intersection was the North Star saloon. The hotel had sometime prior received a coat of whitewash; the saloon hadn't. The next biggest building was marked with a sign mounted on top of the porch awning: SIEGLER GENERAL

MERCHANDISE. Joe counted two other saloons and various businesses. Most of the other buildings were small, some with porch awnings and some without. Those without had narrow signs that were attached to the building on one end, and the other to a pole planted in the street beside the boardwalk.

"I'm puttin' you up in the hotel 'til I can get the board together to visit with you. Hopefully Budd's in town," Siegler said. "Give you a chance to clean up a bit."

Joe pulled his Winchester carbine from the scabbard, stepped down from the bay, and untied the saddle bags. Siegler held the hotel door open, and they went inside.

The lobby walls had dark green wallpaper above a dark wood wainscoting. Beyond the desk, a narrow staircase rose to the second floor. A hallway ran past the desk, straight back to a closed door. No one occupied the dining room to the left. To the right was a sitting room with a couch and table with a fancy oil lamp. With wooden floors throughout, every step of their boots could be heard clearly. They approached the desk, and Siegler greeted the neatly dressed man behind it.

"Harvey, this here is Joe Mundy. I'll be paying for his room. Joe, this is Harvey Martin. He's partnered with his brother Harold

47

in the hotel here. Harold's on the town board."

"Mister Martin," Joe said.

"Welcome to Taylorsville, Mister Mundy." Harvey swiveled the register so Joe could sign it.

Siegler produced a fancy gold watch from a vest pocket. "It's half past one now. How about, say, three o'clock? I'll gather up Budd and Harold, and we'll meet you in the dining room here. Should have the room to ourselves. I'll have my man take the horses to the livery."

After receiving the key to room 4, Joe climbed the narrow staircase. The room wasn't large but had plenty of space for one or two people. He leaned the carbine against the wall next to the bed and dropped the saddlebags on a chair. He shaved, washed up in the basin, and brushed dirt and dried blood from his black suit of clothes. When finished, his dirty gray hat returned to its original black. Wiping off his boots and putting on a clean shirt and tie made him feel almost normal again. He looked at the mirror mounted on top of the dresser and inspected the chapped, bright red face that stared back at him. He was tired and looked forward to trying out the bed. The gun belt and coat completed his dress for now. He resisted the temptation to lie down, because he suspected he wouldn't wake up until the following day. Even though the meeting wasn't for another thirty minutes, he decided to go down. He wanted some coffee and a chair with his back to the wall.

Siegler came into the hotel dining room followed by two other men. Joe could pick out Harold because of the resemblance to his brother Harvey, although Harold was a little shorter and heavier than his brother. The third man was wearing a large gray hat and sheepskin-lined leather coat. Joe assumed he was Budd.

"Joe Mundy, I'd like you to meet the other members of our town board," Siegler announced. Joe stood up and shook hands with each as they were introduced. "This is Harold Martin, who owns this hotel with his brother Harvey who you already met. And this is Budd Jarvis. Budd owns the meat market and livery here in town and a ranch about five miles northwest of here on the river. He also owns the sale yards over by his livery, where he sometimes has livestock auctions." Joe supposed the large corrals he'd seen when they came toward town were the sale yards. Jarvis seemed a bit unfriendly, and his quick handshake seemed to confirm Joe's feeling that he wasn't too excited about this meeting. Jarvis had that unlikeable demeanor that reminded him a lot of Hobe Ranswood. After the four men sat down, a waitress brought more coffee and returned to the kitchen.

"I met Joe down at Forsonn's farm. We both got caught by that damned blizzard," Siegler said. "Joe's a lawman by trade, and we need a new one, as you gentlemen know."

"Where were you lawing at, Mister Mundy?" Martin asked.

"Like I told Mister Siegler here, I just came back from Kansas. Worked under Charlie Oster, the city marshal of Baxter Springs. 'Fore that I was a federal deputy under Bill Daily up at Omaha."

Martin nodded approvingly to Siegler. "It seems Mister Mundy is qualified for the job, Byron." Martin's darting eyes and hurried sips from his cup made it appear as though he was about to miss the train.

"I don't think we have great necessity to replace Welby," Jarvis said. "Sheriff Canfield sends someone down when we have need."

"Good God, Budd, hell would freeze over before Canfield would grace us with his presence, and it takes his deputy half a day to get here in good weather. When we have to send someone to fetch him, it takes all

50

damned day to get him here."

"That's true, Budd," Martin said, nodding quickly.

"Why'd you leave Kansas, Mundy?" Jarvis asked.

"Heard there was a job in Willow Springs, but Mister Siegler tells me it's been filled," Joe said.

"Runnin' from something, Mundy?" Joe's first impression of Jarvis hadn't faltered any.

"I don't run, Mister Jarvis," Joe said, and locked onto the man's eyes.

"I've seen your type before and —"

"What type would that be, Mister Jarvis?" Martin's eyes were working overtime, darting from Joe to Jarvis to Siegler and back again.

The rancher broke eye contact first and looked at Siegler. "He's just a gunman. We don't want a killer protecting our women and children in our town," Jarvis said.

"Have you killed before, Joe?" Siegler asked.

"A badge sometimes puts you in unfortunate situations," Joe said.

"I'd have to believe that," Martin said. Siegler nodded.

"Unfortunate for who?" Jarvis asked. The bitterness in his words overpowered the rich scent of the coffee.

Siegler frowned at Jarvis before turning to Joe. "Joe, this is a quiet town, usually. Sometimes outsiders come in and cause trouble. We want them to know they can't come into our town and do whatever they damn well please," Siegler said. He met Jarvis's eyes.

"You're talking about working cowhands like they was outlaws, Byron!" Jarvis said.

"Well, Budd, sometimes they are, and you know it's true! But it ain't only cowhands." The raised voices caught the attention of the waitress, who peeked out of the kitchen.

"How many have you killed, Mundy?" Jarvis asked.

"Budd, that's enough! I think we all understand there's some danger with law work," Siegler said. "I think we approve two to one in hiring Mister Mundy."

Martin nodded again.

"Just be sure and write down in town records that I voted no."

"Okay, then. Joe, about the wages, the town pays fifty dollars a month. Your office is farther down the street on the north side. It has a small sleeping room, if you want to use it. It was built originally as a jail cell, but just before George left, we had one of those new iron cells shipped in from Cincinnati, Ohio."

Joe was surprised at the low pay. In Kansas he got seventy-five dollars plus a percentage for each arrest, but living quarters weren't provided.

"One hundred dollars now, and fifty dollars every first of the month from this day on," Joe said.

"Bullshit if we will!" Jarvis said. "Now he wants to rob us! December first is less than two weeks away. Then he wants another fifty?"

"Well, uh, I'll agree to that. Budd obviously votes no. How about you, Harold?" Siegler asked.

Harold rubbed his chin nervously and considered the offer. "I guess I vote yes."

"Congratulations, Joe. You're the new city marshal of Taylorsville!" Siegler said.

"Bullshit!" Jarvis shoved his chair back and stomped toward the front door.

Martin offered his hand to Joe. "I better get back to work. Nice meeting you, Mister Mundy, uh, Marshal, and welcome." Joe and Siegler watched as he hurried away.

"Sorry about Budd. He sometimes has a burr up his ass," Siegler said. Joe nodded.

"What happened to the last marshal — Welby, was it?" Joe said.

"Yes, George Welby. He was our first. A good man, we thought. Some of the cowmen gave him some trouble, a couple different times. It seemed like he was handling it, though. Then one night, he packed up and rode out. Said nothing to nobody, including his wife."

"Wife?"

"That's the sad part. They have a house, a nice shack really, at the end of main street and south a bit. Sarah was too stubborn, and proud, I suppose, to accept help from those of us who offered. She did mending at her house, but that didn't bring in enough after George left, so she, uh, started working at the Palace Saloon." He looked down into his empty coffee cup. "Since she done that, the other womenfolk won't speak to her. She don't get any more mending work. So, she, uh, just works the saloon."

"How long has Welby been gone?" Joe asked.

"Oh, well over a year now. We've been dependin' on the sheriff since then, but, well, you heard how that's been working out. In the meantime, the cowboys and some coyotes on their way to the Black Hills come through. They know there's no law here, at least none close enough to matter. They do what they want, to whoever they want, and mosey on out of town at their leisure." Siegler pulled a wallet out of his inside coat pocket and counted out one hundred dollars and handed it to Joe.

"We'll see what we can do about that," Joe said.

"Oh, before I forget," Siegler said. With both hands he reached into his two front vest pockets. "Here's two keys to the front door of your office, and you'll need this." He handed Joe a silver, star-shaped badge. Each of the five points was tastefully engraved, and the smooth center portion read, simply, MARSHAL. "We're fortunate enough to have a very good jeweler here in town. German fellow. Real good with fixin' watches and clocks and can do some nice work like that. Since Welby took his when he left, I had this one made last spring and been hopin' to pin it on someone ever since," Siegler said.

"It surely is handsome," Joe said.

"Got to get back to the store. Welcome, Joe," Siegler said. He stood up and put his hat on.

"I'll come along. A few things I need to pick up."

Siegler hesitated. "Ah, Joe. I kinda' went out on a limb here. You won't disappoint us will you." It was a statement and not a question.

Joe pinned the star to his black vest so his suit coat covered it. After retrieving his belongings from the hotel room, he followed Siegler into his store. It was well stocked with everything from seeds to guns. Oil lanterns hung in a row across a rafter. To the left, an old man stood behind a long counter covered with glass cases and jars of candy. His white apron matched his beard and hair.

"Joe, this is Earl. He'll fix you up. Earl, Joe Mundy, our new marshal."

The old man shook Joe's hand. "What can I get you, Marshal?"

"Well, let's see now. I need twenty pounds of flour, ten pounds of sugar, five pounds of salt pork, sack of them beans, three pounds of salt, sack of that coffee, a pound of baking powder, can of molasses, sack of that tobacco, ten pounds onions, potatoes, and dried apples, a bottle of whiskey, jar of that vinegar . . ."

Earl was furiously writing down the order in between glances at Siegler, who had started toward his little office in the back of the store but stopped as Joe's list grew.

He turned around.

"Don't mean to stick my nose where it don't belong, Joe, but you must not cook much. You couldn't go through all those supplies in a year," Siegler said. He scratched his head as he watched Earl finish writing.

Joe looked at Siegler and then back to Earl. "Did you get that?"

"Uh, yes, sir."

Joe took the glass top off each of the three candy jars on the counter and removed a small handful of each flavor. Earl looked at Siegler again. Joe laid the candy on the counter and replaced the lids. "Give me that set of dishes, that doll, that pocket knife, and that little toy wagon," he said, pointing into two different glass cases.

"Uh, Marshal, that dish set is twelve dollars," Earl said quietly. Joe nodded.

Siegler's mind raced. He was mystified at this point and became worried that they had hired a jester for a marshal. He would never be able to live this down, being's he was the one who brought Mundy to town and recommended him. It was true, he didn't really know him, but felt he was the man they needed, until now. He didn't want to imagine the grief he'd suffer from Jarvis if Mundy turned out to be some sort of a crackpot.

Joe turned to him. "What kind of gun does Lars Forsonn have?"

Siegler was caught off guard, and then he realized what Joe was doing. He felt ashamed for his earlier panic and doubt. A big smile creased each side of his face as he got his thoughts in order. "Uh, oh, a shotgun, a front loader. I sold it to him two summers ago, when we first opened for business."

"A pound of powder, shot, and tin of caps there, Earl." The clerk jerked out of his daze and reached back to the shelf behind him. "Tie up some nice red ribbon on the crates, and I'd like this all delivered to the Forsonns in plenty of time for Christmas. How much do I owe you, Earl, with delivery?"

"Joe Mundy. You're a very engaging man," Siegler said. He smiled at Joe as Earl began adding up the order. "Don't worry about the delivery charge, I'll have my man do it first thing in the morning, least I can do."

"Mighty good of you, Mister Siegler," Joe said.

"Ah, Marshal, that'll be twenty-five dollars and fifty cents," Earl said. The old man stared as Joe pulled out some of the bills Siegler had just given him and counted out what was owed.

# CHAPTER FIVE

Joe looked over the main street of Taylorsville as he walked toward the northwest.
Traffic in the street had turned the new
snow into a soft mire. His destination was
the fourth building in, on the north side of
the street. The small gray building, wedged
between a drugstore and a shoe repair shop,
featured a sign on the awning that read
CITY MARSHAL & JAIL. Joe stepped up
onto the boardwalk and scraped most of
the mud from his boots. He propped the
carbine on his left arm and dropped his
saddlebags at the front door, which was
centered between two narrow windows. The
key snapped the lock, and he pushed the
door open. Once inside, he laid his carbine
and bags on the desk. The only source of
natural light was those front windows and
the door window. Near the corner to the
right was a flat-iron jail cage equipped with
two bunks. The rear office door was barred

by a heavy plank. He placed his Winchester on the gun rack behind the desk. Only a double-barrel shotgun occupied the rack. He took it down, broke it open, and looked into the cavernous ten-gauge holes. The barrels were slightly longer than the short ones carried on stagecoaches. Snapping the gun closed again, he tested the hammers and triggers. It seemed to work fine. On the side of the receiver, it said "Baker, Rochester N.Y."

To his left, just past the desk, was a narrow room made of heavy wooden timbers. This, Siegler had explained, was the original jail cell. The thick door had a narrow slit cut in the middle. Inside, a cot and a table with a wash basin pretty much filled the room. After stowing his gear, Joe sat down behind the desk and looked through the drawers. Other than the cell door keys, handcuffs, leg irons, and some old Wanted posters, there wasn't much of anything very interesting in the top drawer. Inside the lower right-hand drawer was a half-full bottle of whiskey and four shot glasses. After pouring a glass full and downing it, he sat there several minutes watching dust particles float through the fading rays of light coming through the windows. The meeting with the town board had gone well. Siegler and the Martins seemed like decent folks, but he'd have to find out why Jarvis was against hiring a new marshal. A chore that came under the heading of self-preservation. The man reminded him in far too many ways of the late Hobe Ranswood.

He thought back to Baxter Springs and the few friends he'd left there. Charlie hated to lose him, he knew that. But Alice was angry. She'd assumed he would go to work for her father in his dry-goods business, but when told he'd be looking for another law job, she wouldn't speak to him further. He'd held the bay to a slow walk when he left town, hoping she'd come out to say good-bye. She hadn't. Joe didn't bother to tell her of the reason for his devotion to enforcing the law. He figured standing up for those who couldn't do it themselves was important work, and he had good reason to feel that way. Thoughts of Russ Pickard, the foolish cowhand who'd attempted to avenge the death of his friend, caused a malingering sadness. Joe guessed the sadness was due to how close he'd come to killing Pickard. He'd given the cowboy more rope than he should have. If it had been most anyone else, he would have killed them the moment they squared off in the saloon in Mahaska. The occurrences in Joe's life had taught him that the slightest hesitation meant death. All the same, he hoped Pickard would find a good outfit to work for again.

The light had nearly faded when Joe pushed away the past, so he lit a couple of the oil lamps in the office and walked out. Time to start earning his money.

Joe grabbed at door knobs as he walked down the boardwalk. The town was preparing for darkness. Lamplight slipped out of a few windows along main street. Although the sun offered some warmth during the day, when it went down, so did the temperature. He checked on the bay at Jarvis's livery and came back to Main Street. At the corner, he stepped off the walk, crunching through the frozen muck that a few hours ago had been mud. The saloons were still open at ten o'clock, of course, and he could hear chatter and the occasional loud voice from the North Star. The establishment was long and narrow, with the bar at the left and a single line of tables along the right wall. A good-sized heating stove sat in the middle of the tables. Joe was surprised at how many people were inside.

Four men played poker at one of the tables. The loudest voice came from there. Joe walked past and stopped at the bar.

"Got any coffee?"

"Sure thing. You must be, Mundy?" the bartender said. "I'm Gib Hadley, owner of the North Star."

"Nice to meet you, Gib," Joe said.

The barkeeper leaned in close to Joe and lowered his voice. "Could ya' stick around a bit? That big farmer's been drinking a lot and gettin' bolder in complaining about his poor luck." Joe nodded. Hadley walked away and came back with a heavy porcelain mug of steaming coffee.

Joe took a couple steps over so he could see the card game in the mirror behind the bar. He couldn't see any shady dealing. It looked like a game of locals. The loud one was a fair-sized fellow in dirty clothes. As Joe took another sip, the loud one threw his cards at the others.

"You cheatin' sons-a-bitches, you'll have it now!" The big man swayed when he stood and produced a Bowie knife. The card player in a dirty gray slouch hat across from him pulled a nickel-plated British Bulldog revolver.

"Put that pistol down!" Joe said.

The big man, with his back to Joe, whipped around as if to defend himself.

"I'm Marshal Mundy. Drop the knife." Joe pulled his coat open to show the badge.

"Hell I will! Them sons-a —" The big man turned his head back to the table as he spoke, and Joe used that as his opportunity. He pulled Hobe's cavalry Colt from his left side and laid it across the man's head. There was no noticeable reaction to the *thud* that everyone heard, which made Joe wonder if he'd have to shoot him. He turned slowly toward Joe with the knife still in hand. His eyes looked like the fake glass eyes used by doctors. The man took a slow step backward, gradually tipped over, and fell onto the card table, smashing it flat to the floor.

"You three," Joe said, pointing at the remaining card players. "Carry him down to the jail. Keys are on the desk." They decided against arguing and walked reluctantly around to pick up the unconscious farmer. Joe jerked the pistol from the man who still held it. "When I say to drop it, you do just that." The man was angered, but when he looked at Joe, he let it go.

Joe tossed the pistol to Gib. "You can pick it up when you're ready to call it a night."

As the group stumbled out the door, Joe turned back to the bar. Gib sat a glass in front of Joe and poured. "On the house."

When Joe left the North Star, he glanced up and down the street. The only other lights were at the Palace Saloon.

When Joe walked in, he could sense a different atmosphere. The name didn't faithfully describe the establishment. It was a little wider and not as deep as the North Star, and not as clean. Apart from the normal smell of smoke and liquor, there was an ingrained stench of sweat and horses. Joe liked the smell of a horse, but in this combination assaulting the senses, it just plain stunk. And the clientele was different. Although he'd not met anyone here before, these folks could smell a lawman.

Though his badge was covered by his coat, the crowd hushed when Joe walked in. Most appeared to be cowboys, along with some farmers and other laborers. Once the initial inspection was over, the noise commenced, but at a noticeably lower tone.

Joe stepped around a dark brown puddle near a spittoon and walked to the far end of the bar. He stopped and leaned against it. The bartender moved over and looked at him but said nothing. He had a mustache and a little patch of hair on his chin. The rings under each of his half-open eyes had the look of an eternally sad human being.

"Coffee?" Joe asked.

The bartender walked away without a word and brought the coffee back. He wore a dirty brown derby. The apron he was wearing had been white, many years ago. Even though the coffee was better here than at the North Star, Joe hoped they didn't offer him any food. The coffee was good. Joe took his time and savored it.

Surveying the crowd, he saw a narrow stairway that led to three doors on a second-floor balcony. He wondered how many of the men here worked for Budd Jarvis. A sandy-haired woman, plain but acceptable, in a very low-cut dress, mingled through the crowd. Her breasts were prominently on display. She provided an entertaining view until he noticed the face coming down the narrow stairs. It fit the place like a diamond in a cow pie. The woman had dark brown hair, hung partly over her ears, and eyes to match. The drunken cowboy following her down the stairs brought the scene into focus. Joe glanced at the bartender, who was watching him as he wiped down the bar. The two women met near a back table, and Joe could see the plain one say something to the other and nod toward the bar. The brown-haired woman gradually worked her way to the bar and stopped beside him.

"I'm Queenie. Haven't seen you in here before." Her smooth face and deep brown eyes were a genuine treat to look at, and Joe thought he could spend a great deal of time doing just that. Her friendly expression appeared to be slightly forced.

"Good reason for that. Haven't been in here before," Joe said. He couldn't help a quick glance at the woman's cleavage.

"Two bucks, and you can see a lot more than that." Joe felt a flush pour over him that he hadn't felt for awhile. "I'll be. I made a man blush," Queenie said.

"How about I buy you drink?" Joe said.

"That'll be fine, uh . . ."

"Mundy, Joe Mundy."

"Okay, Joe Mundy, I'll have what you're having."

"Barkeep, another coffee," Joe said. The barkeeper looked at him like he'd just set himself on fire.

"Yes, Smiley, *a coffee,* on Mister Mundy here," Queenie said. Joe gave Smiley a nickel for the coffee when he brought it, and ignored the stare he gave both of them.

"Would you care to sit down?"

She was studying him like some extinct artifact. "I would. I would indeed." They walked to a table past the bar that had just been vacated by three card players.

"So, Joe Mundy, what brings you to our big city, or are you just passing through?"

"Not passing through," Joe said.

"So, you live here? I've never seen you before."

"Rode in recently."

"What line of work would you be in? I can see by your clothes you're no cowhand. Businessman?" she asked.

"You might say I have an interest in this town."

"Oh, mysterious, huh? You want me to guess?" Queenie said.

"What I want is . . . to buy you breakfast," Joe said, not expecting those exact words to jump out.

"Sorry, I don't do overnight work." Her answer seemed automatic.

It was obvious to Joe that she'd been asked that before. "Oh, uh, I don't mean that. I mean I'd like you to have breakfast with me at the hotel in the morning."

A laugh burst out like a belch, drawing the attention of a few men nearby. She swallowed the laughter and looked closely at Joe. Her smile slipped away.

"You're serious?"

"I am."

"I . . . I can't," Queenie said.

"Why not?"

She leaned over to him and spoke softly. "Women in my line of work . . . you do know what my line of work is, right? They don't go into the hotel to take a meal."

"What's your real name? You know mine," Joe said.

She had to swallow another burst of laughter. "You're a bold one, Joe Mundy!"

"You're Sarah. Sarah Welby, aren't you?" Her grin went flat. "Hello, Sarah, I'm Joe Mundy. See, now we're properly introduced."

She frowned at him. "Who are you, and what do you want?" Her playful tone turned cold.

"I'm the new city marshal, and what I want is to take you to breakfast."

"What! You think this is funny? You take my husband's job, and you assume his abandoned wife's bed is yours?"

"No. That's not it. That's not it at all," Joe said, remembering that the mysteries of women were alive and well.

"Well, Mister Mundy, or should I call you 'Marshal,' what *is* it . . . exactly? What do you want?" Sarah demanded.

"Where do you live, I'll stop by at, say, eight o'clock? Or, if you'd feel better about it, meet me in front of the drugstore."

"I get all kinds of offers, not breakfast at the hotel, but all kinds of offers. What makes you think I'd accept yours?"

Joe stood up and dropped some cash on

the table. "Because that's *all* I'm asking of you, Sarah." She watched with an open mouth as Joe made his way to the front door.

Joe stood in front of the small mirror near his cot and clipped wild mustache hairs. He felt foolish about his nervousness. He stepped into the office and buckled on his gun belt. While reaching for his coat, which hung from a nearby peg, he heard a noise. He drew the Colt and had it aimed toward the cell. The farmer was starting to wake up and unscrewed himself from the bunk, which was too short. Joe shook his head and mumbled to himself for forgetting his prisoner. He holstered the Colt and grabbed up the cell key. The farmer stood up carefully, holding his head.

"Rough night," Joe said.

"What happened?"

"You were about to get yourself shot down at the North Star. Had to put a lump on your head to get your attention," Joe said.

"Marshal, I don't got no money for a fine," the big man said and looked down.

"Oh, in that case, it'd be ten days."

"I got hogs and chickens to feed, and my wife . . . and Mary and Lacy and Jake," his voice drifted off. His eyes held steady on the floor and he continued to rub the knot on his head.

"You got a wife and children? What the hell ya' doin' gambling away your money?"

The man didn't raise his head. "My wife's gonna be awful sore. I'm sorry, Marshal."

"Don't help nothin' apologizin' to me. Ain't nothin' to me," Joe said. "What's your name?"

"Booth, folks call me Booth."

"Go home, Booth. Don't drink so much. It'll get you killed with your temper," Joe said and unlocked the cell door.

The big man raised his head and looked at Joe. His eyes glassed over and were on the verge of dropping a tear. "Thank you, Marshal. I won't never be forgettin' this."

After Booth left, Joe hurriedly brushed off his clothes and looked at the Regulator. It was 8:10. He stepped out of the marshal's office and looked toward the drugstore next door. A woman was standing there, facing away. He was close when she turned around.

"Do you always keep a lady waiting, Joe Mundy?" she said.

"I try not to," Joe said.

"Well, I'll forgive you this time." She was wearing a dark green wool parlor skirt with a matching black wool paletote and velvet neck ribbon with a cameo brooch. Her dark

71

hair was piled and pinned at the back of her head. Joe thought she was very comely.

"I can't go to the hotel. How about the chop house? The food there is edible."

"No," Joe said. He offered his arm, and she reluctantly took it. They didn't speak on the way to the hotel. Joe opened the front door for her, and she walked inside.

Four of the six tables were occupied, and the conversations ceased when they entered. Joe pulled back a chair and waited for Sarah to sit down. He pulled off his hat, laid it on an extra chair, and sat down. He met the stares of the other diners until they returned to their own meals. The waitress, who had served him during the meeting with the town board members, arrived at their table.

"What will you have, Marshal?" she asked. Joe looked at Sarah, who fidgeted and stared with fright at the table top.

"Give us both the special and coffees." The waitress nodded and glanced at Sarah, who still hadn't blinked. The waitress returned to the kitchen to turn in their order.

"What is it you want, Mister Mundy?" Sarah said.

"First, call me Joe. Second, this *is* what I want. Nothing else, nothing uninscrutable going on here, Sarah. Just a nice breakfast."

"How did you know who I was?"

"I didn't at first. I guess I surmised, as I watched everyone in the saloon," Joe said.

"Someone must have told you about me."

"My job requires I listen to folks. Never know when those things might come in handy," Joe said.

"Did you know my husband?"

"No."

She still eyed him suspiciously as the waitress brought their breakfast. Joe dug right in. Not being able to detect any deviousness to his plan, she began to eat as well.

"You know, I'm still a married woman?" Sarah said, in place of anything else she could think of.

Joe stopped chewing, and the normal remote friendliness, which with effort he could manage, faded away. His cold blue eyes met hers. "If your husband returns and is desirous to complain, send him right to me."

She found his response both chilling and exciting. Something she'd never felt with George. "I don't ask you to stand up for me."

They both noticed that some of the customers had finished their meals and left. Joe and Sarah had been there barely half an hour by the time all the others had vacated the dining room.

Byron Siegler came in with his wife. They were inside the doorway to the dining room before they recognized Sarah. Siegler's wife held his arm until he convinced her to approach the table with him.

"Ah, Joe," Siegler said, taking his hat off. "I'd like you to meet my wife, Fern. Dear, this is Joe Mundy, our new marshal."

"Marshal Mundy," she said. A curt nod was all the acknowledgement Joe would get. She ignored Sarah.

"Good morning, Mister Siegler, ma'am," Joe said, standing. "I guess you know Sarah."

"Ah, Sarah," Siegler said. His voice barely carried across the table. The Sieglers retreated to a table near the front of the room, and Joe could see by the quiet disagreement that Fern didn't want to stay. To Byron's credit, he insisted.

After finishing breakfast, Joe tried to talk Sarah into another cup of coffee, but she refused. He thought better of pushing the matter, and nodded at the Sieglers on their way out.

In front of the hotel on the boardwalk, Sarah spoke. "Thank you for breakfast. I'll see myself home now."

"It's a gentleman's responsibility to walk a lady home," Joe said.

She spun toward him. "I'm not a lady, Marshal. I'm a whore. And if there's any question about that, just ask these upstanding citizens. It's what I do. Now if you want to see me again, bring two bucks!" Tears filled her eyes before she stormed away.

Joe found women difficult to figure, and that feeling hadn't wavered any.

The day after the breakfast with Sarah, Joe took the bay for a ride. When he returned to the office, he found Harold Martin sitting in a chair in front of his desk.

"Afternoon, Mister Martin. Hope you haven't been waiting too long?" Joe said. He pulled off his hat and overcoat and hung them from the wooden pegs on the wall.

"Oh, don't worry about that, Marshal, haven't been here long." Harold sat erect, with his hat resting on his lap. He seemed nervous as usual.

"Say, I heard about what you did for poor ol' Booth. That sure was nice of you, letting him go like you done. Booth doesn't have the brains God gave a cow, but he's got a beautiful family. Yes, sir, he does, uh huh." Joe hadn't heard Harold talk this much during or since the meeting with the board.

"Coffee?" Joe asked.

"Oh, no, no thank you, Marshal. I won't take much of your time."

Joe poured himself a cup from the pot on the heating stove, which had gone cold, and sat down behind the desk. "Good thing you didn't accept. Coffee's cold. What can I do for you, Mister Martin?" Joe said.

"Oh, uh . . . Well, Marshal, it's just that . . . Well, we depend, my brother Harvey and I, that is, we depend on satisfied clientele. If the customer's room isn't to his satisfaction, or he doesn't get the right dinner order, well, that's bad."

"Some folks are a might high on bein' particular, I s'pose," Joe said.

"Ah, yes. I suppose some of them are high on that, yes. Well, Marshal, I just wanted . . . my, this is difficult to say. I wouldn't want to give you the wrong impression of us . . . my brother Harvey and I, that is . . . or the folks here in town . . . for that matter."

Joe knew where Martin's conversation was heading, but let him sweat through every inch of it.

"Well, you see, Marshal, we've had some complaints, you see, ah . . ."

"Someone get some bad food, Mister Martin?" Joe asked. "I ate breakfast there

76

yesterday morning, and it was fine. I didn't have no complaints."

This seemed to confuse Martin, but he recovered. "No, Marshal, nothing like that. It's just that, well, you brought Sarah Welby in . . . in your company, and well, she's a married woman. And she's not married to you . . . you see." Even though the office was next to uncomfortably cool, Martin whipped out a handkerchief and dabbed at the beads of sweat on his forehead.

"You're right about that. If I'd a married her, well, that is something I believe I would have remembered," Joe said with no facial expression.

"Uh, Marshal." Harold was confused again. "Well, you understand, don't you? The way it looks?"

"Mister Martin, you and I, and the whole town, for that matter, know her husband left her high and dry. Well over a year ago, I believe?"

"Close to two years, yes, that's right," Martin added, before catching himself. "But see, Marshal, it still, well, it still isn't right. You know, in . . . in the eyes of the Lord."

"The real reason is that she's a sporting lady now, isn't that right, Mister Martin? And some of them God-fearin' folks didn't like swallowin' their bacon with a sporting lady in their midst, isn't that right?" His tone was firm but not unfriendly. Martin swiped at his forehead again.

"Marshal, well, yes, I suppose that could be it, too. But they said that if she comes in again, they'd stop eating there. They'd go elsewhere." Martin's voice drifted into a whine.

"Mister Martin, there's not a big choice in this town. There's the hotel, the chop house, and a few things at the saloons. But folks wouldn't take their meals at a saloon, would they? So that leaves the chop house. They may stop comin' for awhile, but they'll be back. Ain't no two ways about it," Joe said. He turned his lips into his barely perceptible smile. Martin looked down and slid his shoe back and forth, as if he were trying to scrape a mud clod off the floor.

"Mister Martin, let me ask you something, and I want an honest answer. You're a businessman, correct? Do you really care if Sarah Welby, or anyone else, spends their money at your business?" Joe could see that this made Martin even more uncomfortable.

After several moments of soul-searching, Martin opened his mouth. "Well, no, I guess not. If you put it all out that way. No, I don't. As long as they pay their bill and don't cause a fuss and don't break anything, no, I don't care!" Martin seemed relieved at verbalizing his core beliefs as a businessman.

"And I respect your opinion, Mister Martin," Joe said. "If God looks on me favorably, and I'm privileged to escort Sarah Welby to a meal at your fine establishment again, or anywhere else for that matter, other folks are gonna have to get used to it. And they will after a spell."

"You're right, of course, Marshal. God looks at all of his children in the same light . . . I guess."

# CHAPTER SIX

The next couple of weeks were relatively uneventful. One fistfight between two cowhands had started in the Palace Saloon. Joe made them take it out into the street, but they forgot what they were fighting about in the frigid air and soon lost interest. The participants shook hands and scurried inside next to the stove.

Joe had seen Sarah once in the saloon and once on her way home. He wanted to call on her at home but talked himself out of it.

It was midafternoon on the Saturday before Christmas. Joe was standing at a front office window watching big snowflakes drift down from the low, dark gray clouds. He sipped steaming coffee from a tin cup. Thanks to Adam Carr, the heating stove was crackling and a fresh bucket of firewood sat next to it. Carr was Siegler's handyman, but Siegler didn't have enough work to employ him full-time, so he took any odd jobs he could find. Joe paid him to keep the stove burning, the oil lamps full, and the slop buckets emptied. When Joe had prisoners, Carr would see to it they got fed. A young man of twenty-six years, he was slightly taller than average and muscular. He owned one suit of dark green clothes with a striped shirt.

Carr was most proud of his new short-brimmed, black hat, similar to Joe's, that he was able to buy with the extra income from the marshal. Joe's hat had a slanted crown with a slightly rolled and curled brim, and Carr's hat was almost flat-brimmed. Siegler had sold it to him at cost. Carr had delivered Joe's gifts to the Forsonns, and he also helped clean stalls at Jarvis's livery.

Those parts of the ground that had melted off from the last snow were being covered again. A bitter cold spell had had a death grip on Nebraska for most of the time since the breakfast with Sarah. *Fitting somehow.*

Brave souls were starting to move about. Some carried packages. Few stood around to visit. Two cowhands walked out of the hotel, mounted their horses, and trotted west past the marshal's office. Two youngsters came out of the barbershop across the street and took off running east down the boardwalk. When they got to Siegler's store they stopped and hurried inside. A moment later, a man, maybe the children's father, came out of the barbershop as well and walked down to Siegler's.

Joe watched the freight wagon coming in from the east. It made its weekly trip from Willow Springs on Fridays bringing freight and mail to the budding town. It was then loaded with items being sent back to Willow Springs. The wagon stopped in front of Siegler's store, where the two teamsters jumped down from the seat. The store also served as the post office.

A white-painted sign was tied with ropes to the outside of the wagon. It read JARVIS MEAT MARKET in big red letters. Joe wondered what Budd Jarvis's next business venture would be. He thought he must be doing pretty well with the ranch, livery, livestock sales, meat market, and soon-to-open saloon. Siegler was right, the town was growing. Barrels of beer and whiskey were unloaded onto the boardwalk to wait for hands to roll them down to the North Star and the Palace. A few wooden crates went into Siegler's store. Joe was always amazed at how many supplies were packed onto the wagon. The man from Jarvis's livery would come and get the team, while the freighters checked into the hotel. They would start back for Willow Springs at first light.

Earl came down the street with a small bundle of mail for the marshal's office. Usually reward posters, advertisements for guns, handcuffs, and goods made up the contents of the weekly mail.

"Morning, Marshal," Earl said and closed the door behind him.

"Mornin', Earl. You surely didn't have to bring my mail, but thanks," Joe said.

"Had to stop in the shoe shop anyway!" Earl said on the way out.

Joe refilled his cup and sat down at the desk to sift through the mail. The count this week was four new reward posters, one advertisement, and a large letter envelope. The envelope was addressed "Joe Mundy, City Marshal's Office, Willow Springs, Nebraska." Someone had scratched out "Willow Springs" and written "Taylorsville." Joe opened it with his thumb and pulled out another reward poster, this one with a letter. He read the letter first.

*Baxter Springs, Kansas*
*Nov. 9, 1876*

*Dear Joe,*
*How are you? Hope this finds you, and finds you well. Wanted to git this off to*

*worn you. A few days after you left Thad Green and wife Callie and baby killed shot outside their cabin. You remember them? Lived on the Neosho?*

*Doc Whelan stayed the night was still inside and witnessed. He identified Lute Kinney was won who dun it. I rode out to Rockin R with Sherif Watson to git him but Lyman said he wasn't there. One of the RR cowhands talked to me on the sly and said Missus R sent him to find you. Gets $500 for killing you. He knows you went to Willow Springs so wach out for him.*

*I seen the bodies Joe. Thad was shot in face. Little babys head almost blowed off in her mamas arms. Callie shot in back as she ran back to cabin. Joe, I ain't never seen no worse.*

*Your friend,*
*Charlie Oster*

Joe read the letter a second time, then laid it on the desk. He felt a quick wave of nausea. He picked up the poster that came with the letter and unfolded it. "REWARD" was printed in bold letters across the top. Lute Kinney was wanted for three murders and a reward of $750 had been posted by the Baxter Springs Businessmen's Association. The poster featured a poor sketch that didn't much look like Kinney, describing him as five and three-quarter feet tall, brown hair, dark eyes. No other identifiers were listed. It was signed "William R. Watson, Sheriff, Cherokee County, Kansas."

Joe dropped it on the desk and leaned back in his chair. He closed his eyes and saw the Greens. He had met them several times when the family came to town on Saturdays. They had moved west from Tennessee with intentions of buying a farm in Colorado, but when they found a beautiful spot on the Neosho River, they filed on it and put down roots. Hobe Ranswood felt it was attached to his property and fought them in court. The Greens won.

And now they were dead.

Joe could ride out and search for Kinney, but the chances of missing him were too great. Joe knew where he was headed; the best thing would be to sit tight and wait for Kinney to find him. He would deal with him then.

The door rattled when it opened, and Joe grabbed the handle of his Colt.

A man slammed it shut before noticing. "Don't shoot, Marshal! It took this town a long time to find me. Be a damned sight longer to find a replacement, I reckon."

■ ■ ■ ■

The man wore a buffalo robe overcoat that almost reached the floor, and he carried a basket covered with cloth. A furry cap provided warmth for his head. He peered at Joe over narrow gold-framed glasses, the lenses of which had fogged over upon entering the office. His bushy gray fan-tail beard was an eye catcher. After sitting the basket down beside the door, he offered a hand to Joe, who still eyed him suspiciously.

"Cadwallen Christmas Evans, at your service, sir!" he announced.

Joe stood up and shook his hand, knowing not much more than he did when the stranger first entered. "Joe Mundy. Let me guess, you're selling one of those miracle cure-all patent medicines, and if you can tell folks the marshal bought your goods, well . . ." Joe said, letting his words hang in the air. He reseated himself and looked up.

"Oh, goodness no!" the stranger said. "I am the Lord's representative who delivers the gospel and guides the poor souls of this community from an eternity in hell. I would like to initiate this conversation by asking your forgiveness, Marshal, in that I haven't paid you a visit since your arrival."

"You're Taylorville's preacher?"

"Precisely! I can see that nothing much gets by you, Marshal!" The man pulled off the coat and hat and hung them on a peg. He wore a black shirt and vest with a white-banded collar.

"Help yourself to the coffee and pull up a chair," Joe said, wondering if he'd been slighted by the preacher's comment. "And, uh, sorry for thinkin' you was a hawker."

Evans poured a cup and sat down in front of Joe's desk. "Think nothing of it, Marshal. My enthusiasm is to blame, I'm quite sure," he said, and sipped at the steaming cup.

"That's quite a handle. What do folks call you?" Joe said.

" 'Preacher' or 'Pastor,' mostly. 'Christmas' is fine as well. My family hails from Wales, where my grandfather studied under the great Christmas Evans. Never knew my father, but my future calling was assured at an early age because of my grandfather." Evans shot a huge grin at Joe.

"Who is this Christmas Evans fella?" asked Joe.

"Born on the Lord's glorious birthday, as one might reasonably assume. He was a one-eyed Baptist minister who was considered one of the greatest preachers in the history of Wales. Why, he was equipped with such a vigorous imagination, he was dubbed the Bunyan of Wales."

"And I take it you two are related?" Joe said.

"A common supposition, but unfortunately, no. At least not that my family was ever aware of," Evans said. "I like to think that I, as well as my grandfather, shared the great one's enthusiasm for the infectious spread of the gospel, however."

"So, you're of Baptist persuasion then?"

"We came to America when I was young. I studied in New York, first at a Presbyterian college, but left for an assistant Methodist ministership position. Then in sixty-one I was invited to join the Seventy-Eighth New York Infantry. I did so with great intentions," Evans said, his cheerful voice taking on less enthusiasm. "Did you serve in the great conflagration, Marshal?"

"First Nebraska Volunteers. Fought in Tennessee. Then they changed us over to cavalry and sent us back here to Fort Kearny to fight the Sioux and Cheyenne," Joe said. He pulled open the bottom desk drawer and pulled out the whiskey bottle and two shot glasses. "Do you imbibe, Christmas?"

"I most certainly do, privately, of course!" Evans said.

"Of course," Joe said and poured. "That was a miserable time. Americans killin' each other."

"My duties as chaplain unfortunately consisted mostly of helping at the field hospitals. One can only toss so many human appendages into a wagon before your beliefs become a bit shaky. I hang my shingle solely on the Bible now." Evans looked sullenly at the glass and downed the whiskey without rebuke. Joe poured another.

"So what brought you to this little town?" Joe said.

"Looking for a place requiring my services, much the same as yourself, I presume, Marshal."

Joe nodded.

"Our first church should be finished soon, God willing and the river doesn't rise. You know where it is? Just a shake south of the main street. Like to see you there," Evans said.

"I'll try to make it when I can."

"Been holding services in that saloon that closed up last summer. The one toward the east end of town. The new owner is anxious to reopen, so our new home is none too soon in coming," Evans said. "Have you met Budd Jarvis? He's the owner. Been patient with us while the church is being finished."

"Yes, I've met Mister Jarvis," Joe said.

"My tardiness in coming in to meet you was due to being delayed by the weather. I try to cover a circuit of country folks a few times during the year and try to plan for one before Christmas. My last stop before returning was at the Forsonn farm. Your generosity was inspiring. Those folks, like many, have struggled since seventy-three. But the smiles on their faces, especially Hadda and the children, I wish you could have seen them, Marshal."

Joe could feel a flush in his face. "Those folks saved me from freezin' to death . . . least I could do," he said.

"Well, my hat's off to you, sir." Evans stepped to the basket by the door, picked it up, and placed it on Joe's desk. "Before I take my leave, this is from the Forsonns, a small thank-you until they can properly thank you in person. Appreciate the drink and the conversation, Marshal." Evans pulled the bulky coat over him, replaced the cap, and was gone.

Joe had found the conversation enjoyable and interesting. Now he stared at the basket, wondering what the Forsonns could afford to give him. He pulled off the cloth covering. The cloth was a hand-stitched bandana, always a useful item. Inside he found two loaves of bread, gingersnaps, berry jam, and an apple pie. Next to the pie was something wrapped in old newspaper. He removed the paper and found a dark brown horse not quite two inches tall, as well as a little man wearing black clothing and hat, slightly taller than the horse. Both had been hand-carved from wood. Joe guessed the horse had been stained in tea or coffee for coloring but wasn't sure how the man was colored — with bootblack, maybe. Gifts from Nada and Jorund. The surfaces were smooth and well carved. He carefully slipped them into the upper vest pocket opposite his watch and patted them.

His thoughts returned to Lute Kinney and Charlie's letter. Joe scratched down a quick reply to his former boss, to let him know where he was and that he had gotten his letter. He would send it with the teamsters, for relay to the telegraph office in Willow Springs.

At Siegler's, Joe gave Earl the message for Willow Springs. "Mister Siegler in his office, Earl?"

"Sure is, Marshal, go on back."

Joe knocked on the partially open door. "Come on in, Joe, just finishing some paperwork." The office was small, outfitted with a desk, shelving, and a couple of chairs. Papers were piled all over the desk, making Joe wonder how Siegler could find anything.

"Please sit down," Siegler said. "Excuse the mess."

Joe looked up at a gilt-framed painting of a man. "My father. Had a successful mercantile business in Chicago, which I inherited upon his death. I wanted out of that city, so we came west," Siegler said. "What can I do for you?"

"Nothing really, just wanted you to be aware of somethin', should it ever come to pass." Joe told Siegler about the shooting in Baxter Springs and being followed by and meeting with Russ Pickard.

"I wanted you to see this, came today," Joe said and pulled out the letter and Wanted poster from Charlie Oster. The normal pleasant expression on Siegler's face slid away as he read.

"Good God, he shot down that family, and now he's coming here for you?" Siegler returned the papers to Joe and leaned back in his chair. "You didn't tell me about this before . . . why not?"

"Didn't expect anything more to come of it. Didn't know about him coming 'til now," Joe said. "Would the shootin' down there have changed your mind on hirin' me?"

"Well, no . . . I guess not. I think the board accepted the fact that the job had its problems. No. But I'm not too happy to hear that a hired killer is heading our way and could be here anytime."

"Not too enthused in that regard myself. But if he shows up, I'll handle it."

"Is that a good likeness of him?" Siegler said, pointing to Joe's jacket pocket where the letter and poster were tucked away.

"No, not really."

"So, how will we spot him if he comes in?" Siegler asked.

"That's my job, Mister Siegler. Don't want no folks gettin' mixed in."

# CHAPTER SEVEN

It was just after noon when Joe knocked at the door and listened. He heard floorboards squeaking, so someone was home. He knew he was taking a hell of a chance coming unannounced, but that was what he'd decided to do. He did wonder what to say if a customer was with her.

The door opened, and Joe held up two silver dollars. Sarah Welby stared at him. Her face gave away the pleased look she tried to conceal. She was wearing a long muslin chemise with a wool lap blanket around her shoulders and brown wool socks. Stepping aside so he could enter, she noticed the basket in his other hand. Joe took his hat off as she closed the door.

"Little cold to be going on a picnic, isn't it, Marshal?" Joe handed her the basket.

"This is for you." Joe had kept one of the two loaves of bread at the office and left the rest in the basket that the Forsonns had sent.

"Oh. Well, that's very nice. Are you a baker too?" Sarah said.

"Not hardly. Missus Forsonn made all these."

"As a thank-you, I understand. I heard about what you did for them. That was very kind." Sarah's dark brown hair hung to her shoulders, and she wore no rouge. It was obvious that she didn't need any.

The house was small and tidy. The parlor had a heating stove, a very worn area rug with a settee, table, and two straight-backed chairs. In the front corner of the room was a treadle sewing machine. Through a doorway to the left was a tiny bedroom, and to the right was a small kitchen with cooking stove and table. Lace curtains adorned the windows, and every impression was that this was a warm home and not just living quarters.

Sarah dropped the blanket onto one of the chairs and began to pull at the ties of her chemise. That wasn't why Joe had visited, but he found his voice gone while watching her. When the final tie pulled free, he forced a sound.

"Uh, Sarah, uh, I didn't come here for that. I wanted to see you and, uh . . ." He had trouble removing his gaze from the slender form of her body and the vertical line of bare skin visible where the chemise gapped. Her breasts pushed against the thin material. "Invite you to accompany me to church tomorrow evening. Pastor Evans wanted to have the first service at the new church to be on Christmas Eve. It's finished enough for a service. I'll be by just before seven o'clock." With that he positioned the black hat atop his head and turned toward the door.

Sarah gathered the chemise and held it closed in front of her. "You just won't quit, will you?" she said, and handed him his two silver dollars.

Joe turned to face her, ignoring the money. "Not likely."

"Do you know that I was informed by the ladies of this community that I was not welcome at their church anymore?"

"I do," Joe said. He walked out and closed the door behind him.

The new church was a rectangular, unpainted, wood-frame building, with a pitched roof. A two-foot-tall wooden cross was mounted above the front door at the roof peak. Three windows on either side allowed light in during the day. The oil lamps, mounted on the walls inside and at the altar, were lit when Sarah and Joe stepped in from the darkness. It was very plain but a triumph for a small town. It would serve as a schoolhouse and community gathering place as well. To the right of the altar was a door that Joe assumed led into the preacher's quarters. To the left was a large heating stove, compliments of Siegler's general store, which radiated warmth for those in the first several rows. Flat benches without backs served as pews. Only about half of those needed had been completed. Those were offered to the elderly and women.

Sarah and Joe stood at the back with the others and drew several quick glances. Harold and Harvey Martin greeted them both, as did Byron Siegler. His wife was pretty much speechless, even though Joe was extra friendly to her.

"I don't know why I let you talk me into this. I really don't," Sarah whispered to Joe.

Joe looked over the mass of faces that filled the new church, to see how many he recognized. Budd Jarvis and his wife were the last to arrive. They walked in and stood beside Joe, without looking to see who they were next to.

"Mister Jarvis," Joe said and nodded. "Ma'am." Jarvis turned his head as his wife did the same.

"Mundy," he said, and recognized Sarah. Instead of acknowledging her, the Jarvises stepped over to the other side of the aisle.

Sarah said, "This is humiliating. Is that your intent, to humiliate me?"

At seven o'clock on the dot, Pastor Evans stepped behind the cross-adorned lectern, and everyone hushed. He stood there for a moment, quietly surveying the crowd.

"Welcome. Welcome everyone into the house of God! How fortunate can we be, for this gift? And all of us here together, friends, neighbors, acquaintances, together to worship the Lord," he said, and raised his hands. "Praise the Lord!" The people joined in, repeating his chant, and the sermon got under way.

Joe watched a man three rows ahead of him lean toward a couple of cowboys, who still had their hats on. They shot a surprised look at the man and quickly pulled them off.

"*. . . Blessed is he who considers the poor, the Lord deliver him in time of trouble!*"

Sarah gently took hold of Joe's right hand. He turned his head and looked down at her. She didn't notice. Her concentration was firmly locked onto the sermon that Cadwallen Christmas Evans was so eloquently delivering. Joe wondered if she knew that she was holding his hand. Packed in the crowd, he didn't think anyone noticed. He liked it.

*". . . all have sinned, and come short of the glory of God."* Evans had the crowd spellbound. *"But the ruin is not hopeless. What was lost in Adam is restored in Christ!"* Several of the cowhands were so taken by the sermon that they blurted out, "Amen!" A few chuckled, and the cowhands looked a little embarrassed. Sarah smiled slightly, and then realized she was holding Joe's hand. She quickly jerked it away and shot him an angry glance.

After a while, Evans wrapped up the sermon: *"Let us be strong in the Lord, and in the power of his might, that we be able to stand in the evil day."* He walked up the middle aisle, leading the congregation in song. *"Amazing grace, how great thou art — !"*

Evans stood inside the front door and shook hands with each worshipper as they left the church.

"Glad to see you, Marshal, Missus Welby. Hope you'll come back," he said.

"Lively sermon, Christmas, thank you," Joe said.

Sarah no longer held his hand but walked close to his side. Snowflakes were falling, and occasional wind gusts blew them into their faces. Joe pulled his hat down tighter. The wind made an otherwise tolerable temperature bitter.

"If you want some coffee and pie, I just happen to have some. Can't eat it all myself." Sarah didn't look at Joe as they walked toward her house.

"That sounds fine."

As they rounded the corner of Sarah's house, they heard a voice calling out.

"Marshal! Marshal Mundy!" Adam Carr ran up, almost out of breath. Joe noticed a small bloody scrape mark on his left cheek.

"Ma'am," he said, touching his hat brim. "Marshal, thought you'd want to know that two fellers' come a-drivin' a freight wagon to the livery. They assed where they could buy a whore, beggin' your pardon, ma'am, and I told 'em where the Palace was. Then they said some awful things about what they was gonna do to one when they got one. These two are som' bitches, Marshal. And they stunk."

"They aren't the freighters from Willow Springs?" Joe asked.

"Oh, no sir, these ain't them. Them fellers' is okay, these ain't. They assed if we got a lawdog here. I guess that meant you. I tol' 'em, 'Yeah, we got a marshal, and he don't

put up with no shenanigans neither,' "
Adam said. "That's when one of 'em
grabbed me up against a stall and hurt my
back. He backhanded me a couple times
. . . he said for talkin' back to 'em. They
said I better take care of their team, or *I'd
be pullin' their wagon!*"

"All right, Adam, thanks. You git back to
the livery now. I'll take care of it," Joe said.

"Lucy's working by herself tonight. I'm
coming with you!" Sarah said.

"You stay here. This is *my* business." Joe
took off for the office to get his guns.

While strapping on the gun belt, Joe glanced
at the shotgun. He pulled two brass shells
from a box in a desk drawer and grabbed it
off the rack. With two shells dropped into
place, he snapped the barrels closed.

Joe trotted quickly down the boardwalk to
the corner and turned north. He slowed to
a normal pace as he entered the Palace
Saloon doors. The bartender and owner,
John "Smiley" Wilkie, stood sullenly behind
the bar as usual. There were about twenty
customers drinking at the tables and a half
dozen at the bar. *Surprising,* Joe thought, *on
Christmas Eve.* He heard the screams as
soon as he entered. Smiley acted as though
he didn't hear them, allowing Joe to believe

101

they weren't the first.

The screams came from upstairs. With the shotgun in his right hand, Joe jumped the steps two at a time. The screams guided him to the middle room. The door was locked, so he stepped back and kicked it open. A man in a dirty white union suit was riding Lucy and backhanding her across the face with hard blows. Her face, pillow, and mattress were covered with blood. She appeared next to unconscious. His partner was on the other side of the bed with a Bowie knife in his hand. Joe smashed the butt of the shotgun into the first one's face as hard as he could, knocking him off Lucy and onto the floor. The other man had to dodge him as he fell. The partner then raised his left hand, with the knife, and let it fall to the bed.

"Don't shoot, don't shoot!" he yelled. As the knife fell toward Lucy, he drew a Navy Colt from a holster on the table and hastily fired a round that hit the door sill. Joe's attention had been momentarily diverted, watching the knife. The ten-gauge roared, tearing half the man's head off. His body arched backward into the wall, bounced off the bed, and fell on top of his friend. The small room was full of smoke, which, combined with the human stench of body fluid and tissue, made for a putrid aroma. Joe's ears were ringing from the shotgun blast.

Once sure there was no further resistance, he turned to lean the shotgun against the wall and saw Sarah standing in the doorway with her hands over her open mouth as if in a silent scream. Adam stood behind her with his eyes fixed on the blood and tissue running down the wall. "Somebody get the doc!"

"Doc Sullivan's comin', Marshal," Adam said, his eyes still on the bloody wall.

Joe sat down on the bed and pulled the sheet up to cover Lucy. He gently wiped some blood out of her eyes. "Sarah. Sarah! Need some help here!" Joe shouted, snapping her out of a trance. She looked at Joe and pulled out a handkerchief and sat on the bed in front of him. Next to Lucy, she wiped softly where Joe had left off. "Lucy, Lucy, honey, can you hear me?"

Joe assumed that the red-haired man carrying a leather bag was the doctor. The man, stopped momentarily by the huge stain on the wall, pushed both Joe and Sarah out of the way and sat down on the bed. "Get me some hot water!" Joe nodded at Adam who responded immediately. "I saw you and Sarah at church earlier but didn't get a chance to introduce myself. I'm Thomas

Sullivan." The doctor poured alcohol on a cloth and wiped at Lucy's face so he could see the extent of her injuries.

"Sorry it has to be under these circumstances, Doc," Joe said.

"It appears that you weren't a second too soon in arriving here, Marshal," he said. "Poor Lucy. I was here for the routine exam that I insist on, only this morning, and she was in fine spirits."

"She'll be all right, won't she, Doc?" Sarah said.

"Early to tell. I hope so. I hope so."

The man on the floor started to groan, and Joe thought about shooting him in the head. The man squirmed around enough to recognize that his friend, or what was left of his friend, was lying on top of him, dripping blood all over his union suit. "Ahhhh!!"

"Shut the hell up!" Joe stepped over and grabbed him by his long dirty black hair and dragged him around toward the door. When he noticed Sarah, Doc, and Adam watching him, he released his grip. "Get your clothes on."

The man blubbered, spitting blood that ran from his badly smashed nose and mouth. Joe gathered up a gun belt that held a knife and a Colt Police model revolver, and hung it over his shoulder. He threw the dirty clothes at the man, who groaned. Blood was dripping out of his mouth onto the floor. "You get dressed, or by God, I'll drag your ass to jail in your underwear!"

The man managed to look up at the source of the voice and saw the badge. Mumbling something that probably would have got him hit again, if Mundy had understood it, the man pulled the clothes closer and started to dress.

"I should have a look at him when I'm through here," Doc Sullivan said.

Joe looked him in the eyes. "I'll let you know if he needs your attention, Doc. You save her," Joe said, nodding at Lucy. His voice was calm and steady. The doctor met his eyes for a moment and then returned his attention to Lucy. Joe picked up the Navy Colt and Bowie and slid them into his belt.

Sarah looked at Joe. "You probably saved her life."

"Little early to predict," Sullivan said. "I hope you're right. I'll need help moving her to my place. Keep a close watch on her for the next twenty-four hours. If she makes it that long, she should be all right."

Joe sat at his desk and stared at the man in the cell. He lay on the bottom bunk holding a wet rag to his face, moaning. At times, he'd lean over and spit a wad of blood into the slop bucket. It looked like he no longer had any front teeth, but Joe didn't much care.

Piled on his desk were two brass powder flasks, gun belts with pouches for ball ammunition and percussion caps, the two Colt revolvers, and the two knives. Joe stepped out back in the alley with one of the seized revolvers in each hand and fired them into the ground until empty. Since they were loaded by forcing a .36-caliber round lead ball into each chamber of the cylinder, on top of a charge of black powder, instead of using cartridges like his gun, this was the only way they could be unloaded. Before he turned to go back inside, the door of the outhouse a dozen yards away swung open, and someone took off running west as fast as they could go. Joe managed a partial smile.

Back at his desk, he looked the guns over. Their finishes were worn, but they had been oiled and kept clean. They had been taken care of, so they would work when needed. Joe wondered how much these two had used them.

Adam burst through the front door, stopped, and looked wild-eyed at Joe. "Are you okay, Marshal? I heard the shots!"

"Come in and close the door, Adam. Everything's fine. Just emptied these pistols out back," Joe said.

"Scared hell out of us, Marshal. Thought he might have jumped you. Missus Welby and us was just getting Lucy into Doc's place. I said I'd run up and see if you needed help."

Joe was a little surprised at the concern. He hadn't given it a thought. "Get some coffee and take a chair. Been a tough night."

Joe could still see the panic in Adam's eyes as he sat and drank from a cup. The prisoner moaned again, and Adam glanced at him.

"You know how to tear these apart?" Joe asked, pointing at the revolvers on his desk.

"Sure do," Adam said.

"They'll be in this drawer. When you have time, give 'em a good cleanin', would you?"

"Sure will, Marshal." Adam calmed down as he thought about the chore. "The undertaker got some boys to help haul out this un's buddy. Smiley made sure they picked up all the pieces that went with him. He weren't too happy about the mess. Had 'em pickin' bone pieces out of the wall. Said you'd have to pay to have it cleaned up. Assed if I wanted the job, but I respectively declined. He weren't too happy about that neither."

"Well, Adam, my guess is Smiley ain't all that happy a person," Joe said.

"That's sure enough," Adam's grin showed Joe he was relaxing a bit. They stopped talking while the Regulator struck ten bells.

Joe noticed Byron Siegler brushing snow off his coat before coming into the office. "Evening, Joe. Adam."

"Adam, why don't you go down and assure Missus Welby and Doc Sullivan that everything's peaceful as a church," Joe said. "See Missus Welby home when she's ready."

"Oh yeah. Plum forgot they'd still be wonderin'. I sure will, Marshal. Thanks for the coffee." Adam finished the cup, buttoned up his coat, and went out. The snow was coming down harder, and the wind had picked up. Joe walked over to the stove and shoved another short log inside.

"You okay, Joe?" Siegler asked.

"Course. Why do you ask?" Joe said.

"I heard what happened. Just come from the Palace. God! That dead feller got a shot off at you!"

"He missed. I didn't," Joe said, and returned to the desk.

"I'm glad it worked out that way. Damn ol' Smiley said he'd submit a bill to you for cleanup of the room," Siegler said. "Told him to forget it."

"Good advice," Joe said and waved toward the coffeepot. Siegler shook his head and sat down on the chair Adam had left. The prisoner coughed up and spit into the bucket again. He moaned and rolled over on his back, still holding the bloody cloth. Byron's face got pasty white when he looked at him.

"Adam told me about these two right after church. He's a good man. When I got to the Palace, I heard the screaming from upstairs. Smiley stood behind the bar like he didn't hear nothin'," Joe said. Siegler shook his head slowly.

"I meant to tell you that we'll have a justice of the peace here in town come next week," Siegler said. "The board agreed to appoint him."

"Just in time," Joe said.

"Elsworth Worden. He's a retired lawyer and judge from Broken Bow. I convinced him to move here and hang out a shingle. I think he liked the idea of being the only lawyer in town."

" 'Spect he would," Joe said. "I'll meet with him when he comes in. He can hear the charges against my prisoner."

"He's buying the office across southeast

of the hotel. Has living quarters upstairs like Fern and I have."

"Joe, some of Budd's hands were in the saloon when this happened. You'll probably hear from him about this."

" 'Spect I will."

# CHAPTER EIGHT

Joe opened his eyes and waited for them to focus. His face felt cold, but he was warm under the blanket. The fire was about out in the stove. Exhaling, he could see his breath. After quickly dressing, he stepped out into the office and glanced at the prisoner. The man was curled up in a ball on the lower bunk, shivering. A thin arc of snow had formed on the floor by the office door.

With the stove roaring to life and coffee boiling, Joe poured himself a cup.

"I meed shome offee," the prisoner said. He had trouble talking due to the missing teeth and swelling. The stringy black hair that surrounded his face was caked with dried blood.

"What's your name?" Joe said.

"Gimme shome offee, ya' bashtard! I get out I'm gonna kill you!" Joe ignored him and walked to a front window and looked out.

"Carlshon, Bob Carlshon. Now gimme shome offee!"

Joe saw Adam coming with a basket and opened the door for him.

"Mornin', Marshal, and happy Christmas!"

"You, too, Adam," Joe said. "That his breakfast?"

"Yes, sir, and yours, too, compliments of the Martins."

"Right nice of them." Joe watched as Adam uncovered a tin plate with some bacon and biscuits. He poured a cup of steaming coffee and turned toward the cell.

"Hold it, Adam," Joe said. "Just give him the plate for now. Let that coffee sit awhile." Adam looked puzzled but did as he was told. "We don't want to give Mister Bob Carlson there a chance to throw hot coffee in our faces, do we?" Adam's face paled.

"That's a good idea, Marshal." He reached into the basket, took out another plate that was heaped with eggs, bacon, and diced potatoes and placed it on Joe's desk.

"You eaten?" Joe said.

"Mine's been promised as soon as I return this basket. I'll stop back after I do some chores at the livery." Joe nodded as Adam left.

By the time Joe finished eating, the prison-

112

er's coffee was cold. The marshal opened the cell door, held out his hand for the empty plate, and then gave the prisoner the coffee. With a fresh cup for himself, he returned to a front window and looked out at the deserted town. Although the windows were mostly covered by frost, there were spaces at the top of each pane clear enough to see through. The only tracks in the snow were those left by Adam crossing the street. The stove made the office comfortable again, and the rich smell of the coffee almost overpowered the rancid stench of the prisoner's blood and body odor.

Joe thought about Christmas day in Baxter Springs, and his standing dinner invitation with Charlie Oster and his wife. After dinner, the missus would clean up while the two men would sit in the parlor, smoke cigars, and visit. Until Charlie fell asleep, that is. They were good times, and Joe missed them.

When Adam came back to the office, Joe asked him to keep an eye on the prisoner. He walked east down the boardwalk, which had about half as much snow as the street. He crossed over to the hotel and continued south. At Doc's house, he knocked gently on the door and waited. When it opened, Sullivan showed him inside. The house

113

wasn't fancy, but it was nicer than Sarah's. A homemade examination table sat against the wall to the left, and a curtain hung down that could be pulled to close off that area. Joe guessed that the wooden cabinet contained medical supplies. To the right was a desk piled with books and papers, a nice green upholstered chair, an eating table, and straight-backed wooden chairs. Beyond was a tiny kitchen area flanked by two doors. *A lot packed into a small house.*

"Thought I'd drop by and see how Lucy was doing, Doc."

"Glad to see you, Marshal."

"Call me Joe."

"Okay, Joe. She's awake and seems to be doing well, considering the beating she took last night. Her vision is blurry. I'm concerned about that," Sullivan said.

"Will it clear up?" Joe said.

"Maybe. Maybe not."

"Can I see her?"

"Sure, this way, but be prepared. Her face is almost all black from bruising, and her eyes look shut, but she can see a little," Sullivan said. "I set her broken nose — as well as I could anyway."

Sullivan opened one of the doors, and Joe walked in. There were two single beds and a small table in the tiny room. Lucy rolled over toward Joe when he sat down on the edge of the bed. Her cheeks up to the forehead were dark, and her eyelids puffed outward unnaturally. Her nose, though a blue color with a split across the bridge, looked almost straight.

"Hello, Lucy. I'm Marshal Mundy. How are you feelin'?"

"I know who you are, Marshal. Thank you for what you done. I think they meant to kill me." It looked to Joe like her eyes were mostly closed, but she reached out and touched his hand. "I want them to pay for what they done to me!" Tears squeezed out and ran toward her ears.

"Take it easy, Lucy. There's only one left alive to pay, but he will. A judge is coming and will hear the case, probably next week. Do you think you'll feel up to takin' your oath and tellin' him what happened?" Joe said.

"I sure as hell will!"

"Okay, you relax and get some rest. Looks like you're in good hands here."

At the front door, Doc Sullivan assured Joe that he was keeping a close eye on her, and he thought she'd recover. Joe walked through the snow about a hundred yards due west toward Sarah's house. About halfway there, he saw a cowhand step out of the front door, turn back as if to say something, then put his hat on and walk toward Main Street. Joe felt an unusual twist in his gut, something he hadn't felt before. He stopped and stood for a few minutes. After talking himself into continuing, he walked up to her door.

When it opened, "I said no — Oh, it's you," Sarah said, surprised.

"You were expecting someone else?" Joe pulled his hat off.

"Merry Christmas to you, too," she said. "Come by for that pie and coffee?"

"I just stopped by to see if you were okay, and tell you I checked on Lucy. Looks like she's doing better than Doc expected." Joe wasn't sure why his tone was firm and businesslike, but it annoyed him not being able to control it. Sarah closed the door behind him.

She stared without saying anything at first. "You saw that man leave, didn't you?"

"That's none of my business, Sarah," Joe said. She was wearing the chemise again with a blanket over her shoulders. He thought it best to look down at his boots.

"You're damn right it's none of your business!"

"I should get back to the office," Joe said. He thought better of trying to continue the conversation. When he reached for the doorknob, Sarah placed her hand against the door and slid the locking bolt.

"I'm sorry, I shouldn't have bitten your head off like that. It is none of your business, however."

"Didn't mean to seem like it was."

"Sit down. I can't eat all of that pie myself," she said. He took a chair and watched her pour two cups of coffee and make three slices in the pie.

Joe finished his piece first and sipped from a porcelain cup. He still felt queer about how the visit had started and wished it would have gone better. When she finished, she laid her plate on the little table that separated them.

"The man you saw, he was here for, uh, business, just as you assumed he was," Sarah said and looked at Joe. He began to speak, but she cut in. "I told him no, for now. Not that I never do business here, but I told him no."

"Did he give you any trouble?" Joe said.

"No, he didn't. He's a hand at Jarvis's ranch. A decent enough man. I had some thinking to do, and it's Christmas! The boys have to be randy on Christmas, too?" She shook her head. "Anyway, I decided I'm not going back to the Palace. Smiley stopped by earlier and told me to get to work, that he had customers. I told him to go to hell . . . the way he just stood there doin' nothing while those bastards almost killed Lucy. I ain't stupid, I know that could have been me up in that room." Her tone rose, and her eyes were glassy. Joe let her talk it out, whatever *it* was. "If it was me, up there in that room . . . you'd a killed both of 'em, wouldn't you?"

"Probable," Joe said.

Sarah looked into his eyes. Joe detected a bit of fear, maybe because she saw the level of violence he was capable of.

"I'll have to keep working here. I don't know what else to do. Ben, the man that just left, said when Budd Jarvis reopens the old saloon, he's going to hire some ladies. I don't care much for him, either, but he'd be better to work for than that snake Smiley. And he don't like Smiley much. This is what I *have* to do to survive. You understand that, don't you? This is what I am now."

*Got one thing in common with Jarvis, I guess.* "Maybe you could do some other kind of work. Maybe some dressmaking?" Joe said.

"And sell them to who? Cowhands, so they could dress up on Saturday nights?" Sarah said. Joe tried not to picture that im-

118

age. "And I won't be paraded around town by you or anyone else, to be the brunt of their stares and snickers."

"Maybe with all that's happened, water under the bridge, you might get your mending business goin' again," Joe said. He wished he had a better suggestion. He too, thought *what if* it had been her up in that room.

"Great idea, as long as I stop eating."

They sat in silence for several minutes. Joe could feel her eyes on him. He didn't know what else to say. She stood up and walked to his chair. He looked up, and she let the blanket fall and put her hand out. When he reached for it, she placed his two silver dollars into his hand, and led him to the bed.

He was on his back, trying to catch his breath. As cold as it had been, Joe was surprised at how much he was sweating. The bed was more comfortable than the one at the office. Sarah's naked body felt good against his. She rested her head on his shoulder and caressed his chest while his hand glided over the smoothness of her back and thigh.

"That wasn't the first time, was it?" Sarah said.

"Well, hell no, course not!" Joe said. He turned his head to look at her, taken aback by the question.

"I mean at the Palace."

"Oh . . . you mean the first time I killed a man?"

"Yes."

"No," Joe said. His mind began to drift.

"Does it bother you, killing that man in the Palace?"

"Not much."

"When was the first time?"

Joe started to protest.

"Tell me. Please." He turned again and looked her in the eyes. "Please."

Joe laid his head back on the pillow and stared at the ceiling. He felt something for her. It would be easier to tell her about Baxter Springs, but somewhere along the line, he'd decided that he wouldn't lie to her, about anything. But this was something he hadn't thought about for a long, long time. Since he was a kid.

He laid there wondering where to start, the memories of his father and mother came flooding back. So long ago. He caressed her back. She slid a leg across his. When he began, he told her everything that he could remember about the summer of 1852.

"I was five years old when my baby

brother died and father sold the farm in Iowa and moved our family to Nebraska Territory. He claimed about a hundred acres outside of Brownville near the Missouri River. He struggled with the farm, but was more successful breeding and selling horses. Until the stealing started . . ."

*Joseph woke up when he heard the riders stop in front of the log cabin his father had built. He peeked out of the window and saw men with long rifles. He could tell they weren't soldiers, as they had different kinds of clothes on. He could hear a sharp conversation between his mother and father, so he walked out of his room to see what was wrong.*

*"Joseph, you get right back to bed!" his mother said. His father laid the muzzle-loading shotgun on the table that they ate at and sat down on one of the chairs.*

*"Did we wake you, little man?"*

*Joseph wasn't afraid of his father. "Are you leaving again?"*

*Mr. Mundy patted his leg and let him sit on a knee. "I'll be back tomorrow. Nothin' for you to worry about."*

*"But my birthday. Will you be home for my birthday?" Joseph said.*

*"Well, course I will. You're going to be, let's see, twenty years old?"*

"Naw, Father. You know it's eleven! I'll be eleven. I'm almost growed," Joseph said.

"You sure are. And I'm mighty proud of how you're turning out. But you need to get your sleep, so off you go."

Joseph didn't move. "Why do you go out at night with your gun and them other men, Father?"

"Those other men, Joseph, we taught you better than that!" Joseph's mother said. Jules looked at her and smiled.

"It's just business, Joseph. Nothin' to concern yourself about."

"What's this pin for? Mister Jacobson and Mister Belford have the same ones." Joseph pointed at the horseshoe-shaped pin on his father's lapel.

"Jules Mundy, your son needs his sleep!" Joseph's mother crossed her arms to show that she meant business.

"Just a minute, Mother. I think Joseph is old enough now to know what's happening." Jules studied his son's face for moment. "Joseph, there are men, bad men who come and steal from us, and our neighbors, including Mister Jacobson and Mister Belford that you mentioned, as well as others. The men I'm talking about steal horses. Today I found three of ours missing. This pin is for an organization of citizens who get together to right a wrong. To get our horses back. It's called the Anti–Horse Thief Association. When a member of this group has a horse stolen, we band together and go after those that done it and hand them over to the law. Do you understand, little man?"

Joseph did, but he was scared something would happen to his father. He always waited anxiously for his return.

The next morning he awoke to another sharp conversation. The sun was starting to rise, and his father had returned home. Joseph listened through a crack in the door.

"Tell me what happened, Jules. Lord, tell me what happened!" Joseph could hear his father pacing back and forth beside the table.

"We found two of them. Willoughby says there's a gang of five, but we found two and gave chase. We caught one on my gray. The other got away. Everyone was so worked up by that time . . . oh, Jesus!" Jules said.

"What happened?"

"Mother, I tried to stop them, I tried!"

Joseph was too scared to move. He had never heard his father this upset and it frightened him.

"Before I knew it, they had a rope around the man's neck. My God, what was his name? I don't even know his name! I tried to stop them. I reminded them what our purpose was, to turn them over to the law. They wouldn't listen. That man is still hanging out there by the Nemaha."

That day, Joseph's eleventh birthday, was a solemn one.

A week later four riders came up to the cabin as the Mundys were sitting down for dinner. Jules went outside. Few words had been said when two of them jumped him and tied his hands and feet with rope. One of the two wore a dirty, crushed stovepipe hat with a long black coat, and the other, a dirty straw hat with a wide brim. They dragged Jules behind one of their horses to an elm tree nearby, where they put another rope around his neck and pulled him up. One of the mounted men tied off the rope to the branch so it couldn't be reached. Jules kicked his legs back and forth, turning himself on the rope. Joseph's mother screamed. She picked up the corn knife that Joseph pretended was a pirate's sword and ran toward the riders. She swung it wildly at the closest one, causing his horse to shy and him to fall. One of the other riders ran his horse into her, knocking her down. The man on the ground grabbed the corn knife and tossed it aside. They tied another rope around her neck and pulled her up on the branch next to Jules. She tore at her neck and kicked her legs wildly. Tears ran down Joseph's cheeks, *ashamed, but he knew if he ran out there, they wouldn't let him help his parents. They gazed at the grisly scene for a few short moments, then spurred their horses and rode away.*

*As soon as they were out of sight, Joseph ran to them. Jules had stopped kicking, but his mother's legs still moved a little. Pushing up on the bottom of her feet was no use. He grabbed the corn knife and tried climbing the tree. He couldn't do it with the knife in one hand, so he slid it inside his waistband and pushed it through the side of his pants. He scratched and tore at the tree until he got up to the branch. Joseph pulled the corn knife out, straddled the branch and worked himself down to where his father's rope was tied off. The panicked, wild swings almost sent the knife flying to the ground. He concentrated harder and struck at the rope until it broke. Sliding farther out to where his mother was, Joseph hacked at the rope. When she fell, he dropped the knife, swung down from the branch and let go. He scrambled to his father and gradually worked the rope loose. Jules didn't move. He did the same for his mother, but she was still as well. He dragged their bodies together close enough to hold and laid there until morning when he could no longer cry.*

*Joseph was to be sent to relatives in Council*

Bluffs after the double funeral. He had no intention of going, however, as he had a job to do. Joseph had overheard conversations between his father and some of the association members that the gang of five horse thieves, which now numbered four, used an old Indian cave by the Missouri River as a hideout. Jules had showed him the cave last year when they were hunting. He was only eleven years old, but he would avenge the deaths of his parents. He knew that his parents would not approve of his plan. But he had no family anymore, and the decisions of life were now his to make. Good or bad, they were his. If he died in the process, he didn't care.

When Joseph got home, he went straight to the drawer where his father kept the gun. He liked this gun better than the shotgun. It was big and heavy, a Colt Dragoon .44 caliber revolver that Joseph called "the dragon." His father had taught him to load and shoot it when they were hunting together. If his mother had known, she would never have allowed it. Because of the weight, he could only shoot it once or twice while gripping the big wooden handles with both hands before he had to wear gloves and hold it like a rifle. His father had used light loads, so the recoil wouldn't scare him. Jules felt every man should know *how to use a firearm for hunting and to protect himself.*

*Joseph stuffed some bread and dried meat into a cloth sack. It was midafternoon when he set out for the river, the Dragoon in one hand, the corn knife and sack in the other. By dark he was close to the cave. He hid in some heavy brush and went to sleep.*

*The next day, he waited and watched. That evening as the sun sank, he heard riders. There were four of them heading toward the cave. He recognized the crushed stovepipe hat and long black coat. Another of the riders he remembered wore the dirty, wide-brimmed straw hat. They were leading three horses. After a brief conversation, two of the riders left, turning south along the river with the extra horses. The other two rode on to the cave. Joseph slept a little more, and when the moon was high, he awoke, picked up the Colt and the corn knife, and crept toward the cave.*

*It took a long time, but he was careful and patient. Their campfire was just outside the mouth of the cave. He could hear bird noises that any other time would have frightened him. Being this far from home by himself, in the dark, would have frightened him as well. But he felt no fear. He hadn't cried at the funeral or any time since that night he held his parents. He quietly wondered if he'd lost all feeling.*

*The men lay on the ground on each side of the fire, one on Joseph's side, and one on the far side. Short rifles and knives lay next to each man. He waited until they were both snoring. Kneeling over the closest man, he raised the corn knife high. It struck the man's neck with all the force Joseph could muster. The sound was like a chopping knife striking a roast. A red spray shot into the fire. The man grabbed at his throat, wild-eyed, gagging, not yet realizing that he was dying. The other man stirred and rolled over. Joseph left the knife in the dying man's throat and shifted the heavy pistol to his right hand. He cocked the hammer with the palm of his left hand. By the time the other man was awake, Joseph had the .44 aimed at his chest.*

*"What the hell's . . . ?" The gun roared, twisting up in Joseph's hands, and he nearly dropped it. He hadn't considered that his father would have it primed with a full load. The .44 ball struck the man on the right side of his chest, rolling him over. He pushed and struggled against himself and turned back around. The man stared at his attacker with disbelief. Joseph had the hammer cocked again and pulled the trigger. After the echo of the gunshot died away, he looked at the*

*bodies and wondered why he didn't feel bad for what he'd done.*

Sarah was propped up on an elbow, exposing a breast, when Joe stopped talking. Although they had been lying there long enough for the sweat to dry up, his forehead was wet.

"My God . . . Joe . . . I'm so sorry."

"You wanted to know, so I told you. Never told nobody else," Joe said.

"And only . . . eleven years old," Sarah said.

"Don't need your sympathy. You wanted to know. It's just between you and me." She rested her head on his shoulder and hugged him. They didn't talk anymore.

# CHAPTER NINE

On the Thursday after Christmas, Joe, Adam, and some others helped Judge Worden move into his office across the street from the side door of the hotel. The judge had arrived with a large freight wagon full of his belongings. The men's breath could easily be seen as they puffed under the weight of a wooden platform that came in two sections. When nailed together, the judge's desk and chair would be positioned on top of it giving him an eight-inch elevation above others in the courtroom.

The snow allowed for plenty of slipping and sliding while unloading the wagon. Worden continuously issued stern words of caution against dropping this or banging into that. He was particularly protective of a fancy Baltimore lamp.

The office wasn't large, but it had enough room to uncomfortably squeeze in a dozen people for court if the need arose. If a larger trial was held, they would use one of the saloons. Joe knew that about two seconds after the judge announced, "Court adjourned," the saloonkeeper would announce to the crowd, "Bar's open!"

Joe nailed up a short sign beside the front door that Worden brought with him from Broken Bow. It was painted dark green with faded gold letters that read HON. ELSWORTH T. WORDEN, ATTORNEY AT LAW, JUSTICE OF THE PEACE.

Judge Worden was old, but the way he toted a crateful of law books told anyone watching that he was far from used up. He was a good four inches shorter than Joe, with a white beard and soon-to-match hair. Tufts of hair protruded from both sides of his head and on top, which combined with the beard, covered all of the points of a compass. He wore a black vest and a worn Prince Albert coat with a small, low-crowned black hat. The clothes weren't shabby, but neither were they new.

"Judge Worden, I'm holding a prisoner for nearly killin' a lady at the Palace Saloon on Christmas Eve. Wondered when we could have a trial?" Joe asked. He wanted to get court set up for Carlson before heading back to the office.

"A *nymphe du prairie,* eh?" Worden said.

"Excuse me?" Joe said.

"A prairie nymph, Marshal," Worden said with a sly grin. "Went to law school in Baltimore. The only two good things about Baltimore were the whores . . . and I can't remember what the other thing was."

"Lucy's a nice girl, Judge. My prisoner and his partner almost beat her to death."

"His partner escape the iron hand of justice, Marshal?" Worden asked. He stepped onto the platform and sat down at the desk, mopping his brow with a handkerchief.

"In a manner of speaking. He jerked a trigger without aimin'," Joe said. "I helped him avoid all the court bother."

"Ahh. Well, then, we'll have a hearing on Monday at one o'clock. Should have everything here in order by then. We'll need the prosecutor and another attorney to represent the accused, of course."

"I'll send word to Gracie Flats, the county seat," Joe said.

On the way back to the office, Joe wondered what kind of judge Worden would be. He had many years of experience and seemed to have a strict personality, despite his quirky sense of humor. Joe walked by the hotel and was almost past Siegler's store when a voice called his name.

"Joe! Joe, I was looking for you." It was Doc Sullivan, who was just leaving the store. "I have some bad news, I'm afraid."

"Is it Lucy? Is she okay?"

"Yes, she'll be fine, except maybe for her vision," Doc hesitated. "But — she's not going to testify."

"What are ya' talkin' about, Doc? Sure, she is."

"Let's go to your office and I'll explain."

"No privacy there with the prisoner. Let's go to the hotel," Joe said. Sullivan nodded.

There were only three other customers in the dining room, and they were able to pick a table away from them. Joe waved off the waitress when she approached.

"What's this all about, Doc?" Joe said.

"That son-of-a-bitch Smiley came to see how Lucy was, asked to speak to her alone. After he left I went in to check on her, and she was crying. Well, she asked me to deliver a message to you. Said to tell you that she doesn't want any trouble and it was a misunderstanding. She won't testify against that cretin."

Joe stared at Sullivan, trying to understand. "What the hell did he say to her, Doc? Did he threaten her? You can't threaten a witness," Joe said.

"I never heard any raised voices, but what

else could he have done?"

"I'll go talk to her. She'll testify," Joe said.

"No. Joe, I tried to persuade her, but it is set. She said to tell you she's sorry, but she's not about to change her mind. Said she's goin' back to work Monday. I told her about the new judge in town. She's gonna tell him on Monday that she won't testify. I think she's scared of Smiley."

"Goin back to the Palace? So next time some animal beats on her, Smiley can just stand there wiping down the bar? Bullshit!" Joe said. The other three customers turned to look.

"I agree with how you feel, Joe, but women, well out here, they have a different perspective on survival," Sullivan said, in a low voice. "Men sometimes don't know how good we have it."

Adam was sitting behind the desk, book in hand, studying intently, when Joe returned to the office. He jumped up, startled, when Joe entered. "Sit down, Adam. I don't mind," Joe said smiling to himself.

"Thanks, Marshal. Did you get your legal business done with Judge Worden?"

Joe tried not to show his sour mood. "Yep, sure did. Care for some coffee?"

"No, thanks, Marshal. Matter of fact I gotta go and get rid of some," Adam said.

He stepped out through the back door.

Joe looked at Carlson. "What do you boys do? You freighters?"

Adam had given the prisoner a fresh wet cloth, and he used it to wipe off some of the dried blood around his face. It appeared the bleeding had almost stopped. The swelling was still evident, though.

Carlson stared coldly for a few moments, and Joe wondered if he'd decided not to talk.

"Yeah, freighters," Carlson said. He could speak only slightly better than he had been. "We haul minin' supplies to them Black Hills."

Joe nodded.

Adam came back, picked up his book from the desk, and sat down in the chair by the stove.

"What ya' readin' Adam?" Joe asked.

"Missus Siegler gave me this book as a Christmas present. It's to practice up on my readin' skills," Adam said. He looked at the cover and read. "It's 'Howard's Book of Con-an-drums, Rid-dels, and A-musing Sells.' Marshal, what is a con-an-drum?"

"Conundrum. I don't know, maybe sort of a puzzle."

"Oh. Con-nun-drum," Adam said and looked at Joe for approval.

135

"Believe you got it."

"Con-nun-drum. I like the way it sounds. I think this book will be a con-nun-drum! Listen to this." Adam opened the book and turned a couple of pages. "But twist the meaning out, by hook or crook. Of ev-ry plea-sant mystery in our book."

"You're doin' pretty good," Joe said.

Adam snapped the book shut and slid it into a coat pocket. "Well, gotta' go finish up some work at Mister Siegler's before din-nertime. See ya' later."

Joe sat behind the desk wishing there was some way to send Carlson to prison. He decided to walk the town and think about it. That snake could at least stay in jail until Lucy notified Judge Worden that she wouldn't testify.

Joe walked east down the boardwalk until it ended, then headed around the north side of town, which didn't take long. A few inches of snow still covered the ground, and the air was cold enough to freeze the inside of his nose when he inhaled. As he headed south toward the livery, he noticed that the new sign for the meat market had been installed. He also noticed the wagon behind the livery. The wagon belonged to the freighters and might be worth a look.

He didn't see anyone in the livery as he

walked through. The bay shook his head up and down in approval after receiving a sugar cube from Joe. He looked over the stall, food, and water, and was satisfied that his horse was being taken care of. Out back, Joe started to pull back the canvas that covered the goods in the wagon.

"What ya' think you're doin'?"

Joe turned and saw a man in a shabby brown coat and tall crowned hat approach.

"You the manager here?" Joe said.

"That's right. That ain't your wagon so get the hell away from it."

"It's okay, I'm Marshal Mundy. It belongs to my prisoner."

"I don't give a shit who you are . . ." The man grabbed Joe's arm. In one swift move, Joe turned and spun the man into the wagon and pulled his arm up behind his back.

"Ahh, that hurts, damn it!"

"Bet it does," Joe said. "Now let's start over. I'm Joe Mundy. What's your name?"

"Ace. Ace Todd, I work for Budd Jarvis. Now lemme go!" Joe released him, and Todd stood rubbing his shoulder. The marshal could see by the lump under the coat that Todd was wearing a gun. He watched a moment to see if Todd would settle down or pursue the matter further.

Todd seemed content to nurse his shoulder. The man was clean shaven, which made his prominent cheekbones stand out. The intense eyes and thin lips that turned down at the sides betrayed the look of an unhappy person.

"What is it you're lookin' for exactly, or just anything that suits your fancy?" Todd said, not hiding his sarcasm.

"Curious to see what they need in the Black Hills," Joe said and pulled back the canvas. He looked over several wooden crates marked with various manufacturers' names from the East. There were a couple of whiskey kegs and two cases of Winchester ammunition, one of .44–40 cartridges and one of .56–50 cartridges. Four large bags of grain were stamped QUALITY MILLS-LOUP CITY, NEB. A large bundle on the floor wrapped in canvas caught Joe's attention.

"That'll be all, Mister Todd. Glad you're keeping such a close eye on things." Joe eyed the manager, who grumbled something before he walked back to the livery office.

Joe pulled the end of the bundle open and found several branding irons. He could see ten for sure. He recognized the straight bar ends of two as running irons. These were used by rustlers to alter existing brands on animals they stole. There were other irons as well, with legitimate-looking brands. He covered them and headed back through the livery, stopping to give the bay another sugar cube.

"So, what do you think? You think those two are rustlers?" Sarah asked and wiped her mouth with a napkin.

Joe swallowed a bite of fried chicken before answering. He enjoyed sharing a meal with Sarah in the privacy of her home. She was a terrific cook. Adam had agreed to sit with the prisoner while he was gone, so there was no reason to hurry.

"Well, it sure wasn't mining supplies like Carlson said. They don't use branding irons in mines, far as I know."

"Wonder where they were headed?" Sarah said.

"Hard to say, maybe western Nebraska, or up in Dakota," Joe said. He finished the last of his chicken and took a drink of coffee. "May have to follow him a ways and see where he goes." Joe could see the concern in her face when he said that. "Wish I didn't have to let him go," Joe said. He gently swirled his cup and watched the coffee churn.

"Yes. But Joe, don't blame Lucy. She's got

no family and no other way to make a living. Doc Sullivan was right what he told you. It ain't the same for women as it is for men out here. Maybe Budd Jarvis will hire her at his new saloon."

"If I could prove to Judge Worden that he threatened her . . ." Joe said.

"Joe, he didn't have to threaten her outright. She lives in that room at the Palace. All he had to do was remind her that she'd be out on the street with no money, no food, and no options."

"What does Smiley pay, anyway?" Joe said.

"She gets a dollar a turn, gives Smiley eighty cents of it, since she has the room, and still has to pay for her food and drinks. She has no way out." Sarah took a sip from her cup. "I get two dollars, as you know, and I keep seventy-five cents."

Trying to ignore Sarah's additional information, he replied, "Guess you're right, but I may have to offer Smiley my opinion on the matter."

# CHAPTER TEN

It was Sunday evening, and the activity in town was light. Saturday night had been quiet except for Sanderson's pigs getting out and running around on Main Street. Joe sent two drunken cowhands back into the North Star without their pistols after they tried shooting them.

Joe passed by Jarvis's new saloon, which looked about ready to reopen. After checking in at the North Star, he walked across to the Palace. Both establishments had a half dozen customers, some of them playing poker.

When he walked through the door, Smiley gave him a short stare. Joe continued down to the far end of the bar and leaned an elbow on it. He didn't plan on ordering anything, and Smiley accommodated him by not offering. Mugs and shot glasses littered some of the vacant tables. The odor of the place hadn't improved any, and it seemed to have an eternal smoke cloud hanging in the air.

After several minutes of watching a card game, Joe thought about leaving. As if on cue, Smiley walked over and placed both hands against the bar.

"Almost forgot, Mundy, you owe me three dollars for cleaning that room you messed up. That stinkin' whore ain't been back to work yet, and money's tight."

Joe forced a grin, turned, and leaned both arms on the bar. He slowly looked up and met Smiley's bloodshot eyes. In an instant, Joe reached across, grabbed the man's shirt, and pulled him onto the bar. He slapped Smiley hard across the face, sending the barkeeper's hat flying. "If someone lays a hand on her again, and you do nothing, I'll give you what she got!"

Conversations ceased, and the customers turned to look. A few who were there the night of the shooting upstairs grabbed their chairs, ready to dive to safety should there be a repeat performance.

"You can't hit me, you son-of-a-bitch!" Smiley said.

Joe slapped him harder this time. "Do we have an understanding, Smiley, or do we continue the lesson?"

"Okay, okay. If it happens again, I'll . . ."

Smiley's voice drifted off.

Joe slapped him again.

"Okay, I'll send for you, damn it." Joe pushed him backward off the bar, and he stumbled back a few steps to catch his balance.

"You catch on real quick, Smiley. Be sure you don't forget," Joe said.

# CHAPTER ELEVEN

The sun was bright on Monday morning with the temperature slightly warmer than it had been. The snow in the street hadn't melted much, only mashed around by horses' hooves, human feet, and the occasional wagon. Joe sat at his desk and half-cocked his pistol, opened the loading gate, and used the ejector rod to remove each cartridge. That done, he loosened the screw at the front of his Colt's frame and pulled out the cylinder pin, letting the cylinder slide out. The cleaning rod went smoothly through each cylinder chamber and then the barrel. He wiped a lightly oiled rag over each of the parts, then reassembled and reloaded the gun with six cartridges. Some men left one chamber under the hammer empty for safety reasons, in case the gun was dropped. Joe felt that anyone who dropped their gun deserved to get shot by it or their opponent. Besides, he wanted all six if he needed to shoot. Joe had finished the cavalry Colt when Adam walked in.

"Mornin', Marshal."

"Mornin' to you, Adam," Joe said.

"I come with a message from Judge Worden," Adam said, and sat down in the chair across from the desk. "He wants to see you."

Joe was expecting that, of course. He nodded at Adam.

"I'll stay here 'til you get back," Adam said.

"Thanks."

"Was them shooters cleaned okay?" Adam said.

Joe pulled open the drawer, took out the two confiscated cap and ball revolvers, and inspected them closely. "Looks like they're clean as a whistle, Adam, thanks." Joe finished his coffee, pulled on his black overcoat and hat, and headed out to see Judge Worden. Adam took Joe's place behind the desk and pulled out his book of conundrums.

When Joe walked into Worden's office, the judge was sitting at a table off to the side of the bench, where he did his paperwork. He didn't look up when Joe walked in.

Worden finally put down the paper he was reading. "Good morning, Marshal."

"Judge."

"Had a visitor bright and early."

"Lucy," Joe said flatly.

"You knew she was dropping charges?"

"Heard she might."

"She looks like hell, Marshal. Kept rubbing her eyes, poor thing. Looks like her balance is off a bit, too."

"Doc says her vision is blurred from the beating. May not improve," Joe said. "Isn't there any way we can make that cur pay for what he did?"

"I understand your anger, but if she refuses to tell what happened, we won't get a conviction," Worden said and set a match to his pipe. He puffed several times before producing a great cloud of smoke.

"I can sure as hell tell what I saw, him on top of her, beating her," Joe said. He tried to keep his voice from rising.

"We could try that, but if she isn't interested enough to testify, and being a whore, we'd never get a conviction. Might not even if she *did* testify." Worden sucked gently on the pipe and eased the smoke from his mouth. "I wish there was a better solution, Marshal, I truly do, but I don't see it." Worden stared vacantly out the front window. *"Men must work and women must weep."*

Joe thought he understood the drift of

that, but wasn't sure.

After a moment the judge regained his attention to the matter at hand. "This is to make it proper," he said, and handed Joe a sheet of paper. It was a handwritten order to release the prisoner.

"It is not to my taste, either, Marshal, but without law, we have chaos. Remember, *let all things be done decently and in order.*"

Joe swallowed hard, folded the paper, and tucked it into his coat pocket.

He wondered how many new legal papers he'd see now that they had a judge in town.

*Too many.* He was pretty sure about that.

Joe hung his coat and hat on pegs and poured a cup of coffee. Adam could see the solemn look on his face so held back on any conversation. Byron Siegler was sitting next to the stove with a cup.

"Mister Siegler," Joe said.

"Mornin', Joe. Came by to beg a cup while Missus Jarvis is picking up some things. Hope you don't mind."

"Not at all," Joe said. "Figured you'd take care of Missus Jarvis personally."

"Ahh, Earl has everything well in hand," Siegler said. His face flushed slightly. "He is, how shall I put this? He has the required temperament to assist Missus Jarvis."

Joe nodded.

Letting the prisoner go free was the last thing Joe wanted to do and knew it wasn't right. But right, and the law, didn't always cohabitate. He dropped Judge Worden's order on his desk.

"Hand me the keys, Adam," Joe said.

Joe walked to the cell, unlocked the door, and swung it open. Carlson stood slowly grabbing onto the flat metal straps that made up the cell. He looked at Joe cautiously.

"You threatened to kill me, remember?" Joe said, and waited for a response.

"Damn right I did!" Carlson said. A bubble of spit flew from his mouth when he answered.

"You're free to go. But know this, if you step foot in this town again, I'll kill you. Won't be any warnin'. Won't be any talk. You'll just be dead," Joe said and waited for a response. "Do you understand me?"

"Yeah," Carlson said.

"Git," Joe said.

"You ain't gonna shoot me in the back, are ya?"

"That's a thought," Joe replied. He held up the paper in front of Carlson's face. "Can you read?"

"Naw."

"Adam, read this to him, will ya?" Joe

148

handed it to Adam and sat down behind the desk.

Adam looked dubiously at the paper, glanced at Siegler, and then at Joe.

"I'd better be getting back. Thanks for the coffee," Siegler said, and hurried out the door.

"Go ahead, Adam, you're readin' is comin' along fine. You can do it," Joe said encouragingly, seeing Adam's worried look.

"Uh, this here says, 'Tow-it. . . . hereas . . . bein' no charges . . . hereby founded on Robert Carlson, that Robert Carlson is cur-rent-ly . . . in-car-cen-nated in the city jail of Tay-lors-ville, Nebraska, that Robert Carlson be released upon . . . re-cept . . . by the city marshal of said city. Judge Els-worth P. Worden, Justice of the Peace.' "

"Thanks, Adam," Joe said. He turned to Carlson. "Now git."

"You gonna gimme my knife and gun back?" Carlson asked.

"Which part, exactly, of *git,* is it, that you don't understand?" Joe looked at him.

Carlson slowly edged over to the door, not turning his back on Joe. He stepped out and hurried west toward the livery.

"Adam, go saddle the bay. Take my carbine and saddlebags," Joe said. "Wait 'til Carlson has headed out, though. I'll be down there as soon as I talk to Mister Siegler."

"Where you goin', Marshal?" Adam said.

"Carlson's wagon had some odd cargo for a mining operation. A bunch of branding irons for one thing. Think I'll trail him a ways to see where he's headed."

"But what about the town?"

"I'd like you to keep an eye on things," Joe said. "I'll be back tonight."

"You mean, I'd be your deputy?" Adam said hopefully.

"Only unofficially, like a secret deputy. If there's any problem, don't do nothing, just go tell Mister Siegler about it."

"I'm not too dumb to be your deputy."

"Course you're not. Didn't mean to imply that, if I did. It's only that the town board would have to authorize the money for me to employ one, you understand?" Joe said. "I won't be gone long, and maybe we can talk about it later. And don't tell anyone what I'm doin'."

In Siegler's office at the back of his store, Joe told him about Carlson.

"Sorry you had to let him go," Siegler said.

"Yeah. If Smiley hadn't threatened Lucy, she'd have testified. Carlson said they was haulin' minin' supplies to the Black Hills. I took a look and found ammunition, whiskey, some other crates, and a pile of branding

150

irons, including runnin' irons."

"That's a bit odd. What's a running iron?" Siegler said.

"Used to make bars, or the straight line parts of brands, but they're also used by rustlers to alter good brands. Don't know why they should be haulin' irons of different brands, and they all been used," Joe said. "Ace was a bit protective. Didn't like me lookin' in the wagon. Had to twist his arm a bit, but he came around."

"I suppose we should notify Sheriff Canfield and let him look into it."

"Carlson would be long gone by that time. I plan to be back tonight. Follow him long enough to see what direction he heads. If he goes north, I may swing over to Gracie Flats and talk to the sheriff."

"Okay, but be careful out there, Joe," Siegler said.

"Always. I told Adam to keep an eye on things in town and tell you if there's any trouble," Joe said. Siegler nodded. "He wanted to be my deputy while I was gone. Told him the board would have to approve that."

"I suppose we could pay a little, but only for special occasions. You think he's up to it?"

"He's a good man, honest. I won't let him

do much but watch prisoners right now, which I pay him for out of my pocket. After he's been around it long enough, he'll be okay."

When Joe got to the livery, Adam and Ace were standing inside next to the bay, talking. The horse was ready to go and started walking when he saw Joe. Ace didn't seem friendly, and Adam looked a little dejected.

"Where ya' headed, Marshal?" Ace asked. He was nosy enough to act friendly.

"Gotta' go up to Gracie Flats on official business. Be back tonight," Joe said and glanced at Adam. Ace opened the door, and Joe walked the bay outside. After he closed it, Joe mounted up.

"Something on your mind, Adam?"

He looked back to make sure Ace had remained inside. "He tol' me I was fired. I don't think he likes me working for you. I needed that money."

"Don't worry about it, I'll help you whenever you need it. Talk to you when I get back," Joe said. "You have the extra key to the office. Stay there as much as you like."

"You don't trust Ace, do you?" Adam asked.

"Don't trust many."

The wagon tracks were easy to follow in the

snow, which was only fetlock deep. They continued north until they met the Loup River and then followed it. Joe took his time, not wanting to get so close that he was easy to see. The bay was giddy, wanting to step it up a bit. Clouds had filled the sky and prematurely darkened the day, which, by Joe's reckoning, had about five hours left.

It wasn't long before he caught sight of the wagon. Joe stopped and pulled out the spyglass from a saddlebag, extended it, and took a look. Carlson didn't seem to be concerned with watching his back. Joe sat still for several minutes and watched the wagon slowly ford the river. It continued north, leaving the river behind, until it went over a hill and dropped out of sight.

The bay splashed through the cold water, soaking Joe's lower pant legs. The tracks were so easy to follow that he forced himself to stay vigilant for ambush. About two hours later, he stopped on the upside of a hill, at a point where only his head was exposed. Through the spyglass he could see Carlson starting down another hill. He collapsed the glass and pulled out his watch. It was almost four o'clock. He waited to see the wagon make the incline on the next hill. By four thirty, it hadn't. Joe wondered if this was Carlson's destination or if he had only stopped for the day. He was losing daylight, so he decided to take advantage of what light was left.

An hour later he was approaching the hill he had last seen the wagon on. He dismounted and ground-hitched the bay. With the Winchester in one hand and the spyglass in the other, Joe tromped through the snow to the top. He could smell the smoke before he reached the top of the hill. Joe eased up to the hilltop, staying low. The glass revealed a small soddy and corral built into the south side of the next hill. It was almost unnoticeable unless you knew where it was or happened on it by accident. Carlson and three other men had finished unhitching the team and were unloading the wagon. The tiny soddy had to be cramped with four people and the newly arrived provisions. One section of the corral had four horses and another held a dozen longhorn cattle, which Joe wanted to get a closer look at. It was getting cold, but he waited to move until after the men went inside. Joe returned to the bay and rode west and north, then turned back toward the soddy and dismounted on the north side of the hill. He carefully made his way to the corral. Light was starting to fade from the gray sky. It wouldn't be long before the livestock would be difficult to see.

Joe kneeled down above the corral, which was cut into the hill. The front had a gate made of skinny wood rails. He took a leatherbound notepad from his overcoat pocket and jotted down four different brands that he could see without disturbing the cattle. One of the steers let out a loud bawl while he looked over the horses. He didn't see any brands on them. A moment later the cabin door opened, and one of the men, armed with a rifle, came outside to look around. Joe took off his hat, threw it behind him, and hunkered down with his face almost in the snow. The man walked over to the corral, looked around, and leaned the rifle against the gate. He hiked up his coat, unbuttoned his pants, and urinated. When finished, he went back inside. By then the smell of frying pork swirled from the chimney.

It was dark when Joe got back to the bay. He figured that riding easterly would take him to Gracie Flats. He would give the information he had to Sheriff Canfield and let Canfield take care of it from there.

# CHAPTER TWELVE

The men carried in the last crate and piled it in the corner of the tiny soddy. The bundle of branding irons was leaned in a corner. Heat radiated from a small stove, and two oil lamps brightened the inside of the soddy. The men who occupied it were used to the stink of body odor and coal oil. The short, sickly-looking one with a cloth cap dropped four slabs of pork into a frying pan on the stove and went about making coffee.

"Okay, Bob, we're all unloaded. You gonna tell us where Darnell is, or is it still some kinda secret?"

"Ain't no secret. Jus' wanted to get unloaded and in here where it's warm," Carlson said.

"Well, are ya' comfortable 'nuff . . . ?" Peering more closely, the bear-sized man went silent, grabbed a lamp, and held it up to Carlson's face. "What in hell happened to you?"

"Darnell and me, well, we's needin' a woman, bad, you know? So we stopped in Taylorsville," Carlson said.

"You dumb som' bitch, the boss tol' ya' no stops after you snatched the stuff at Loup City. You's to come straight here."

"Luther, I knowed that. It's just that we *really* needed some, been too long," Carlson said. "We's up in the room with the whore doin' our business when this tin star kicks in the door and feeds me the butt stock of his gun. Next thing I knowed, I'm on the floor feelin' starry-eyed, chokin' on my teeth, and then I heared gunshots. One small one and one big one that hurt my head. Musta' been dazed a second, 'cuz when I come to, there's Darnell and his brains was spillin' out on me!"

"Darnell's kilt?" Luther asked. The scrawny cook turned and silently watched for Carlson's answer.

"Christ! Ain't ya' been listenin'? Hell yes, he's kilt," Carlson said. "And then some! Then the tin star drags me to jail, and we wasn't doin' nothin' but our business why we came for in the first place."

"He done that, and you two wasn't doin' nothin' wrong?" asked Luther.

"Swears to God, that's the truth, best I

157

can recollect!"

"Well, we gotta go down there and set that som' bitch straight on a few things," Luther said.

The fourth man had been reclining on the crates, smoking a cigarette and listening to the conversation. Without getting up, he joined in. "We ain't goin' nowhere less the boss says we do. He'll be up here in a day or so to tell us where these steers go. You can tell him about it then."

"We ain't gonna let that tin star get away with that, are we Tyler?" Luther said.

"Until the boss says otherwise. Those two idiots were told not to stop anywhere. What they found was their dumb luck."

"What was that? Did you hear something?" Luther said. The men were silent. The pork sizzling in the pan and some snaps from the fire in the stove were the only sounds.

" 'Less I'm mistaken, that was a steer bellerin', but if you're so worried, maybe you better go check," Tyler said.

Luther pulled on his coat and hat. "Think I will. You better not a' let anybody follow you here, you dumb bastard!"

Carlson shook his head.

Three tiny lights in the distance off to Joe's

right told him he was well north of a town, probably Gracie Flats. From only a nudge to the shoulder with the left boot, the bay turned south. A gentle touch with the spurs moved him into a trot.

Lamps were burning inside the houses Joe passed as he entered town. A dog was barking behind one of them. Farther on were more businesses than houses. From what he could see, the town was barely twice as large as Taylorsville. Most of the businesses were closed, except for the saloons, of course. Joe dismounted at the first one he came to — the sign read J. HOOVER SALOON — and tied up the bay.

He stood on the boardwalk in the light of the window for a minute, to let his eyes adjust before going in. His pocket watch showed almost eight o'clock. The saloon was about half full, and a small man in a white shirt and black vest hammered away on a piano. The man was good, and Joe enjoyed it. He hadn't heard any music for some time. At the bar, he ordered coffee and asked the bartender where he could find the sheriff.

The county courthouse was two blocks east of the saloon. It was a two-story, wood-frame building smaller than Harold and Harvey Martin's hotel. Joe went through a front door and into a narrow hallway. Light came through the door window of only one office. Above the door was a small hanging sign: SHERIFF. He tried the knob, but it was locked. A few knocks brought a man from an inside door that looked like the jail area.

"What is it?"

"Sheriff Canfield?" Joe said, and introduced himself.

"No, I'm his deputy. Sheriff's at supper, be back shortly. Come on in," the man said in a monotone. The deputy wore a tan cloth vest over a blue shirt and red floral tie with a black coat and trousers. He was about thirty and of average size, with what Joe thought was prematurely graying hair. His mustache hung just past the sides of his mouth, and a small patch of hair perched under his lower lip. The deputy was unassuming — in fact there was nothing striking about the man at all, except for his eyes, which seemed to bulge slightly. And the fact that he hardly ever blinked. He looked like he would be right at home in front of a schoolroom chalkboard. A short-barreled revolver with bone handles rested snugly in a cross-draw holster under his suit coat. The handles were of a shape Joe didn't recognize.

Joe could hear some merry singing from

behind the jail door.

The deputy went over and opened it. "Shut up or I'll kick ole' Susanna up between yur' ass cheeks!" he said, in a voice that barely approached a yell. He received a lower volume for his effort.

Push come to shove, Joe wondered if he could actually back up a threat like that.

"Care for some coffee?" the deputy said. The deadpan voice returned.

Joe was about to answer when the front door opened, and another man walked in.

"Sheriff, we got a visitor," the deputy said.

"I'm Joe Mundy, city marshal in Taylorsville," Joe said and extended a hand.

"Wick Canfield, Marshal, heard they hired a new man. Good to meet you. Been trying to get down there. If I had a second deputy . . ." The sheriff pulled off his coat and a brown, wide-brimmed hat and hung them on a rack inside the door. He was as tall as Charlie Oster but not as heavy. The sheriff had a tall forehead and thick black hair that was centered more toward the back of his head. Not quite collar length, wild bunches of it protruded backward giving the effect that he was facing a terrific headwind. His heavy mustache drooped outward and off from the jawline, and the eyebrows each made an upward arch, which offered a permanent look of scrutiny. It looked like his huge hands had seen years of hard work.

"What are ya' doin' up here so late?" Canfield said.

Joe told Canfield the whole story, starting with his killing of one and arrest of the other "freighter" in the Palace Saloon. He finished with the little hideout and corral full of cattle wearing various brands that he found northwest of Gracie Flats.

Now sitting at his desk, Canfield stroked his mustache. He shot a quick glance at his deputy. "We haven't heard of any stock thievin' goin' on 'round here for a spell. You remember any since them was took last fall?"

The deputy shrugged. "Nope." He continued to build a fresh pot of coffee.

"You remember any of the brands?" Canfield said.

"Wrote down a few that I could see without bein' discovered," Joe said. He slipped the little notebook from an inside coat pocket, opened it, and handed it over.

"Hmm, the TO Bar, the Block S, the Lazy 2, the Circle A. Don't recognize any from around here. The Lazy 2 might be up at Long Pine. Budd Jarvis had any stock go missing?" Canfield said. He picked up a pencil and copied the brands down on a piece of paper before he handed the note-book back to Joe.

"Hope not," Joe said.

"You know Jarvis then?"

"He's on the town board. Wasn't very tied to the idea of hiring a new marshal."

"He's got a nice ranch. Little standoffish, but a hard-workin' fellow, I understand," Canfield said. He stood up and walked to a county map tacked to the wall. "Can you point out where you saw 'em?"

Joe studied the map and made a small circle with his index finger in the northwest part of the county. "Ain't exact, but that's close. Not much for landmarks out there. I came across the Calamus River here, where two big trees sit right across from each other, and turned south to get here."

"The irons you saw in the wagon match any of these?" Canfield said and looked at his notes.

"None that I recall," Joe said.

"By God, we'll head out that way at dawn. Appreciate you bringing this to me."

"Be glad to help," Joe said. "There's four of them fellers out there."

"Thanks, but I can get a couple others to ride along to discourage any foolishness," Canfield grinned. "We should be able to pick up your tracks and follow 'em in."

"In that case I better head back," Joe said.

"You goin' back this late? Won't get there 'til three or after," Canfield said. "I can get you a good rate at the hotel."

"Thanks, but I better be gettin' back. Appreciate your time, Sheriff," Joe said.

Other than the noted lack of presence around Taylorsville, Joe thought, the sheriff seemed a diligent sort. But Budd Jarvis seemed to be the only town board member to show any confidence in Canfield. It wasn't Joe's intent, but maybe hiring a new marshal somehow reflected badly on Canfield and the job he'd been doing for the county. If he and Jarvis were friendly, it might explain why Jarvis didn't like Joe.

When Joe tried the door of his office, it was locked. He could see Adam tilted back in his chair, feet on the desk, fast asleep. He used his key and went inside as quietly as he could. The Regulator said 3:25.

"Glad you're back, Marshal," Adam said, his eyes still closed.

"You can see through closed eyes?" Joe asked. Adam smiled and sat up.

"All quiet in town?" Joe said.

"Quiet as a church mouse," Adam said. "Oh, Missus Welby came by to surprise you with a basket supper she cooked, so we, her

164

and I, ate it. Hope you don't mind."

"Course not, Adam. I was only out on the frozen prairie, wind blowin', cold and hungry, no food in sight . . ." Joe's lips turned up slightly at the corners.

Adam hesitated for a moment and then grinned. "Find out where that Carlson went?"

"Followed him north across the river a spell where him and three others have a soddy northwest of Gracie Flats. They had some cattle there, and the place looked more like a hideout than anything else. Told Sheriff Canfield about it."

Joe pulled the cavalry Colt from his left side, placed it on the table, and hung his gun belt on the peg next to his bed. It felt good to pull off the boots and vest and stretch out for some sleep.

"Help yourself to a bunk in the cell, Adam," Joe said.

"Don't mind if I do."

It seemed to Joe that he had just drifted off to sleep when knocking on the front office door woke him. Wondering at first who it could be at that hour, he gradually pulled himself up. He glanced out and saw Siegler standing there with his nose pressed against the glass. Joe was too tired to care that he was in stocking feet and shirtsleeves when unlocking the door. The cell was empty, and the Regulator said it was 9:03.

"Morning, Joe. Long night?"

"Might say it was a short one," Joe said. "Coffee? I see Adam made some already." Siegler sat quietly as Joe filled him in on the night's activities, including his visit with Sheriff Canfield.

"Hope he looks into it. Sometimes I think the great sheriff has grown too important for the likes of us. And, I might be a bit hard on the man. He does have only one deputy. Well, you told him what you found, up to him what he does about it," Siegler said.

"How long's he been sheriff?" Joe said.

"About two years. I guess he went broke ranching down at Plum Creek before that. Remember I said you might hear from Jarvis? Well, our regular board meeting is at my place at ten. He wants you there. Don't know his intentions, but I guess I'll see you there."

Joe rinsed his face in the wash basin and dried with an old towel. After the clean shirt, vest, and boots, he strapped on the gun belt and replaced the cavalry Colt in his waistband. He knew he'd find out what Jarvis wanted soon enough, so he didn't dwell on it during the walk down the street. The air was brisk, and no thawing of snow was evident.

Harold Martin, Budd Jarvis, and Byron Siegler were seated around the small table by the stove that usually held a checker game. Harold had a ledger book in front of him, and Byron was looking over some papers.

"Gentlemen," Joe said, and sat down in the extra chair beside Harold. Byron and Harold greeted him in return. Joe noticed Judge Worden, Christmas Evans, and two other men he didn't know leaning against the long counter.

"We'll call the meeting to order," Siegler said. "We have a few items of general business to cover, but we'll start with Budd, who has something he wants to say."

"What I got to say is on the actions of our new marshal. He's been here less than a month and already killed a man. We had no killin' here before he came, and then he beats the man's partner half to death and arrests him. Then he lets him go for lack of charges. If that's not enough, he beats Smiley in his own establishment for no reason at all. What kind of example is that for the town marshal to set? I'll tell you. He shows us the kind of example he sets by taking a whore to a meal at the hotel, and then to church! Why, the women are so disgusted by all these actions that they want him gone, pronto!"

Siegler could see Joe stiffen and his face reddening and gave him an almost undetectable shake of his head.

"Are any of the women coming in to complain, Budd?" Siegler said.

"What? Hell no, they won't, you know that!" Jarvis said. "They complained to me as a member of the town board."

"Harold, have you received any complaints on Marshal Mundy?" Siegler asked.

"Huh, well. Some of those ladies, well, you know, about the . . . ah, Missus Welby taking a meal in the hotel," Harold said.

"Don't you have a complaint about that, Harold?" Jarvis asked and stared at him.

Harold squirmed in his chair and checked each face at the table. When he met Joe's stare, he quickly turned back. "Well, no. I'm in business. Be foolish to turn down business."

"Joe, can you account for the . . . uh . . . incident with Smiley, uh, Mister Wilkie?" Siegler said.

"He asked me to pay for a room cleanin', and I had to point out the error of his thinkin' in not summoning help for Lucy when she was gettin' beat. He was a little slow on the uptake at first."

"So you beat him?" Jarvis said.

Siegler nodded for Joe to answer him.

"I slapped him a couple times to aid him with the understandin' process," Joe said.

"Did Mister Wilkie complain to you, Budd, or, Harold?" Harold shook his head.

"No, but I was told by two of my boys what he done to him," Jarvis said.

"In that case, I will say, it was not in town's best interest to handle Mister Wilkie's . . . lack of understanding, in that manner, and I'd ask Marshal Mundy to refrain from physical violence unless necessary," Siegler said. "As for the killing and the arrest of the deceased's partner, Judge Worden, could you address that?"

"He beat Miz Lucy at the Palace, but she declined to testify against the man afterward. That's why I ordered the marshal to release him from custody."

"And as to the complaint of Missus Welby attending church, have you a complaint about that, Pastor Evans?"

"Goodness gracious, no. All of God's children are welcome in the Lord's house, and if I may —"

"Thank you, Pastor, that's all we need for now," Siegler said.

"Yesterday, Mundy left town and his duties, poking his nose in business outside of town limits. I motion to fire Mundy as city marshal," Jarvis said.

Joe could see that Siegler was exasperated with Jarvis, but did his best to give an even accounting of his protests.

"Budd, Joe told me before he left what he was doing and that he would be back later in the night. I had no objection with that," Siegler said. "His actions were aimed at possibly avoiding further problems from those folks here in town. I vote no firing, there being no grounds for such a move. Harold?"

Harold shook his head, "No, for firing." He carefully avoided Jarvis's eyes and made notes in the book.

"Motion fails on two to one vote against firing," Siegler said.

"If that's all that pertains to me, I have work to do," Joe said. He met Jarvis's stare as he stood and walked out. The store was silent except for Joe's spurs raking across the wooden floor. He accepted the dressing down that Siegler had given him, but knew he would deal with Smiley the same way if it happened again. It seemed to Joe that Sheriff Canfield might have voiced a complaint to Budd about sticking his nose in county business. Canfield let on like they weren't close, but maybe they were. Joe wondered if a rider could have followed him back to town — a rider who talked to Budd or someone else.

# CHAPTER THIRTEEN

The low eastern sun made the white barren landscape sparkle as far as the eye could see. The only sound for miles was the hooves of two horses crunching through the snow. The horses puffed clouds of vapor with nearly every step. When they stopped, the riders looked down at their destination. It was time to signal as they approached.

"Hello the camp!"

A few moments later a man stepped out of the soddy and waved his hat.

"Good to see ya', boss," the cook said, and took their horses.

The men inside didn't have a chance for a greeting.

"Let's play a guessin' game, shall we?" the big man said as soon as he and his partner entered. His partner carried a sawed-off shotgun pointed at the roof.

Luther and Carlson looked at each other. Tyler watched the boss.

"Guess who followed the professor here, right back to this spot?" He nodded at Carlson.

"Too hard for you? How about this. If you dumb bastards go up behind the corral, guess whose footprints you'll find?" Luther and Carlson looked at each other again. "After bein' here and findin' this place, guess who came to my office last night and told me all about it?" Everyone was silent. "You buncha' dumb bastards! The answer is, the same person that splattered Darnell's brains on the wall of a whore's crib in Taylorsville."

"That tin star in Taylorsville?" Luther asked.

"Well, hell, we have us a damn winner! How 'bout explaining yourself, Carlson? Since Darnell can't add to the conversation!"

Carlson's bruised, puffy face turned pale.

"I'm waiting. I'm waiting to hear why you stopped in that town when you were told to come straight here. I remember telling you good, so's you'd hear me and understand. I know you did, 'cuz you and Darnell both said you did. So, that means that you just decided ol' Wick didn't know what the hell he was talking about. That about it, Robert?"

Carlson looked faint. "Uh, na, no, Mister Canfield, that ain't it at all . . ."

"Why don't you tell me what *it* is then, Robert."

"Wah, wah, well, I was tellin' the boys here," he motioned with his hand to each of his pals to stall the inevitable haranguing he knew was coming. "We both had such a horn on, we had to stop for a dip. It was just eatin' us fierce. I didn't mean for Darnell to go gettin' kilt," Carlson said. "And that damned marshal threatened to kill me if I set foot back there too!"

"I don't give buffalo shit about Darnell, you dumb ass! That tin star *knows* about this place now and suspects you all as cattle thieves!"

"Bah, but, boss, we *is* cattle thieves," Carlson said.

Canfield slowly shook his head. "You couldn't track a fat squaw through a snowdrift, could ya?"

Because of the silence that followed, Carlson thought he was expected to answer.

"Wah, well, yeah, if she was fat enough, I —"

Canfield looked at his deputy. "Shoot him!"

The deputy lowered and cocked a barrel of the shotgun in one smooth motion. The blast shook dirt loose from the roof of the soddy, and it streaked downward onto them all. Carlson lunged backward into the stove and knocked the chimney pipe loose. He came to rest face down on the dirt floor.

"There ends today's lesson. Any questions?" Canfield said.

# CHAPTER FOURTEEN

Steam drifted upward from the tub water. The warmth soaked deeply into the parts of Joe that were in it. A person could either slide down into the water so it covered the torso and expose most of the legs, or sit up and cover most of the legs and not the torso, but not both. Not unless one was *very* short. The four-foot-long bathtub was made of heavy tin with a wooden bottom. It was painted blue on the outside and adorned with a narrow gilt stripe.

The bathing room had no windows and was about eight feet square. Heat was not evident, but as long as the tub water was hot, it was comfortable. Entry was through a door in the hallway, but the door off the kitchen made it easy for the cook to carry in a bucket of boiling water straight from the stove. In addition to the tub, wooden boxes and small barrels were stacked against the walls, and canned foods occupied six shelves of the storeroom.

Joe's gunbelt and both Colts rested on a chair next to the tub. A fifty-cent payment had been tendered to Harvey Martin, who let him use the tub normally reserved only for hotel guests. As it was late, there wouldn't be any conflict with guests.

He finished scrubbing with lye soap and leaned back to relax a few minutes. Thoughts drifted in and out, but one caught, and he centered on it. Lute Kinney.

Joe didn't look forward to the prospect, but if there was ever anyone in desperate need of killing, it was Kinney. He pictured Thad and Callie Green walking out of their cabin on the Neosho River to see what Lute Kinney wanted. They knew him and who he worked for and no doubt expected more foul talk and threats.

Joe knew that there had been hard feelings between Hobe Ranswood and the Greens since the court battle over the land that they had settled on, and he knew of no other reason for paying them a call. It was simple — Ranswood wanted them to abandon their land. He sent Kinney to convince them to leave.

Callie evidently had the baby in her arms. No doubt Thad wasn't armed. They weren't the violent type. Joe believed the only gun

Thad owned was a muzzle-loading rifle that he used for hunting. The words exchanged were lost, but the actions were witnessed. Kinney pulled out one of his Smith & Wesson revolvers and shot Thad in the face and then shot the baby in the head. Callie would have screamed as she ran back to the cabin, covered in her baby's blood, before the final bullet tore into her back. Charlie Oster's words came back to Joe like a recurring nightmare, *I ain't never seen no worse.* Oster had tried repeatedly to find a Wanted flyer on Kinney, and even wired the Pinkerton National Detective Agency in Chicago, but with no luck.

Unfortunately, though, for Kinney, his murders were witnessed by Doc Whelan, who easily knew him by sight, having stitched up a stab wound to Kinney's leg on one occasion. Kinney had picked a fight with a gambler and knocked him down with a whiskey bottle, slicing the man's scalp. The gambler, on his hands and knees, drove a knife into Kinney's leg. Kinney had pulled a pistol and shot him in the forehead. The court had ruled self-defense.

Kinney was a predator who killed without hesitation, for more than just survival. From the talk Joe had heard, the man was oblivious to danger, or maybe *needed it.* Some thought he was from Missouri or Arkansas. Other than being employed by Hobe Ranswood, that was all that was known of Lute Kinney. And now Joe had the honor of being his prey. Valuable prey. Joe wondered when Kinney would arrive in Willow Springs and who would direct him to Taylorsville. Considering riding time, he should have arrived by now.

The water started to turn chilly so Joe got out of the tub. He was expected at Sarah's house and looked forward to the visit. No silver dollars needed.

"I thought you'd stop by yesterday to celebrate. I bought this special," Sarah said. She held up a small bottle of brandy and smiled.

"It wasn't your birthday, was it?"

Sarah shook her head. "For your information, Marshal Mundy, we're in the second day of a brand new year. Eighteen-seventy-seven, can you believe it?"

"Plum forgot about that. I guess it is. Was gone trailin' Carlson and then rode to Gracie Flats," Joe said.

"And I brought a dinner to the office, and you weren't there, so Adam and I ate it. He was very good company. Read some to me from his book."

"He told me. If I knew you were comin'
. . ." Joe said.

"You'd still have rode off following that
man, right?"

"S'pose so."

She poured and handed Joe a tumbler.
"To the new year and better times." Joe
touched his glass against hers and downed
the brandy.

"No, no, no! This ain't whiskey. You're
supposed to sip brandy and enjoy it!"

"Oh," Joe said. He held the tumbler out
with both hands. "Please, may I have another?" She smiled at his poor English accent and poured.

"That was pitiful." She held up the bottle
and walked toward the bedroom. "How
about we start on those better times?"

"To better times."


Joe enjoyed lying next to Sarah after sex
*almost* as much as the act itself. Troubles
seemed far away. He liked it when she slid
her bare leg over his, and he liked the feel
of her skin under his hands.

"Tell me about you. I don't even know
where you were born, or when you came
out here or . . ."

"Okay. I was born on a farm in Indiana.
My sister and I helped mother in the house,

180

and my brother fed the chickens and pigs. Had a pony to ride for awhile."

"When did you meet George?" Joe asked.

Sarah was silent for several moments. Joe wondered if she was reflecting on bad, or maybe good, memories. Then he began to wonder if she was going to answer him at all. Finally she spoke. "For a couple years our farm served as a stage stop. His family lived about three miles west of ours, and one time he came through on his way home."

"Fell in love on the spot?"

"Not exactly, but we married when I was eighteen. Father walked in on us one evening in our barn, at an awkward time."

"George offered to marry you then?" Joe said.

"Father offered him to marry me or else."

"How'd you end up here?" He kissed her on the forehead.

"George wanted to be a lawyer. Parents all gave us what money they could, and we moved to St. Louis, where he worked in his uncle's law office. George couldn't handle being cooped up in an office, so we moved to Omaha, and he took a job on the railroad. That didn't work, either. He heard this new town was going to need a marshal, so here we are."

"Do you know why he lit out without sayin' nothin'?" Joe said.

"Next time I see him, I'll ask." Sarah's tone was coated in sarcasm. Joe thought he'd like to ask him, too, but at the same time was glad he'd left.

"Just because I'm tellin' you all this don't mean that anything's changed in what I have to do, you know, to earn a living."

"Never occurred to me that it would," Joe said. He felt the atmosphere cool.

"I talked to Judge Worden, and he said he'd help me to dissolve the marriage legally. He said that it could be done on the grounds of abandonment."

Joe thought he heard a bit of sadness in her voice. "That's good. Glad to hear it," he said. "Is that him?" He pointed to a framed photograph on the wall, wondering at the same time why she hadn't taken it down yet.

"Yes. Taken when we were in St. Louis."

"I guess a woman would consider him smart-lookin'."

"George was the best-looking man I've ever seen. Course, that doesn't beat a manly ruggedness," Sarah said and smiled at Joe.

Joe ignored the smile. "You still love him?"

A few too many moments passed before she answered. "Loved that bastard a long time."

Joe left Sarah's house about one-thirty and decided to walk through town before turning in for the night. He pulled his collar up to block a frigid breeze as he crunched through the snow. When he approached Doc Sullivan's house, he saw lights on, and as he got closer could see the doctor moving about inside.

When Sullivan opened the door, Joe said, "Saw the lights on, Doc."

"Come on in, Joe. Just going to have some coffee, I'll get another cup."

"Keepin' late hours, aren't you?" Joe's question had just left his lips when he heard crying in the patient room.

"Sanderson's six-year-old is very sick. The missus brought her in yesterday and is staying with her," Sullivan explained. "Excuse me." He got up and went into the patient room. While the door was open, Joe could see Missus Sanderson holding the little girl's hand and daubing a cloth on her forehead with the other hand. Sullivan slipped the thermometer out of her mouth and examined it. When he returned to his seat at the small dining room table, Joe saw wrinkles around the doctor's eyes that he hadn't noticed before.

"Her temperature is up to a hundred and two." Sullivan sipped at his cup, and they both listened to the little girl wail. Education aside, Joe could see how difficult a doctor's life could be.

"What's wrong with her, Doc?" Joe said.

"First thought maybe typhoid, but I'm bettin' on influenza," He said. "Had some experience with it back east, and I think that's what we have here. On that occasion I helped care for twenty-four with the sickness, and seven of them died."

"Is that worse than typhoid?" Joe asked.

"Neither is good. As long as there's no complications, a person *can* survive. It can be very serious, but they can survive." Joe thought the Doc was trying to talk himself into believing it.

"But . . ." Sullivan's words stopped, and he looked down into his coffee. "The very young and older people have a tougher time with it. And if there's an outbreak —"

"Doc!" Missus Sanderson screamed.

Sullivan hurried back into the room and came back a few minutes later carrying a bloody cloth. "Complications." He poured hot water into a pan and rinsed the cloth.

"Doc, is there anything I can do, or go get for you?" Joe stood up preparing to leave.

"Any extra prayers would be good about now, Joe," Sullivan said. He went back into the room, and Joe headed to his office.

The next morning Joe went down to the North Star for coffee. The saloon seemed to be an informal meeting place before businesses opened up for the day. It was a chance to share gossip and news as well as coffee.

Joe closed the door behind him and saw Byron Siegler, Harvey Martin, Budd Jarvis, Christmas Evans, and Gib Hadley, owner of the North Star, seated at the second table.

"Mornin', Marshal, I'll get you a cup." Hadley served Joe and sat down again. The others, except Jarvis, greeted Joe and continued their conversation. Something in the *Omaha Daily Bee* seemed to be the topic for the morning.

"I still say it stinks to high heaven, excuse me, Pastor, but stinks just the damn same. Governor Hayes is a veteran of the late war and he won fair and square. Why don't they commence with swearin' him in?" Hadley pounded a fist on the table.

"It sounds like some of those Southern states don't know how to count their votes correctly. What do they want to do, keep recountin' 'em 'til they turn out how they want 'em?" Martin said. "I agree with Gib, it stinks."

"I recollect like it was yesterday, our ironclad, ringing like a bell from hell, the ringing in our damned ears never stopped. The *Carondelet* was sneaking by Island Number Ten, but the reb batteries saw us when our stacks caught afire, marking us like glowing ducks in a pond," Hadley said.

Jarvis said, "Gib, just what in hell does that have to do with anything we're talkin' about here?"

"The war. Somebody mentioned the war!"

"I believe *you did,* Gib, if you don't mind me pointing that out," Martin said. Hadley's head twitched slightly as he ignored Martin.

"According to this," Siegler said, his right forefinger slid across the page. "Governor Tilden won the popular vote. It's the electoral votes that are in question."

"Samuel Tilden is a scoundrel of the highest order!" Evans said. His tone rose all the way to the end, and then he raised his eyebrows as if he'd surprised himself. The men looked over at him, expecting a sermon of some sort to follow.

"Pastor, do you know something we don't?" Siegler said.

"I was still in New York back in sixty-eight, and that skunk was state Democratic chairman. He allowed his illustrious members to engage in fraudulent voting schemes."

"What did they do to him, Pastor?" Martin asked.

"They were unable to prove up the charges, I'm afraid."

Siegler continued, "It appears that a special commission has been appointed to settle the matter."

"Governor Hayes fought in the war and was wounded several times. I do not recall any such service, meritorious or other, on the part of that scalawag Tilden!" Evans said. "I do not believe he is the type of man we want as our president!"

"Why, Pastor, I do believe we found a subject outside of the Almighty that raises a rankle," Gib said. The men laughed.

"Chortle to your hearts' content, gentlemen, as I assure you, your joviality will become a rare commodity, indeed, with that one leading the country!" Evans said.

Before the last chuckle died out, a young boy ran into the saloon. "I found a man in the street. He looks dead! Come quick!" All faces turned to Joe as he stood and followed the boy.

"What the hell now?" Jarvis demanded for

Joe's benefit. The rest of the men followed Joe and the boy.

Straight north of the saloon, at the edge of the town's boundary, a man lay face down in the middle of the street. The North Star group gathered around to look. It seemed to have cooled down even more after the sun came up, and the men's breaths were visible.

"See, Marshal, I told you!" The wide-eyed boy stood pointing a sharp index finger.

Joe turned the rigid body over on its back. The blue skin and coating of frost made it obvious the man was dead. The massive blood stains on his shirt made it certain that he'd met a violent end. The mangled hands and several missing fingers indicated a futile attempt to block the attack. There was no blood or tissue of any kind on the road. The body had been dumped there. Joe recognized him immediately, but Siegler beat him to the announcement.

"Joe, isn't that the man you had in jail. What was his name?"

"Yeah. Robert Carlson." He squatted and looked over the body.

"Son, would you go fetch the undertaker for me?" Joe asked.

"Sure thing, Marshal, right away!" The

boy turned and sprinted across the back lots.

Harvey Martin turned pale and stepped back. "I better be getting back to the hotel."

"So, this would be the man you supposedly followed on your little trip out of town?" Jarvis's tone was accusatory. "Did you decide you'd give him the justice you figured he wrangled out of? That it?"

"Budd, that's enough jumping to conclusions. Joe didn't kill this man. He followed him to a hideout, then rode to Gracie Flats and told Sheriff Canfield about it," Siegler said.

"That's what he *said.* Did you see him follow this man?" Jarvis said.

"You know I didn't, and I won't continue this conversation! Feel free to ask Canfield if you ever see him around."

"How many times was he shot?" Hadley said.

"Shotgun, maybe just once," Joe said. He was glad to ignore Jarvis's ranting.

Except for Siegler, the men turned away, one by one, and walked back toward Main Street. Hadley turned back to take one last look. Christmas Evans had remained silent. Jarvis brought up the rear of the entourage.

Siegler glanced down the street to make sure the others were out of hearing distance.

"Joe, look me in the eyes and tell me you had nothing to do with this man's death, please."

"You, too, Mister Siegler?" Joe said.

"The only reason I ask, if you remember, I was in your office the day you let him go. And . . . uh, you threatened to kill him! Did you mean it?"

"Don't joke about somethin' like that. But, I said I'd kill him if he came back to Taylorsville, and he didn't. Not 'til now." Joe stood up and looked directly at Siegler. "I didn't kill him, Mister Siegler. Would have if he'd come back alive."

"That's good enough for me, Joe. I guess." Siegler looked down the street again and saw the undertaker driving his wagon toward them. "Who do you suppose did him in? And why drop him here?"

"I'd guess his cronies weren't happy with Robert drawing attention to themselves in town, and losing a man, I s'pose," Joe said. "Why they dropped him here is a good question."

## CHAPTER FIFTEEN

That afternoon Joe walked down to Mac-Nab's to see Robert Carlson's corpse. The undertaker, Iain MacNab, was a tiny man with flaming red hair and beard. He'd started his business in Iowa before moving it to Taylorsville. As in many other towns, the business of furniture making and funeral directing were often a combined enterprise. The sign painted directly on the front of the building read FURNITURE MAKER, with UNDERTAKER below in smaller letters. It was the last building at the east end of Main Street. A coffin displayed in one of the front windows, along with a small table and chairs, made a somewhat curious offering for window shoppers.

Joe entered the narrow store and walked past the completed furniture, through a shop area, and into a back room. Inside, Carlson's body lay on a wooden table stained over the years by body fluids. Without his clothes, and with the blood washed away, the body was an odd combination of colors. The torso, legs, and arms were lily white, while his face, neck, and hands were dark-toned. His mouth was partially open, and Joe could see several broken and missing teeth, on the top as well as the bottom row. Some dried blood was still evident around his mouth. Carlson's chest area looked like it was caved in. It had large chunks of skin missing, and semicircular edges could be seen at the border of the largest wound. A couple of pellets had spread out, making their own holes. It was a shotgun blast all right, at fairly close range. Death would have been quick. The final week of Robert Carlson's life had been a tough one.

MacNab told Joe that he had agreed with Siegler's request to use the cheapest pine box he had, since the town was paying for the burial. The funeral would take place the next day in the small cemetery behind the church, and Pastor Evans had insisted on saying a few words.

Joe was glad that Carlson hadn't been killed in town, because then he would have been obligated to try and find his killer. Still, he was a lawman, and a murder had been committed somewhere. The best guess was still that Carlson's buddies at the hideout did him in. With any luck, Sheriff Canfield and his posse may have them locked away in his jail by now. Joe would send word to him and see if any of his prisoners would 'fess up to killing Carlson. That would be a good chore for Adam.

Joe wrote a letter to Sheriff Canfield that Carlson's body had been dumped, that a shotgun had killed him, and asked him to see if he could get the dead man's associates to confess. Adam left for Gracie Flats on Siegler's Appaloosa in the early afternoon with the letter. He was expected back by ten o'clock.

That done, Joe walked the town, saw Sarah for a few minutes, and headed to the North Star. Gib Hadley usually had beans and bacon available if folks wanted something to eat with their drinks, but on this night he was offering fried liver and bacon. Joe had a plate with some beer.

After finishing dinner, Joe headed to the Palace. He walked to the end of the bar and leaned an elbow on it as usual. Smiley gave Joe a withering look when he came in and continued wiping off the whiskey bottles he was pulling from a crate. Most of the tables were occupied, two with poker games in progress. Joe glanced again at Smiley, who now was looking at the crowd. Smiley's grin showed up on his mouth but not on the rest of his face. When he chuckled, Joe looked back over at the tables and saw Lucy picking herself up from the floor. Joe had seen her sitting at a table when he came in. After getting to her feet, she walked between the tables, bumping into each chair back as she went. She had a hard time keeping her balance and forced a smile with each step. The flimsy low-cut dress exposed most of her breasts. She tripped on a chair leg and almost fell again. One of the few cowhands who wasn't laughing caught her arm and kept her from falling.

"How much has she had to drink?" Joe asked.

Smiley's grin ceased when he heard Joe's question. "Why, Marshal, she ain't had a drop all day." Part of his grin reappeared. "That's the God's honest truth, too. She's a bit wobbly on her feet, but as luck would have it, she's steady on her back." He stepped away from the bar and out of reach as he said it.

"You son-of-a-bitch." As Joe left the bar and headed toward Lucy, he heard Smiley again.

"You ain't got no call to curse me like

that!" Smiley was grinning again.

"Lucy, come and sit down with me a minute, like to talk to you." Joe took her arm, and they walked to an empty table. She bumped into three chairs as they went.

"Want to do some business, Marshal?" Lucy asked. "Only a buck. But I owe you, I'd do you for free if ya' want?" She looked hopeful.

"No, Lucy, no thanks. I wanted to see how you were gettin' along. You know, how you're feelin'," Joe said.

Her eyes filled with tears, and she looked down. "I'm doin' better all the time, Marshal. On a good day, I don't fall down but twice." Her voice was thick with emotion. She raised her head and looked at Joe. The tears streaked down both cheeks.

"Have you talked to Doc Sullivan lately?" Joe said.

"This mornin', a checkup, down there, ya' know." Lucy pointed to her lap and wiped the tears away with the back of her hand.

"Did he say anything about the dizziness or your eyesight?"

"Not much. He doesn't know if it will ever get better." She forced a smile and looked at Joe. "I know, you're probably mad because I didn't go through with charges —"

"Don't worry about that," Joe interrupted.

"No, let me finish. I know it was the right thing to do, but I don't have anywhere to go. Smiley would have fired me. He told me."

"It's okay, Lucy. Both those animals got their comeuppance, after a fashion. The other one is laying out at MacNab's," Joe informed her.

She looked him in the eye. "Did you . . . ?"

"Did I kill him? No. But both of 'em are dead now, so you can put that behind you."

"Can't put all of it behind me, can I? I better get back to work."

"Where you from Lucy?" Joe asked.

This brought more tears and she wiped them away with the back of each hand. "Small town in Mississippi, just below Memphis."

"Any family there?"

"My daddy and brothers drowned in the big river when their raft broke up. Momma died havin' me. Ain't nobody else left."

Joe had hoped that he could figure out someone to take Lucy and care for her. Now he regretted asking.

"Here, for your time. Give Smiley one, and you keep the rest," Joe said. He slid four silver dollars across the table.

Lucy looked at him and started to say

something.

"Gotta finish my rounds. Let me know if you need anything." Joe watched her squint and paw repeatedly near each coin before she found them and picked them up.

# CHAPTER SIXTEEN

"He the one, Luther? In the black hat and coat with the whore? Can't see no badge on him. Is that him?"

"Keep your voice down, Cookie," Luther warned. "Yeah, that's him. Seen him once before when I was playing cards at the North Star. I was bilkin' some dumb farmer real good 'til he got mad. The marshal buffaloed 'im and we had to haul 'im down to the jail." Luther grinned. He sipped beer from his mug and watched Joe and Lucy three tables away.

"We friends, ain't we, Luther? I been thinkin', listen to me, just listen and see if I don't make sense," Cookie said in a low voice. Luther looked at him and waited.

"Maybe the boss won't be mad at us no longer if we kilt the marshal, but that's odds I ain't particular fond of. I don't want the boss or his damned deputy shootin' me for no reason like they done Carlson. Instead of killin' this tin star, let's go tell 'im we saw them kill Carlson right in front of us. That way, he'd go arrest *them* for murderin' Bob, and we won't have to worry about 'em no more."

"Cookie, are you drunk? You think that tin star could arrest Canfield and his deputy? And besides that, we'd have to testify on what we seen."

"I thought about that, too," Cookie said. "Listen, if we kilt the marshal, the law would be after us, maybe not the sheriff, but somebody would come after us, since it'd be a lawman we kilt. But, instead of doin' that, the two of us could testify, and they'd hang them two, and our worries would be over. Hell, the marshal cain't pin any thievin' on us without proof."

Luther stared at his friend and took a long swig of beer. He lowered his head and looked at the table top. "Sure wish I had some of your corn dodgers right about now." He rubbed his chin whiskers. "Might make sense. I sure don't like thinkin' about watchin' my backside all the time, expectin' the law to catch up."

"It does make sense, Luther. Why in hell ya' think Tyler lit out and went back to Montana where he come from? Tell me that," Cookie said. "He lit out 'cuz he didn't want to get shot for no reason by the boss, neither."

Luther chewed at the stub of a fingernail and watched Joe walk out of the saloon.

"Okay, but we'll stay here 'til nine or so. There's an outhouse behind the marshal's office. We'll hide out in it 'til there ain't no folks movin' around. Then we'll knock on the back door of the office and go in without bein' seen and tell him what we know."

"That's fine, jus' fine. I know'd you'd see it my way," Cookie said with a triumphant grin.

"Right now, I'm gonna go have me one with Lucy. Got this dollar I swiped from Tyler 'fore he left." Luther held it up and grinned.

It had only been ten minutes when Luther came back downstairs and returned to their table.

"Wooeee! That was a quick one!" Cookie laughed.

"Shut the hell up, will ya'?" Luther said.

"Shit, Luther, my mood is usually improved afterward. What the hell's wrong?"

"She uses that middle room," Luther said and pointed. "Soon as we walks in, I see a chunk of the wall busted, and there's a big stain. Looks like it's been scrubbed some, but the stain is still there."

"What are ya' talkin' about, Luther? Ya' do your business or not?"

"Hell, no, I didn't! I tried, but once it hit me what that stain was, my wood was limper'n a cooked noodle," Luther said, and downed his warm beer.

"Oh." A look of realization had crossed Cookie's face.

Joe returned to the office after finishing his rounds and relaxed at the desk with a glass of whiskey. The Regulator said 9:30, and he expected Adam to return at any time.

Rereading Charlie's letter served two purposes. First, to consider Lute Kinney, but most of all, it seemed that he found comfort in reading his old friend's letter. His former boss was the only man Joe could remember that he both trusted and respected, other than his father. His commanding officer at Shiloh came close, but Charlie Oster filled the entire bill. *It wouldn't be bad to have him at my side these days, that's for sure. Until Kinney was dealt with at least.*

It was a few minutes before ten o'clock when Joe heard a light knocking at the back door. He slid the cavalry Colt into the front of his trousers and stopped to listen. Whoever it was knocked again. Joe couldn't imagine Lute Kinney precipitating an attack this way, knocking on the back door of the office late at night, but he wasn't taking any chances. He grabbed two brass shells from the desk and pulled down the ten-gauge. After glancing up and down the street through the front windows, he walked to the back door.

"Who's out there?"

"Uh, uh, name's Luther, Marshal. We need to talk to you private, why we came to the back door." The voice was low, almost a whisper.

"Who's we, how many?" Joe said.

"There's jus' me and Cookie, that's all. Can we come in Marshal, 'fore someone sees us?"

"What is it ya' want?" Joe hadn't heard Kinney talk enough to recognize his voice.

"Uh, we know who kilt Bob Carlson, Marshal. We don't want nobody seein' us talkin' to you. Can we come in?"

Joe wondered if this was a trap of some kind. But he was tired of playing games. If these folks, whoever they were, came looking for trouble, they'd find it. He lifted the crossbar from the door, leaned it against the wall, and stepped back. Joe cocked both hammers, and with the ten-gauge at his shoulder, he spoke. "It's unlocked. Come in slowly with your hands out front where I can see 'em. If I don't see 'em, the ball will open!"

The latch snapped, and the door gradually opened. Two hands came through first and then the large grubby-looking man who was connected to them. "Jeesus!" His head ducked reflexively when he saw the shotgun.

"Keep them hands high. They go below shoulder level, this'll be the last thing you ever see," Joe said. The man stepped aside so his friend could enter.

"I'm Luther, Luther Brennan. This is Cookie Jones."

Cookie gasped when he stepped into view of the shotgun. "Marshal, them look like two well pipes stuck together!"

"You boys heeled?" Joe said.

"Oh uh, Marshal, we are. Plum forgot about 'em."

"You first, Luther, slowly with your fingers, drop it in that bucket, then you, Cookie."

They did as they were told and noticed Joe wrinkle his nose and sniff the air.

"Oh, uh, sorry about the smell, we been waitin' in the privy 'til there weren't no one movin' about," Luther explained.

"That the gun you blasted Darnell with, Marshal?" Cookie asked.

"If you mean the cur upstairs at the Palace Saloon, it is. There's chairs over here, sit," Joe said, and motioned them over in front of his desk.

"If ya' wouldn't mind considerable, Marshal, could we stay back here behind the cage, out of sight?" Luther said.

Joe lowered the shotgun and uncocked it. "Okay. What is it you want to tell me?"

Apparently Luther had agreed to be the speaker. "We know who kilt Carlson, but first we want your word on somethin'."

"What?" Joe said.

"We'll testify whenever you call on us, but we don't want to be locked up in a cage. Be too easy gettin' kilt bein' caged like a chicken. We can stay hid right here in town, but nobody 'cept you knows where. Your word?"

"Where you boys gonna be?"

"Oh, uh, okay." Luther looked at Cookie. "Ya' know that little shack the hermit died in last summer?"

"Before my time."

"Oh, uh, it's out behind the undertaker's. A lean-to off the shed he keeps his wagon and horse in," Luther said. "He lets us use it when we come in."

"Let's hear it," Joe said.

Luther and Cookie looked at each other.

Luther commenced to telling how he was standing right beside Carlson when he was killed.

"Sheriff Canfield and his deputy killed him? That's your story? You two drunk?"

"Ha! I asked Cookie that same thing when he said we should tell you about this. God's truth, Marshal, 'cept the sheriff didn't kill Carlson, he told his deputy to do it . . . and he did, just like that!" Luther snapped his finger to emphasize the point.

"I was there, too, when it happened, Marshal," Cookie added. Joe felt like shooting them for being too ignorant to live. What kind of fool did they take him for? Maybe the cell they were standing behind would be the place for them until he sorted out their tale.

"I believe the story is more likely to be they came to arrest you fellas for rustling others' cattle, ain't that right?"

"Arrest us?" Both men looked at each other and laughed. "If they had come to arrest us, we'd be arrested, but we ain't. Been workin' for 'im for nearly two year, why would he arrest us? He was mad at Carlson for him and Darnell causin' the ruckus here in town —"

Cookie interrupted. "And Carlson kept sayin' dumb things that plum angered the sheriff. I think that's why he killed 'im."

"Shut up, Cookie, I'm the one —"

"Well, ya' wasn't tellin' every —"

"Enough!" Joe said, derailing the squabble. "What do you mean you was workin' for him?"

"Well, we come from the Gracie Flats jail, let out by the sheriff once we had an agreement. We'd swipe some critters out a ways and drive them to the holding pen. Sometimes horses, sometimes cattle, or maybe both. We'd get a corral full and sell 'em. The sheriff would get a cut for letting us stay clear of jail."

"What were you locked up for?" Joe was trying to figure if anything they said was true. One thing, though, if Canfield and his deputy had gone to arrest them, he supposed they'd be in jail.

"Well, we had a little fight at the Hoover saloon, with a feller from back east who thought he was gonna be a boxin' champ or something. In the alley, he wanted to take on all four of us, and things got out of hand, and we knocked him around some. Seems he wasn't so tough. The feller died, and that's how we ended up in jail," Luther said.

"Who's the fourth one?" Joe said.

"That was Tyler. He lit out right after they kilt Carlson 'cuz he didn't want to end up that way, neither. That's why we come to you," Cookie said. "We don't want them killin' us for no reason. Fact has it, we lean toward them not killin' us at all."

"We're more afraid of Canfield than we is of you, Marshal," Luther said.

"So you boys are admitting to rustling cattle?" He knew he wasn't able to identify those at the hideout, except for Carlson.

"Marshal, all due respect and all, but you'd need proof, and there ain't none. Them critters are gone. It's just what we said, betwixt the three of us here. And if you arrest us, we'd say we never said any such thing, ain't that right, Cookie?" Cookie nodded, his eyes on Joe.

"So you figure that if the sheriff and his deputy are put away, you don't have to worry about them killin' you?"

"That's it! Ya' hit the nail right on the head," Luther said.

Joe didn't think these two were smart enough to come up with any schemes, but wondered if they were actually telling the truth. That could explain a few things, like Canfield's lack of properly tending to the county. And Jarvis sure seemed to be on his side. Could Jarvis be involved with his little side business? Someone in his position could profit from some *low*-cost livestock.

■ ■ ■ ■

"That's what they told you?" Siegler sounded flabbergasted.

"What they said," Joe said. "I decided to play along and see if they went back to their shack like they said they would. They did. Waited around in the alley for an hour to see if they stayed. Canfield has my letter about finding Carlson's body. Be interesting to see what he does."

They leaned against the long counter in Siegler's store, with only one lamp burning. Earl hadn't arrived yet, so they were able to talk privately.

"I don't have much faith in Sheriff Canfield, as you know, but he's no murderer. And his unimpressive deputy, good God. When *you* walk into a room, you fill the place. If *he* walked in wearing a cowbell, no one would notice."

"My impression, too," Joe said. "Those two idiots were right about one thing, though, I don't have anything to arrest them on, so we'll just see what Judge Worden wants to do. They're not the most credible witnesses we could have."

The sun was about to peek over the horizon and was filling the store with a golden hue. Siegler blew out the lamp. He walked toward a front window, hands on his hips, and looked out. Joe could tell he was deep in thought. Then something caught his eye, and he leaned closer to the window. Coming from the north were two riders. They crossed the intersection and tied up in front of the hotel.

"What is it, Mister Siegler?" Joe asked.

"I'll be damned. I think hell just froze over," Siegler said. "Canfield and his deputy just rode in."

They started for the door and heard a crash upstairs. "It's Fern, she hasn't been feeling well!" Siegler said, and hurried out the back door to the stairs on the rear of the building. Joe followed in case he needed help.

When they entered the Siegler's living quarters above the store, they found Fern lying on the floor next to an overturned parlor table. She had vomited and was try-ing to get up.

"Mother, what are you doing out of bed?" Siegler asked.

Joe placed his hand on her sweaty fore-head. "She's burning up. We need to get her to the Doc's."

"Will you help me? I can't lift much. It's my damned back."

"Get the door." Joe scooped Fern up in his arms and with a grunt lifted her up. Siegler threw a blanket over her as Joe carried her out.

At Doc Sullivan's, Siegler knocked frantically on the door. They heard screaming and crying inside and exchanged glances before entering. Sullivan was holding Missus Sanderson, who was wailing and pounding her fists against his back. Joe and Siegler looked at each other.

Sullivan noticed them. "Put her in that chair for a moment, please."

Joe sat Missus Siegler in the green padded chair, and Siegler pulled the blanket up around her. Fern was mumbling and turning her head from side to side.

Sullivan was able to seat the sobbing lady in a chair at the table. He went into the patient room and a few moments later came out with a wrapped blanket. He placed it on the examining table and pulled the curtain across.

The picture became painfully clear to both Joe and Siegler. Joe remembered seeing Missus Sanderson wiping her daughter's forehead, the crying, and the conversation with the doctor about influenza. *"Complications"* he'd said. Joe's stomach tightened, and he turned his attention to Fern.

As he squeezed Fern through the door into the room, he noticed a young boy in the other bed. He lay on his side quietly crying and rocking back and forth. His hair glistened with sweat. Joe laid Fern on the other bed.

Sullivan came in, sat down on the bed, and felt Fern's forehead. "Marshal, would you get Pastor Evans for me?" He looked up, and Joe saw dark circles around his eyes. It was obvious the doctor hadn't slept much. Joe was shocked at how much older he looked than the first time they'd met.

"You bet," Joe said.

After delivering Evans to the Doc's, Joe walked up to the judge's office to talk to him about Luther and Cookie. When he walked in, he found Sheriff Canfield seated in front of Worden's work table. His deputy leaned against the wall with a sawed-off shotgun under his arm.

"Mornin', Judge, gentlemen," Joe said, and nodded.

"Well, Marshal, we were just talking about you," Canfield said. He hesitated and held his eyes on Joe's coat sleeve. Worden and the deputy looked as well.

Joe glanced down and noticed the vomitus on his shoulder. "Missus Siegler took sick.

Just carried her down to Doc's." Worden nodded.

"What can I do for you, Sheriff?" Joe said. He studied the two lawmen in a different light and tried to see anything that he might have missed before.

"Well, fact is, Mister Carr brought your letter about the body you found and I thought I better look into it," Canfield said. "Now we ain't accusin' you, but we have information that you had this feller in jail and, well, threatened to kill him. You can see we had to talk to you about it."

"Of course."

"Marshal, did you threaten that man?" Worden asked.

"He threatened to kill me when he got out, so I told him, with that in mind, if he came back to town, I'd kill him in self-defense," Joe said. Worden stared at him a moment with raised eyebrows. "He came back, but was already dead, Your Honor."

"Somebody killed him," Canfield said. "Anyone else threaten him besides you?"

Joe studied Canfield and tried to read what was going on behind his dark brown eyes. The sheriff didn't give anything away. "Wouldn't know about that," Joe said. "Did you find them fellas I told you about at the soddy?"

Canfield looked at him. "Seems like luck wasn't on our side. Didn't find squat. In fact, it didn't look like anybody'd been there in quite a spell, ain't that right?" He looked at his deputy.

"That's right." The deputy spoke in a monotone.

It seemed to Joe that the sheriff was attempting to cast doubt on his word. "That's a shame. Well, if you're done with the judge here, I've got some business with him." Joe thought he was a bit stymied by his dismissive attitude but the sheriff recovered quickly.

"We'll head back later, after we visit the deceased. Told Judge Worden here that I'll be talking to the county prosecutor, see what he thinks. You won't be goin' anywhere will you?" Canfield said.

"I'll be here. You know where my office is, Sheriff." Joe struggled to maintain an air of friendliness.

After the two walked out, Joe related to Worden the story he had gotten from Cookie and Luther. The judge let the rest of his cigar burn down without another puff.

"God almighty, son. You're not one of those fellows that troubles follow everywhere they go, are you?"

Joe almost smiled at that. "Not 'til re-

213

cently, it seems."

"I don't know Canfield. Be real disappointing if he's a rotten apple," Worden said. "Know anybody that would vouch for him?"

"Budd Jarvis thinks highly of him, but don't know anyone else that knows him much," Joe said.

"You're not saying you think Jarvis is involved somehow?"

"I don't know, but I don't think Canfield is bein' truthful. Luther and Cookie are hidin' out here, two are dead, and one maybe run off. But he's downplayin' the rustling like it didn't happen. Think his story is taller than it is wide," Joe said.

"Well, I don't want you thinkin' I won't act on anything, but those two sound like the dregs of society, not the best witnesses. Do you have anything other than their story?"

"Nothing, Judge. That's it."

"All right, I want to talk to them. Bring them to my back door at midnight."

After darkness enveloped the town, Joe slipped down the alley and made his way to the lean-to behind the undertaker's, half expecting Luther and Cookie to be gone. But they were still there. He told them to be ready at midnight for a visit with Judge

Worden.

Joe found Adam waiting for him. "Sheriff's trying to blame you for what they done, sounds to me," Adam stated. He was leaning against the cell with a coffee cup in his hand. Joe had finished telling him of the recent events.

"That'd be a pretty good supposal," Joe said. "What'd he have to say when you gave him the letter?"

"He looked at his deputy and said, 'Looks like we got a killin' on our hands,' and that they'd come to town straight away. It almost seemed like it wasn't the first they'd heard of it, but put on like it was. Know what I mean?"

Joe nodded. "You and Mister Siegler were the only ones here when I told Carlson I'd kill him if he came back."

"I didn't tell anybody," Adam said.

"I know you didn't," Joe said. "And Mister Siegler hasn't seen him, so that about adds up to Carlson tellin' the sheriff himself. Maybe Canfield thought that was an interesting whit of information for future use."

"You mean like tryin' to hang his killin' on you?"

"That's what I mean," Joe said. "You know everyone here. You think Jarvis could be involved with Canfield?"

"Hadn't never suspicioned him on anything, but he seems to pull for Canfield at times. Budd's kind of a disagreeable sort, but I guess I would be too with his wife."

"What about his wife?" Joe said.

"Doc Sullivan visits Rosella, uh, Missus Jarvis, out at the ranch, kinda' regular. She's of a fitful nature, and Doc gives her medicine for it. It seems to have gotten worse the past year," Adam said. "Maybe that's why Budd stays in town a lot."

Joe walked to a front window. The buildings he could see were all dark except for the hotel. He thought how easy it would be for someone to shoot him down while he walked the streets at night. Someone like Canfield or his deputy, or Lute Kinney. But Kinney seemed to enjoy killing and didn't mind broad daylight. Wondering when Kinney would appear was starting to wear on Joe. Maybe that was the plan. Any stranger to town would be noticed, so he was fairly certain that Kinney hadn't yet arrived.

"Marshal?" Adam said. That brought Joe back from a stream of runaway thoughts.

"Oh, what'd you say, Adam?"

"I was saying that Canfield and his deputy just quit a card game with Jarvis and a couple others at the North Star when I went by a little bit ago. I waited out of sight and watched 'em ride out headed north. Looked like they was headed back to the Flats."

Adam sat down on a chair next to the stove, and Joe leaned back in his swivel chair and perched his boots on the desk. It was almost eleven o'clock. They didn't have much longer to wait. Joe had instructed Adam to be on lookout when Joe crossed the east end of Main Street with Luther and Cookie.

"Did you hear about Sanderson's little girl passing down at Doc's?" Adam asked after several minutes of listening to the Regulator tick.

"Yeah, terrible thing. Missus Siegler and a young boy are sick, too," Joe said.

"Abe Barton went down tonight, sicker'n a dog with that inflenza. Doc gets anymore, he'll have to lay 'em on the floor," Adam said. "What is that stuff, Marshal?"

"I don't know, disease, I guess. Seems to be as bad as typhoid," Joe said. "Pastor Evans and Sarah are down there lending Doc a hand."

The tapping was soft. Luther looked at Cookie in the dim light. They kept the lantern turned low while they played cards waiting for Marshal Mundy to escort them to see the judge. Cookie pulled out his pocket watch and read 11:10.

"It's early," Cookie whispered.

"Marshal, that you?" Luther asked. He got up and stood by the door.

"Yeah," was the whispered reply.

Luther slid out the bolt that served as a makeshift lock, and slowly pushed the door open. A pistol barrel appeared instantly on the end of his nose. Behind the gun, he could see the bulging eyes of Canfield's deputy. He pushed Luther inside and closed the door behind him.

"Wha, wha, what do you want?" Cookie asked. Luther was afraid to make a sound.

"Sheriff wants to talk. He's waitin' outside kinda' unhappy. Says you don't deserve to look him in the face, so turn around," the deputy ordered. He pulled their pistols and threw them in the dirt behind him. They stood still and stared at the deputy.

"Wa, we, don't want no trouble. . . ." Luther said, finding his voice.

"You won't have any, 'less you don't do what I say." The two men looked at each other and turned away from the deputy.

"Kneel down so I can bring in the sheriff," the deputy ordered. They kneeled down as they were told.

Cookie heard a bang and saw Luther fall onto his face. He didn't hear the second one.

"Did you hear something?"

Adam opened his eyes and waited to reply. "Just that damned dog of Farnham's barking again." They were quiet and listened to the dog.

Joe got up and took his cup to the stove. "More coffee?" Adam shook his head. Joe could see his heavy eyelids.

"Be good to have Judge Worden hear what they got to say. What ya' think he'll do?" Adam asked.

"Could sign arrest warrants for Canfield and his deputy, so they stand trial. But he'll want to be damned sure, since we're talkin' about the county sheriff and his deputy," Joe said. "Or, he might do nothing."

"Not supposed to get away with killin' folks," Adam said. "No matter if they was trash."

"You have a good head for justice, Adam. Hope you ain't disappointed as events develop."

When the Regulator struck the quarter hour, Adam raised his head and opened his eyes. Joe was standing beside his desk.

"Time to rise and shine," Joe said. Adam saw it was eleven forty-five. "Bar the door after I go out the back. Take your position beside MacNab's so you can see the street. Give a wave when it's clear to cross."

Adam nodded.

Joe slipped into the darkness and headed north through the alleyway. Behind the main street buildings were privies and sheds. A narrow walkway ran between the Palace and the corner building. He crossed the street and walked down the alley of the next block. Behind the undertaker, Joe went out and around the wagon shed to the lean-to. He knocked gently on the door.

"Luther. Cookie, it's Marshal Mundy." There was silence. Farnham's dog started barking again. He drew his Colt and pulled the door open. After turning the lamp high, he could see the two rustlers lying face down in the dirt. The back of their heads looked wet in the lamp light. Joe touched them and brought back bloody fingers. He felt them again and found neat little holes that the end of his finger almost fit into.

"Damn it!" He stepped out with the lamp and gave Adam a wave.

When Adam ran up, he stopped and looked over Joe's shoulder. "Gawd, are they killed?"

"They are," Joe said. "Go tell the judge our witnesses have been shot. When you get back, wake up MacNab."

"You suppose Canfield and his deputy did it?" Adam said.

"Surely possible, especially if they got wind that these two were talkin'."

Adam headed to Judge Worden's office. Joe went down the alley and knocked on the side door of the North Star, where Gib Hadley was inside sweeping. Joe saw that the chairs were piled on top of the tables when he went in.

"Sorry to bother you, Gib."

"Joe, you're up late. What can I do for you?" Hadley said.

"Adam said Sheriff Canfield and his deputy were in here playing cards tonight," Joe said.

"Yes, they were. Budd took 'em pretty good."

"Do you remember what time they left?" Joe said.

"Sure do. They kept tryin' to get their winnings back before they headed out. Was belly achin' it was going to be late getting back to the Flats. They called it quits at ten thirty," Hadley said. "Why, what's wrong, Joe?"

"Oh, nothin'. Thought I'd catch 'em before they left."

# CHAPTER SEVENTEEN

"I can't believe it. Those are the first killings in our town, other than, ah, at the
Palace," Siegler said. He slowly shook his
head. Joe and Sarah were sitting at a table
in the hotel with Siegler. All three had bowls
of buffalo stew with homemade bread on
the side, which was the special for the day.
The dining room was full, and most of the
people were minding their own business.

"Those two said Canfield and his deputy
killed that Carlson fella, and they were going to tell the judge, and now they're dead.
And those two so-called lawmen were here
when it happened . . ." Siegler said, and
sighed. "Coincidence?"

"We're not likely to find out with Luther
and Cookie dead," Joe said. He tore off a
piece of bread and dunked it into his stew.

Joe finished chewing, took a drink of coffee, and wiped his mouth with a cloth. "According to Gib, they left at ten thirty. They

could have killed 'em then, or headed out to make it look like they were really leaving, and then doubled back and done it. Either way, there's no proof. No one seems to know anything other than they heard Farnham's dog barking."

"How did they find out those two were here in town?" Sarah said.

Joe shrugged. "Probably followed their tracks here. Hard to hide in a town this small. I shoulda' locked 'em up though. Guess I wasn't real sold on their story." Joe considered that his inaction in that regard had possibly cost the lives of the two hapless thieves. If he would have locked them up, and it was Canfield's intent to see them dead, he wondered if the sheriff would have tried to take them at the jail. That's exactly what Luther had said they were afraid of. The mystery behind Canfield and his deputy might have been resolved with that confrontation.

"I was thinking maybe things would settle down a bit now, but with that fella from Kansas after you . . ." Siegler said, stopping abruptly. Sarah looked at him and then at Joe.

"What's he talking about? What fella from Kansas?"

Joe knew better than to try and talk

around it. "Had to kill three men in Baxter, lawful like. One of them's missus maybe sent a man to find me."

"Three men? All at once?" Sarah said. Joe nodded. "Who is this man? What's he look like?"

"I don't think he's coming, 'cause he should have been here long before now." Joe stuffed the last of his bread into his mouth and started chewing.

"So that explains why you're carrying *that* around," Sarah said, and nodded toward the ten-gauge that was leaning against the wall beside Joe. Lately there was more than one reason to be carrying the shotgun along. Joe didn't care to list them all over lunch. He was only kidding himself if he thought that Kinney wasn't one of them. He wanted every edge he could get with someone like him. Of course, the possibility of a confrontation with the sheriff was another. Joe wasn't sure just when, but he had decided that if Canfield tried to arrest him, he would respectfully decline and invite him to send for the U.S. marshal. He wouldn't be surprised, now that he thought about it some more, if the sheriff tried hanging the killings of Luther and Cookie on him as well — just like he was aiming at with Carlson.

"How's Missus Siegler feeling this morning?" Joe said. He decided a change in conversation might help the taste of the stew.

"Doc says her fever has peaked," Siegler said. "Thinks she'll pull through this just fine. She's a strong woman."

"Kinda guessed that," Joe said, smiling at Siegler. "Glad to hear it."

"Bad news is we've got two more sick ones come into Doc's this morning," Sarah said.

"Doc looked like hell when we took Fern to him," Siegler said.

"Katy Sanderson's death hit him very hard. So young," Sarah said. She sipped from the cup and stared into space. "I thought he'd be used to that sort of thing, being a doc and all."

"Well, he's not an old doc. A thick skin takes a while to grow," Joe said.

"He was born in Boston thirty-two years ago. Served in the medical corps during the last two years of the war, then he went to medical school," Sarah said. Joe and Byron looked at her.

Joe said, "Well, aren't you a fountain of knowledge?"

"We had a chance for coffee in the middle of the night. He proceeded to tell me about himself."

"Doc's a real decent sort," Siegler said. "Joe, have you met Thord Sanderson yet?" Joe shook his head.

"He's a blacksmith, started in business here just before you got here. Nice folks. Friends with the Forsonns. In fact, I believe they came to America together. Little Katy was their only child, and sweet as a sugar plum."

"I better be getting back down there so Pastor Evans can get a little rest before the funeral," Sarah said and smiled at Siegler. The smile evaporated when she looked at Joe. "And, Marshal Mundy. I'll be interested to hear why you felt that you couldn't confide in me about someone coming here to kill you." Joe had no words to offer. Nor did she give him the chance.

They all stood and headed for the door. Many of the customers stared at Joe as he walked by carrying the shotgun.

# CHAPTER EIGHTEEN

Katy Sanderson's tiny coffin was placed in the back of the undertaker's wagon, which was the same wagon that he used to pick up bodies. Today, the businesses in town were closed as the wagon rolled slowly down Main Street. The wagon and harness were draped in black ribbon, and the team wore black feathered plumes. A cedar wreath tied with ribbon lay on top of the coffin. Thord and Dana Sanderson walked behind the wagon. He was dressed in a black suit and carried his hat. He held his wife with his free arm and, at times, seemed to be her only means of support. She wore a black dress and veil. Mrs. Sanderson wiped nervously at her nose with a hankie, and those in the procession could hear her convulsive sobbing.

Behind the grieving parents walked Pastor Evans, Doc Sullivan, the Forsonn family, and then nearly every man, woman, and child of Taylorsville.

As the procession neared the marshal's office, Joe and Adam stepped off the boardwalk and fell into line. Hats in hand, they followed the wagon to the west end of Main Street, where it turned south toward the cemetery. The line of people was still making the turn off Main Street when the wagon inched by Sarah's house.

When the wagon came to a stop, four men eased out the pine box and carried it to the grave. They gently set it on two short poles that were positioned across the open hole.

With Bible in hand, Pastor Evans took up a position at the head of the grave and waited for the line of mourners to arrive. The Sandersons and Forsonns stood alongside the coffin, and others filled in around them. The silence was numbing. The chill of the air was tempered with bright sunshine and a cloudless sky.

Behind Pastor Evans, at the far south end of the cemetery, Joe could see the three fresh graves of Bob, Luther, and Cookie. No funeral for them, just a few words spoken over them by the pastor and a burial. He hoped they got along well, because they were now together for eternity. About twenty yards out, a man in a dirty coat leaned on a shovel and watched. A pickax lay near his feet. Joe didn't envy the gravedigger's job, most particularly in January.

"We are gathered here today to commit the body of Katy Isa Sanderson to the ground, and her soul to God and his glory. Katy, precious daughter of Thord and Dana Sanderson, was aged six years, ten months, and four days, when her lone journey began . . ."

Joe watched as Missus Sanderson's knees buckled, and her husband grabbed her with both arms to keep her from falling down. No one ever wanted to experience the pain that gripped her.

". . . Grasp firmly, the shield of faith. You will need it in your contest with the last enemy, which is death . . ."

Joe felt a nudge at his side and saw Sarah standing next to him. Her eyes were overflowing and solidly fixed on Evans. He pushed gently against her to acknowledge her presence.

". . . I have fought the good fight, I have kept my faith. Laid up for me is a crown of righteousness, which the Lord shall give unto me in that day . . ."

MacNab produced a straight-backed chair and placed it behind Mrs. Sanderson. Hadda Forsonn kept her arm around Mrs.

Sanderson and eased her into it. Thord Sanderson stood solid as a rock, tears streaming down his face. Doc Sullivan stood off to the side and stared blankly at the coffin. At a glance, one might have thought he wore a thin mask due to the dark circles around his eyes. For the first time, Joe noticed that the doctor's clothes hung from him as if draped over a scarecrow. Sullivan had brought Lucy, and he kept his right arm around her waist to keep her from falling down. This was the first time Joe, or anyone else for that matter, had seen Lucy in a dress that was buttoned up to the neck. Though Doc Sullivan held onto her, who was actually supporting whom was not clear.

". . . Yea, though I walk through the valley of the shadow of death, I will fear no evil . . ."

Memories flooded into Joe's mind as he stood there. The words he heard were familiar. He remembered them from that summer of 1852. No tears left to lose for the two split-log coffins sitting side by side.

". . . a table before me in the presence of mine enemies, thou anointest my head with oil, my cup runneth over . . ."

Nada and Jorund Forsonn and a handful of other children walked up one at a time and placed small homemade flowers of paper and cloth on the coffin. One was a paper doll. A young man stepped forward with his son, close in age to Katy, and held him over the coffin so he could place a dried leaf that he brought.

". . . and I will dwell in the house of the Lord forever. Amen."

Pastor Evans closed his Bible and nodded to the four men who had carried Katy's coffin. They picked up the ends of two ropes under the coffin and gently lifted the box while two other men pulled the poles out of the way. They carefully lowered the box into the hole and pulled out the ropes.

Dana Sanderson fell to her hands and knees beside the grave and shrieked. Her husband knelt beside her and tried to ease her back to the chair. Reseated for only a moment, she flung herself down again beside the hole, almost falling in. He didn't try to lift her again. He knelt down and placed his arm around her shoulders.

Many of the people gradually broke away and walked back to town. Joe, Sarah and Adam followed.

# CHAPTER NINETEEN

"What ya' got there?" Joe asked when Adam came into the office. He was carrying a burlap bag.

"MacNab told me to give this stuff to you to hold. Personal things of them two who was killed. I signed a note saying he gave me the stuff."

"Our undertaker is the careful one," Joe said. "Let's see what we have." He turned the bag upside down and emptied the contents on the desk. The two gun belts were nearly worn out. Seams of both holsters were coming apart, and the belts were dry and cracked. Joe laid two pistols aside, one a Union Army Colt .44, and the other a short-barreled .36 with missing loading lever. A cloth bag of tobacco, pad of cigarette paper, a pair of homemade dice, a piece of jerky, and a silver pocket watch comprised the worldly possessions of Luther Brennan and Cookie Jones.

"MacNab said he only kept their clothes that he buried 'em in."

Joe squeezed the tobacco sack and thought about the two. As he worked the sack he felt a piece of paper inside and assumed it was a cigarette paper. He worked the sack open to look inside and found a note. "Looks like they saved a scrap paper to smoke." Joe said. He pulled out the worn, wrinkled paper and unfolded it. *"A has hids to haul out. Be quik bout it."* He read it aloud.

"A has hides to haul out?" Adam said. "That don't make no sense."

"I think A is somebody's initial," Joe said. Adam nodded.

"If they was rustlin', think maybe they was doin' some slaughterin' out there at the soddy? And needed to get rid of some hides?"

"Maybe. If they were, who were they writin' this note to? Who's A?" Joe said. "None of them boys had an A for an initial. Don't know about that Tyler, though."

They thought silently about the note. Adam walked to the front door and looked out. "Freight wagon come in. Mister Siegler has been expectin' one of them new Winchesters. Think I'll head over there."

Joe sat quietly thinking about the note after Adam had gone. Hides meant that they had been doing some slaughtering. Where would they sell the meat without raising questions? A meat market down at Kearney had been caught red-handed with the remains of stolen stock. Joe didn't know about Gracie Flats, but Taylorsville had a meat market. He thought about the initial. The "A" could stand for Ace, as in Ace Todd, who managed the livery and meat market for Budd Jarvis. *The pleasure in arresting them both would be more than any one man deserved.* But first, he'd have to find proof. Joe slipped the note into a vest pocket, rebagged the other items, and dropped the bag into one of the desk drawers. A little snooping around would be in order, but first a stop at Siegler's in case that new rifle did come in.

Inside the store a group of men were standing at the counter. The "oohs" and "ahhs" told Joe that the new rifle was indeed the center of attention.

"Joe, take a look at this," Siegler said, and handed him the gun. "The Winchester model of 1876. They call it the Centennial model, because it came out on our country's one-hundredth birthday."

"It's heavy," Joe said, and took a bead on a window across the street.

One of the onlookers held up a cartridge for him to see. "Look at this, Marshal, it's a damned big one!"

"It's chambered in .45-75. Easily bring down a buffalo or elk, or about any other game animal," Siegler said with pride. "Any one of you fellas can own it for $14.25."

"It looks like a '73, but bigger," Adam said. His eyes were fixed solidly on the rifle.

"Surely is a beauty," Joe said. He handed the rifle back to Siegler, but one of the men intercepted it. "I'll leave you men to fight over it."

# CHAPTER TWENTY

The moon glared down and cast shadows around the buildings of town. It was cold but not bitter as it had been. Joe once again stood against a shed watching the rear of Jarvis's meat market. It was the seventh night in a row that he had held vigil over the business, the third that included getting up in the middle of the night to take a look as well. He calculated it was now about three o'clock and thought about going back to bed. He looked over the small corral behind the market, and the door on the back of the building where the animal entered to be slaughtered. Joe guessed they could bring in only one or two at a time due to the size of the building.

He was thinking that this was probably a waste of time when he heard hooves crushing the thin layer of snow. From the north came two riders herding a steer down the side street in front of them. The back door of the market opened, and a man who resembled Todd came out and opened the gate. The steer was guided into the corral and then inside the building. The door closed, and a moment later Joe heard a thud and the sound of what he thought must be the animal falling to the floor. This activity in the middle of the night was suspicious. Joe picked up the ten-gauge and approached the two mounted men. They were closing the gate behind them when they noticed him.

"Hold up there, I'm Marshal Mundy," Joe said.

In an instant the two riders spurred their horses into a dead run, heading north from where they had come. Joe slipped into the corral and to the back door. As he reached for the handle, the door opened a crack. He jerked it open and shoved the shotgun into a man's face and pushed him inside.

"Nobody move!" Joe said. The man on the end of the shotgun was bald and fat-faced, with wide eyes, and he held a large butcher knife with his right hand. Three lanterns were burning, and Joe saw Ace Todd standing over the dead steer, a bloody sledgehammer lying on the floor nearby.

"Take 'im, Dan!" Ace screamed. "Take 'im, damnit!"

Dan gave a cross-eyed look at the cavernous twin barrels at his nose. "I . . . I . . . I'm just a butcher, Mister Todd, I . . . I ain't no fighter!"

When Todd saw that Dan wouldn't move, he started forward.

"You'll never make it, Todd!" Joe pushed Dan backward and aimed the shotgun at Todd, who froze in midstride. His eyes locked onto a Winchester carbine laying on a counter next to him.

Joe cocked the other hammer and held the shotgun on Todd. "Think about your next move very carefully. It may be your last." Todd eyed Joe, Dan, and the carbine, and Joe again. A few long moments later he straightened up and raised his hands without being told.

"Pull your coat open," Joe said.

"I ain't heeled," Todd said. He opened his coat and then raised his hands again.

"Drop the knife, Dan," Joe said without looking at the butcher. He heard the knife clatter onto the wood floor.

"You ain't got no right to barge in here. We're closed," Todd said.

"Both of you sit down against that wall, keep them hands high. I can't see 'em, I start blastin'!" Both men sat down and held their hands as far above their heads as they could manage. Joe picked up one of the lanterns and held it down by the dead steer's rump. He saw no brand, so moved it slowly up the ribcage and found what he was looking for. The brand was hard to read under the winter hair, so he retrieved a pair of clippers. The brand on the steer became clear as he removed patches of hair.

"Looks like a Circle A brand. You have a bill of sale for this one, Mister Todd?" Joe said. "What's Mister Jarvis's brand?" Todd looked away.

"Mister Jarvis holds the Seventy-Seven brand, Marshal," Dan said. "I ain't no thief. I just butcher what they tell me —"

"Shut up!" Todd said.

"Last chance, Todd, you got a bill of sale or not?" Joe said.

"Go to hell, Mundy!"

"With that attitude, I believe you'll make it there first."

Todd scowled at Joe.

"Both of you stand up," Joe said. "We're gonna take a little stroll down to the jail, and if you're polite about it, I won't have to cut you in half with this shotgun."

When the trio walked into the marshal's office, Adam raised up and banged his head on the upper bunk of the cell. "Damn!

What's goin' on, Marshal?" The clock rang four bells before Joe answered.

"Sorry, Adam, these two are takin' your place." Adam stepped out of the cell and swung the door open wide. Joe patted down their pockets, making sure there were no hidden weapons. He pushed Todd into the cell by himself and closed the door.

"Hey, what about him?" Todd said.

Joe ignored him and walked Dan over to his desk. "Consider yourself under arrest as well, Dan. You'll have to explain yourself to the judge. What's your last name?"

"Loman, Marshal, Dan Loman. I needed the job. I just did what he told me to do," Dan said.

"You're a butcher, then?" Joe said.

"Six years of it up at Omaha. Got fired 'cuz . . . well, 'cuz I drink a bit. Met Ace at a saloon up there, offered me a job here. Hell, I hadn't never even heard of Taylorsville. I just needed the job."

"Be a shame for all that meat to go to waste, wouldn't it?" Joe said. "If I let Adam escort you back down to the market, you do your job quick and without a problem?"

Dan grinned. "I shore will, Marshal. That's too much meat to let rot. I won't be no trouble, give you my word on it."

"His word ain't worth shit!" Todd spat

and glared at Dan. "You keep your mouth shut, ya' dumb bastard! Remember what I said before!"

"Mister Todd, would you be kind enough not to open your mouth again unless you're asked to?" Joe said. "Adam, strap on that Navy Colt you been fawnin' over, take the shotgun, and escort Dan to the market."

Adam looked a little sheepish, surprised that Joe knew he had been wearing the Colt around the office and polishing it whenever he could.

"I will ask Adam to shoot you if you're not cooperatin'," Joe said. "It's loaded, isn't it?"

Adam nodded, wondering how Joe knew he'd reloaded it in case of an emergency.

"There's a carbine layin' on the counter in back, might want to put it up out of the way when you get there."

"Okay," Adam said.

"I won't cause no trouble, Marshal," Dan said.

Joe rummaged through the top desk drawer and brought out a badge. "Adam, I'm appointin' you a temporary special deputy. You may not get any pay for it, but it's legal. Swear to uphold the state's laws and ordinances of Taylorsville?"

"That ain't no problem, Marshal, proud

to. I do!" Adam pinned the badge to the outside of his green coat and cinched up the gun belt over it as well. The belt was too big for his waist, but it fit around the coat.

Joe walked outside with them and closed the office door. "Dan, I need you to tell me right now, with Adam as a witness, just what went on at the meat market. You do, and I'll put in a good word with Judge Worden. If not, you'll stand for the same thievin' charges that Todd will. What'll it be?" Joe said.

"I don't owe him a damn thing," Dan said. "Ace had word out that he'd take beeves to dress out and sell, but only one or two at a time, and only when he was ready for 'em. He'd wrap up a wagon load and head out the same day to Willow Springs, or Broken Bow, or elsewhere. Does it mostly in the winter 'cuz the meat keeps better."

"Who was them two riders that brought in the steer tonight?" Joe said.

"I don't know who any of 'em are, Marshal, that's the God's truth of it. They ain't always the same ones, neither. There's a bunch thievin' cattle up north. Horses, too."

"They all part of the same gang?"

"From what little I hear, I think there's a big gang, but, hell, there's little ones, too," Dan said. "Them ones was killed here in town, I knowed them. Luther, Cookie and Bob. They worked with a man name of Tyler, never met him, though. They brought us beeves too. Them's the only ones I knew."

"Now, this next question is very important, and I want the truth," Joe said, hoping for the chance to nail down Sheriff Canfield once and for all. "Who was Luther and them workin' for?"

"I don't know that they worked for anybody, Marshal, I figured they were working on their own."

Joe grabbed the front of Dan's shirt and pulled him close. "That's bullshit, and you know it! You'll swing right alongside Todd!" Joe threatened. Adam's mouth hung open as he stared at Joe. The vicious change of demeanor scared both Dan and Adam.

"Marshal, I don't want to hang. I'm tellin' ya' what I know. If I knowed who them fellas worked for, I'd tell ya'! I just done my work and didn't ask questions." Dan's eyes were glassy, and his face turned pasty in the cool air. Joe believed he was either telling the truth or was a first-class liar. He leaned toward the former.

"Okay, but I better not find out you've lied to me or held back on anything," Joe said. "One more thing. Is Budd Jarvis involved in this?"

"I can't say certain —"

Joe glared at him.

"I . . . I don't think he is. I say that 'cuz Ace told me regular not to be discussin' our extra sales with *nobody,* or I might not wake up in the mornin' sometime. I think Ace is a little crazy."

"You sell Jarvis's beef at the market, don't you?" Joe asked.

"Yeah, that's what we sell there, just like Mister Jarvis wants," Dan said. "The extra that comes at night, that's Ace's own little business. And he's hauled off some of Jarvis's meat to sell, too. Not much at a time, but it adds up."

"So, you come to work here knowin' you'd be cuttin' up rustled stock?" Joe said.

"No, sir. I was promised the job of butcher and clerk, that's what I was promised."

"Okay. Adam, take him over there, and as soon as he's done, bring 'im right back here. Take a look for any other hides while you're there."

"Yes, sir," Adam said. "Move!" He poked Dan in the back with the shotgun.

# Chapter Twenty-One

"So Judge Worden set trial for next Thursday. I told him Dan Loman was cooperative with my questions. Don't know if he was all truth, but cooperative." Joe leaned against a chair in Siegler's store and gazed at the new Winchester. It hung by itself, prominently displayed in a horizontal rack. It was apparent that no one had yet forked over the $14.25 required to take it home. It was nearing suppertime, and the store was empty except for Joe and Siegler.

"I can't believe what goes on in this town anymore. What's happening?" Siegler said. "You don't think Budd is involved do you?"

"Don't know him very well. What do you think?" Joe said.

Siegler sat in a chair by the checkerboard and considered the question. He worked his mustache and slowly shook his head. "No, I don't. He's abrasive sometimes, as you know, but he's no criminal."

Joe looked through a front window and saw Jarvis coming from the North Star under a full head of steam. He was out of Joe's sight when he landed on the boardwalk in front of the hotel. He could hear Jarvis's boots clunking down the boardwalk before he saw him. Coming into the store, he skipped the formalities of greeting and stomped straight into his mission.

"Byron, have you seen Ace or Dan around town? Those two sons-a-bitches are nowhere to be found!" He paused for a reply. Siegler looked at Joe.

"Mister Jarvis, I'm afraid your two boys are in my jail."

"What the hell's he talking about, Byron?" Jarvis said, ignoring Joe.

"I'm asking you to settle down and hear what Marshal Mundy has to say. You'll want to hear this," Siegler said. "And thanks for asking about Fern, she's back home and doing well." Joe wondered if Siegler's sour tone escaped Jarvis, knowing the rancher was waist deep in poor social graces.

"I'm, ah, sorry, Byron. Glad to hear she's better," Jarvis said, his tone reconciliatory.

The exchange surprised Joe. He'd never have believed the word *sorry* would cross Budd's lips.

Joe told Jarvis what he'd been doing during the last week, culminating in the arrest of Ace and Dan. Jarvis's face got tight when Joe told him about their little side business.

"Adam cut out three other odd brands from hides at the market," Joe said. "And there's a whole beef in the cellar you might want to do something with."

For the first time, Budd Jarvis was quiet. His loss for words amazed Joe.

"I'd like you to step outside where we can talk privately," Joe said.

"You have questions of me?"

"Yes," Joe said.

"Budd, before you go off half-cocked, Joe *is* the duly appointed city marshal here, and he's doing his sworn job right now, however unpleasant it might be for all of us," Siegler said.

"You can ask your questions in front of Byron. I've no secrets," Jarvis said.

"Okay. Did you have any knowledge of Ace or Dan's activities with stolen stock?"

Jarvis flashed an angry look at Joe. "You accusin' me of being a thief?"

"Budd, please, just answer the damned question, get this over with," Siegler said.

"I ain't no rustler, and I don't sell stolen goods. We used to hang rustlers where I come from!"

"Texas?" Joe said.

"That's right. Suppose you think Texans are thieves?"

"Nope. But I need to know your involvement, if any," Joe said.

"I flat out ain't involved with stealin', and don't ask me that again!" He gripped the counter and look down at the surface. "If I'd known those curs were stealin' from me, you'd never got 'em in your jail!"

"Did you know Luther Brennan, Cookie Jones, Robert Carlson, or a man named Tyler?" Joe said.

Jarvis raised his head slowly and turned it. Joe figured he was mad enough to burn down a cottonwood tree with a single glance.

"Heard their names, but didn't know 'em. Carlson's the one dumped in the street. The first two, weren't they the ones killed in that shack?"

Joe nodded. "They were. Know who did it?"

Jarvis whipped around toward Joe. "You accusing me of murder now?"

"Nope. Just wondered if you'd heard anything," Joe said.

Jarvis leaned back against the counter, seemingly exhausted. "I don't know who done it. Ain't that your job, to find out?"

"You'll be called to testify at the trial next

Thursday," Joe said.

"I'll be there," Jarvis said.

The following morning Joe sat at his desk sipping at a fresh cup of coffee. Adam had just returned the prisoners to the cell after taking them one at a time to the privy. He'd already emptied the slop buckets, and it was now time to feed. Joe smiled to himself as he watched Adam pour two cups of coffee and let them sit on the table by the stove before he left to fetch their breakfast. He was happy that his temporary deputy was taking to the job. In time, Adam might make a lawman. Still, Joe had no intention of putting him in the line of fire. His help with the prisoners was as far as Joe was willing to risk Adam's safety. It was true, everybody has to start somewhere, but he refused to put Adam in a position that might get him killed.

He got up and went to the window. The weather continued to embrace the area with a milder temperature, which was rapidly melting the accumulated snow. On the bad side, the streets were transformed into muddy quagmires that could suck the shoes, and maybe even the boots, right off a person's feet.

Joe thought about the previous night and

the supper he'd enjoyed with Sarah. She was still angry with him for not telling her about Lute Kinney. So much so that few words were spoken until they had finished the meal. It didn't help much to explain that he didn't want her to worry about it and that Kinney probably wasn't going to show now anyway. She wasn't dumb, and recognized the potential danger. She asked him the details of the shooting in Baxter Springs, and he told her. She winced at Arliss's age, but recognized that Joe had been given no choice.

Adam returned with the prisoners' breakfasts and served them, including the lukewarm coffees. Joe stayed at the window and watched a young man help a woman through the mud to the boardwalk in front of Siegler's store.

"You know somethin', Carr, that badge don't make you a man," Todd said. He gripped at the iron strapping and looked out of the cage at Adam. "You're nothin'. Nothin' but a common stooge."

Joe listened but didn't turn around. Loman lay on the top bunk and turned his head slightly.

"You ain't much better'n a dung beetle. Only thing is, I ain't never seen a dung beetle with a badge."

Joe had to grit his teeth while he stared out of the window, but he wanted to see how Adam would react to the verbal abuse.

"In fact, it don't much matter how many badges you hang on your coat, all you'll ever be good for is dungin' out stalls, which you're lousy at, by the way."

Adam glanced at Joe and back to Todd.

"Don't be lookin' at him. You know how to talk, don't ya', boy? That's right, *boy*. You ain't no man, that's for damned sure."

Adam remained silent and ignored Todd.

Joe noticed a lone rider coming from the east who reined up his horse in front of the office. Joe didn't recognize him, and he instinctively felt for his Colt.

"Marshal Mundy?" the stranger asked when the door opened.

"I'm Joe Mundy."

"Name's Revis. Marshal Twilliger over at Willow Springs asked me to deliver this note to you, pronto."

Joe ripped open the envelope and read:

*Marshal Mundy,*
*Had a fella here ask about you. Smelled trouble, a bad one I think. I didn't lie, Tole im I didn't know you. He's wearin two guns, unfriendly type. Been gamblin here*

*a lot. Still with it.*
*Marshal Hank Twilliger*
*Willow Spgs.*

"Marshal, what is it? What's the matter?" Adam said. "Marshal?"

"Oh, uh, nothin', Adam, nothing at all," Joe said. "Would you give my regards and thanks to Marshal Twilliger for me?"

Joe knew that he could let Twilliger know who the man was, and that he was wanted in Kansas. It would be an easy way out. Let Marshal Twilliger arrest Kinney, if that's who it was, and it sounded like it. But Joe knew there was a better than average chance that Kinney would kill Twilliger, and Joe didn't want that on his shoulders. Besides, this was between him and Kinney. He would have to deal with Kinney himself.

"Sure will. Good-day," Revis said, and hesitated. "Say, whatever happened to Marshal Welby — George, was it?"

"Yes, George. No one seems to know. Lit out one night and never came back," Joe said.

Revis gave a quick nod, touched his hat brim, and went back out to his horse.

Joe stood for several moments looking at the note. He'd missed his guess about Lute Kinney showing up. He knew the killer liked

252

poker. He must have tied up in some games along the way that he didn't want to hurry through. He also knew that just because Twilliger didn't tell Kinney where Joe was, that didn't mean he wouldn't soon find someone else there who would.

"Marshal, dang it, what's the matter?"

Adam's sudden question startled Joe slightly.

"I can see the look on your face. Somethin's wrong," Adam said.

"No, nothing's wrong."

"That's bull!" Adam came back. "Why won't you tell me? I can see it on your face!"

"Adam, it's not important right now. When it is, I'll tell you, don't worry," Joe said. He stuffed the note in a coat pocket, put on his hat, and started for the door. "Goin' on rounds."

As soon as Joe stepped out, he saw Lucy at the north corner on the boardwalk. There wasn't anything odd about that except that she had not one stitch of clothing on.

Joe had his overcoat in his hand when he trotted down the boardwalk toward Lucy. She was stumbling and wavering, which was now normal for her. The brown whiskey bottle in her hand, however, was affecting her already challenging mobility problems. As Joe approached, she bounced off the corner building and went headlong into the muddy street.

He stepped into the mud beside her, pulled her upright, and sat her on the boardwalk. Gib Hadley came across from the North Star to help. With Joe's overcoat gathered around her, the two struggled to stand her up. Joe hooked one of Lucy's arms over his shoulders with his right arm around her waist. She was crying and mumbling words neither man could understand.

"Go get Sarah — she's helping down at Doc's. I'll take her back to the Palace," Joe said. Gib set off without speaking.

Joe kicked open a door of the Palace Saloon and headed toward the stairs. The place was empty except for Smiley, who appeared to be amused by the sight.

"I told her not to go out without a wrap!" he said, and chuckled.

Joe stopped at the bottom of the staircase, turned, and looked at Smiley. The barkeeper's sickening grin went away as fast as it had appeared. Joe proceeded up the stairs with Lucy. Once she was in her bed, Joe forced himself to take a few extra breaths and used the time to talk himself out of beating Smiley to death. Lucy was shivering, so Joe pulled a blanket over his coat, giving her a double layer of warmth. He sat down next to her and wiped mud from her mouth and nose.

"Lucy, can you hear me? What were you doing out there with no clothes on?"

She mumbled more words that Joe couldn't make out and began sobbing. She started to wretch, so he rolled her over on her side. Sarah took over for Joe when she and Gib arrived.

"Jesus, what's the matter with her? She tryin' to catch her death, Joe?" Hadley said.

"Sure could of, Gib," Joe said. "She's been havin' a real hard time since her beatin'. It really fouled her up."

"I'll clean her up," Sarah said.

Joe and Gib stepped out of Lucy's little room and closed the door. On the way down they saw Smiley standing near the bottom of the stairs. It looked like he wanted to say something, and he did.

"You's up there long enough, Mundy, that'll be a dollar!"

All of Joe's effort in calming himself down instantly vanished. He stepped for Smiley, but as Joe got close enough to land a punch, the barkeeper whipped out a chair rung from behind his leg and swung it. It caught Joe across the side of his face and sent his hat flying. When his chin hit the grungy wood floor, Joe's thoughts and vision were momentarily scrambled.

"How ya' like them apples, you son-of-a-bitch!" Smiley yelled.

Hadley lunged at Smiley a second later, but the barkeeper threw a chair in front of him. Joe staggered to his feet and felt the warm flow of blood down his left cheek.

Joe got to Smiley first and this time successfully ducked the swing of the rung. His fist hit Smiley squarely on the jaw and sent him flying into a table. The dirty glasses left there tumbled to the floor. Smiley grabbed the handle of a broken mug and swung it back and forth. Joe waved Hadley off and kicked the mug out of Smiley's hand. He kicked Smiley in the head and then in the stomach. With a left hand full of apron and vest, Joe pulled him up and drove his fist into the man's nose.

Gib spoke after the fifth punch smashed into Smiley's bloody face. "Joe, hell, you're killin' him! Hold off now!"

He wanted to hit him ten or maybe twenty more times. Joe almost told Gib to leave, but his rage began to recede. He dragged the unconscious Smiley up on top of a table and stepped back to catch his breath.

Gib looked at Smiley and at Joe, and then up at the balcony. He was startled by the beating Joe had carried out so violently. Joe noticed his gaze and looked up at Sarah, who was holding her hands over her mouth like she had at the shooting in Lucy's room.

"Are . . . are you all right?"

"I am," Joe said.

She glanced into Lucy's room and back down. She saw that Joe's knuckles and face were bloody. "Have Doc look at your face?"

"Surely will," Joe said.

"What do ya' wanna' do with him?" Hadley said.

"He's comin' with me." Joe grabbed Smiley by the back of his shirt collar.

Along the way, Harvey Martin, Siegler, and several others stepped out to watch the spectacle of an unconscious man being dragged down the boardwalk by the bloody-faced marshal.

Adam was seated behind the desk reading his book when the door flew open, and Joe dragged Smiley over to the cell.

"Gawd, what happened?"

"Smiley needs a little time to think," Joe said. He took the keys from Adam, unlocked the cell, and shoved Smiley inside.

"Hey, there ain't enough room in here for us two, let alone him! Put 'im somewheres else!" Todd said. "Shit!"

Joe ignored him, and dropped the keys on the desk. "I'll be at Doc's for a bit if ya' need me."

"You okay, Marshal?" Adam said.

"A small headache is all," Joe said, and grinned. Blood dripped off his face onto the floor.

Joe knocked gently on the door, trying not to wake any of the sick who might be managing some sleep. When Doc Sullivan opened it, he stared at Joe's bloody face. Stepping aside, he asked Joe what happened.

"Gib and me found Lucy takin' a drunken stroll on Main Street without any clothes on. We took her back to the Palace, and Smiley suckered me with a chair rung."

"Why the hell did he do that?"

Joe ignored the question. "You need to check on Lucy, Doc. She's not doin' very well."

Joe took another long pull on the bottle as Doc finished wiping the blood from his face. He threaded what looked like a small fishing hook and placed his hand on Joe's forehead. Joe nodded, and Doc forced the needle through the skin, first on one side, then the other side of the cut that ran vertically from the left eyebrow up to his hair line. Blood oozed from the cut and required periodic daubing to keep it out of Joe's eye.

Doc sewed efficiently, like he was repairing a coat seam. Joe couldn't help but wince each time the needle poked through his skin.

"Didn't you have your hat on?" Sullivan said.

"Just carried Lucy upstairs. Pushed it back on my head as Gib and I came down the stairs," Joe said. "Made a nice clear target for him."

"You did that," Sullivan said. "You did that."

Joe could smell a mix of whiskey and onions on Doc's breath. "You have a full house today?" Joe said.

"Luckily down to two with the influenza, but they're both children."

"Don't mind my sayin', Doc, but you look like hell," Joe said. "Dark circles, hell your eyes look worse than mine."

Sullivan stopped in mid-stitch, making Joe wonder why he just didn't keep his mouth shut until the doc was done. Probably the whiskey.

Doc looked Joe in the eye and was about to speak, but didn't. At last, he said, "I'm not dead." Joe wasn't sure, but guessed Doc was referring to the Sanderson girl who had died under his care. And now two more children were down.

"We all do what we can do, Doc. We're all

just human," Joe said. *Damn, there I go again.*

Doc stopped halfway through the last stitch. A flash of anger went across his face, and his eyes glassed over before he lowered his head. He nodded and continued his work.

# CHAPTER TWENTY-TWO

Smiley was wearing handcuffs when Joe escorted him from the jail to Judge Worden's office at ten o'clock Monday morning. Gib Hadley was already seated near the bench, and several onlookers were seated along the side, including Budd Jarvis and Byron Siegler.

Everyone stood when Worden, wearing his black robe, stepped out from the back room and seated himself. "Order!" He rapped the gavel twice, and the room fell silent.

Smiley had refused counsel, so the judge decided to hear the case immediately.

"John Wilkie, you are charged with assault with intention of doing bodily harm to Marshal Joe Mundy. How do you plead?"

Smiley looked at the judge from a swollen, black and blue face, and said nothing.

"Very well, I'll enter a not-guilty plea on your behalf. Mister Hadley, would you take the witness stand please?" Worden said.

Harvey Martin stood up with a Bible, and Hadley placed his hand on it. "Swear to tell the truth, the whole truth and nothing but the truth, so help you God?"

"I do."

"Tell the court what happened yesterday, regarding the arrest of John Wilkie," Worden said.

"Well, I looked out a window from my saloon, the North Star, and saw Lucy, naked as a jay, goin' down the walk. Marshal Mundy had seen her, too, 'cuz he come a runnin' with a coat. I headed across the street to help, but just before we got there, she fell in the street. Why, she was so drunk, she couldn't a hit the ground with her bottle in three tries. We got her picked up, and Joe, ah, Marshal Mundy, helped her back to her room at the Palace. He sent me for Missus Welby, to help 'cuz Lucy was three sheets to the wind. I fetched Missus Welby and took her to Lucy's room, and she said she'd take care of her. The marshal and I come back down the stairs, and Smiley said we'd been upstairs long enough that the marshal owed him a dollar. When Joe stepped closer, Smiley whipped out a chair rung and whacked Joe across the head. Knocked him right down. Then the fight was on, and uh, Smiley got hauled off to jail. That's about it."

"Thank you, Mister Hadley, you may step down."

Joe was called next and gave basically the same story. The onlookers stared at the ugly stitched gash and dark bruising around Joe's eye.

"Mister Wilkie, would you like to testify on your own behalf?" Worden said.

"No, goddamnit! You'll condemn me anyway. That bastard got what he deserved bullying folks —"

"Order! Order!" Worden wrapped the gavel several times, which finally had the desired effect.

"Mister Wilkie, take your oath, and sit down on the witness stand if you desire to testify, or shut the hell up!" Smiley sat still and ignored the judge.

"Very well," Worden said and looked down at Smiley. "I find you guilty as charged and sentence you to sixty days in the county jail!" With that, Worden rapped the gavel. "Court adjourned."

The ride to Gracie Flats was uneventful. Smiley had nothing to say, and Joe was glad of it. He had half expected some trouble out of the saloon man on his way to a two-month stay in the county lockup.

Joe tied the bay to the hitching rail in front of the courthouse but kept hold of the reins of Smiley's mount until he had stepped down from the saddle. Inside, Sheriff Canfield, alone in the office, did a double-take when they walked in. He stood up and gazed at both faces before offering a greeting.

"Marshal Mundy. Can't tell which one of ya' looks worse."

"Afternoon, Sheriff," Joe said, ignoring his inquisitive nature. "Here's a sentencing order from Judge Worden. Mister Wilkie here is good for sixty days." He handed the paper to Canfield and removed Smiley's handcuffs.

Joe studied Wanted posters tacked on the wall while he waited for the sheriff to lock up his new prisoner.

"Marshal, I heard you had two more killings in Taylorsville. Sounds like things are gettin' out of hand, wouldn't you say?"

"You mean Luther and Cookie? That was a shame. Came in to tell me who's behind some rustling goin' on in the county." Joe left it at that to see where Canfield would take it. After a brief lull, it seemed to Joe that the sheriff couldn't help but pursue the matter.

"Did they pass along anything of value?"

Joe thought that the mild wrinkles in Canfield's forehead gave away more than a passing concern and made him look like he was holding wind. The sheriff was probably not much of a poker player.

"Not a lot. Guess they were saving the whole story for Judge Worden," Joe said. His vague answer was meant to worry the sheriff, and it seemed to be working.

"Well, what did they tell you? Maybe I can be of assistance."

"Nothing that's usable for anything, not right now anyway," Joe said. He enjoyed making the sheriff squirm a little. "Still thinking about me for Carlson's killing?"

"Well, you were the only one who threatened his life." Canfield's answer was a poor mixture of fake friendliness and duty.

"Suppose you suspect me of killing Luther and Cookie as well?" Joe said.

"Well, I'd be a liar if I said it didn't cross my mind," Canfield said. "You didn't threaten them, too, did you?" His grin was very slight.

"Did a motive cross your mind?" Joe said.

"I heard those boys all rode together. Maybe they came after you for killin' their friend Carlson?" Canfield said. He leaned back in the swivel chair and lit a cigar. He didn't try to conceal the smirk on his face.

"Course if they tried that, I couldn't blame you for defending yourself."

Joe said, "Sounds possible, if I did. Only one problem, I didn't. Someone got to them before I could take them to see the judge. Someone who didn't much want them talkin' to the judge. Have any idea who that might have been?"

The two stared at each other trying to reach inside and read the other's thoughts. See what exactly the other knew, or thought he knew, and their plans. It was a Mexican standoff of sorts. Joe was certain Canfield and his deputy killed Carlson, Luther, and Cookie, but couldn't prove it. Canfield was trying to corner Joe for killing them, but was having trouble putting a strong enough case together. Other than the fact that Joe had threatened Carlson, he had nothing factual. The sheriff knew he could arrest Joe on that, and might get a conviction. But, he appeared to be treading lightly, concerned about what Luther and Cookie might have told Joe.

"If I could offer anything to help, Marshal, I would," Canfield said. "We should both continue to seek information, as time allows, of course."

Joe studied him for a moment and then stood. "I've got to get back, Sheriff, good day." Canfield gave only a slow nod in return.

"You just missed Mundy," Canfield said as his deputy walked in.

"I seen him."

"*We* have a problem," Canfield said. He puffed on the cigar and pulled it out of his mouth. He looked at it for a moment and continued. "That gawdamn Luther and Cookie must have talked before you got to 'em. He wouldn't say exactly what they said, but the way he eyed me, he knows."

"Shoulda' done it as soon as they hit town," the deputy said.

"We needed the darkness. We can't be doin' that without it," Canfield said.

The deputy poured a cup of coffee and sat down beside the sheriff's desk. "So what do we do with him?"

"Didn't want it to come to this, but I'm afraid Marshal Mundy has become a liability." Canfield puffed on the cigar and stared straight ahead. "Can't let him put a noose around our necks, can we?"

"Guess we're gonna visit that shithole town again," the deputy said.

Canfield nodded slowly as he thought of a plan. "Remember Budd telling us his new saloon was gonna open Friday?"

"Yeah, his piano will be comin' in from Willow Springs. Gonna have a big to-do for opening night."

"He asked for some help in keeping order so the rowdies don't bust up his new place. You head down there Friday morning. Scout a place in an alley where you can take Mundy. After dark. After the hoo-rawin' gets under way. I don't care how you do it, just don't be seen. Once Mundy's out of the way, we can reorganize. Get some new men. Some we can depend on this time, like the pony boys. Get some money coming in again."

The deputy nodded and sipped from his cup. "We gonna do anything to help out Todd?"

"Hell with him. If he's that damned dumb to get caught, he can swing, as far as I care."

"What if he talks?"

"He won't," Canfield said.

"How can you be sure?"

"If he gets prison time instead of a rope, he knows I have friends inside those sandstone walls at Lincoln. Hell, you were one of 'em! If he gets there after runnin' his mouth in court, his life ain't worth two cents, and he knows it. In fact, one ol' boy there would do it for nothin'. And if he gets county time, we'll take care of him 'til his time is served."

"What about Loman?" the deputy asked.

"Loman don't know nothin'," Canfield said.

The deputy nodded.

# CHAPTER TWENTY-THREE

Joe was standing on the boardwalk in front of Siegler's store when the Forsonns pulled their wagon team to a stop. Lars jumped down and helped Hadda step down from the wagon.

"Mister Forsonn, Missus Forsonn," Joe said and touched his hat brim. "It's good to see you. Wish it could have been under better circumstances." Hadda looked at Lars, and he said a few words in their language.

"Joe, by golly, it good to see ya' too. Sorry to be a seein' ya' when we're headin' home," Forsonn said.

"I know you been busy helpin' the Sandersons. Terrible thing losing their child."

"Da missus is takin' it awful bad," Forsonn said. "But we wanted ta t'ank ya' for the kindness ya' showed, Joe. Ya' shouldn't a sent so much to us, but we wanted to t'ank you for it." He reached out his hand and Joe took it. Forsonn nodded at Hadda, and she stepped forward and gave Joe her hand. "T'ank you, Mis-ter Mun-dy." She smiled and stepped back.

Forsonn nodded at the children, and they stepped forward as well.

"T'ank you for the gifts and food, Marshal Mundy," Jorund said and offered his hand. He stood straight as his father.

"You're welcome, Jorund, I'm glad you enjoyed them," Joe said, his face flushing slightly. Jorund stepped back, and Nada stepped forward with a big smile. Joe knelt down, and Nada gave him a hug, saying nothing.

"And I thank you for the basket, and especially these," Joe reached into his vest pocket and showed them the little wooden horse and man. "They are very special, and I carry them with me always."

The children smiled widely and looked up at Lars and Hadda.

"Well, we gotta' be headin' back now. You come see us anytime ya' want, Joe Mundy," Lars said.

"I'll do that, Mister Forsonn. You take care now," Joe said.

Siegler joined Joe on the boardwalk and bid the Forsonns farewell. The two men stood and watched as Lars carefully turned the wagon around and headed out.

"Fine family. Good people," Siegler said.

"Yes, they are."

"Say, Joe, care to walk with me over to Budd's new saloon and take a look?" Siegler said. He pulled his coat tight and buttoned it all the way. "He's having a grand opening Friday night, I think as much to show off his new piano as the saloon itself."

"Sure." Joe said and picked up the ten-gauge that he'd leaned against the storefront. "Didn't know he got a piano."

"It made it to Willow Springs and will be on the freight wagon come Friday," Siegler said. "Being's it'll be the first one in town, I expect a lot a folks to show up. Most haven't heard piano music for some time."

They walked across the refrozen street, and when they stepped onto the boardwalk on the other side, Siegler spoke again. "Joe, Budd told me he asked Sheriff Canfield to send his deputy down Friday to help keep the peace at the opening festivities. I wanted you to be aware of that."

"Thanks, but I think your city marshal can handle it."

"That's what I told Budd, and he said, 'Probably so.' Actually, I think he's easing up on his attitude toward you. Not a lot, but maybe a little," Siegler said. They both saw a canvas covering the new sign on the awning and two men digging large holes in the street.

Joe said, "Uh huh," as he followed Siegler inside. They heard hammering on the balcony but didn't see anyone. A narrow stairway went up the back wall to the middle of the balcony that featured a room on either side.

Jarvis's saloon was wider than the North Star but not as wide as the Palace. It was located in the middle of the block, with the North Star on the west end and the undertaker on the other. A dark wood bar was set to the right, with a plainly designed backbar that was fully stocked with liquor bottles and cigars. A large mirror was mounted above it that was larger than the one at the Palace. No doubt the larger size was on purpose. Hanging above the mirror was a large, framed painting of a naked woman reclining on a couch. Her seductive eyes seemed to follow a person wherever he was in the place. A heating stove was situated in the middle of the tables.

A door off the far end of the bar opened, and Jarvis and another man appeared. The other man, a carpenter, climbed the stairs.

"Byron, 'bout damned time you stopped by for a look," Jarvis said, glancing at Joe. "Mundy." Joe noted that this was the first time that Jarvis had actually offered him a greeting.

"Mister Jarvis."

"Well, what do you think, Byron?" Jarvis said.

"Very nice, Budd. Congratulations. What are those men digging up the street for?"

"Fire pits. Got Sanderson makin' up some grates to cook beef on. He made these rims for the hangin' lights in here, too." He pointed up at the iron rims hanging from chains. Three lamps were affixed to each of the four rims. "I'm cookin' up two beeves and feedin' folks free, long as the meat lasts."

"Well, we haven't had a regular wing-ding like this since the great Centennial celebration last July! Look forward to hearing that piano, too," Siegler said.

"Yep, be here Friday, along with some new employees. Buy you a drink?" Jarvis said.

"By God, I'll take you up on that. Probably the only free drink I'll ever get from you!" Siegler said and laughed.

Jarvis smiled and pointed his finger at Siegler. "That's damned sure!" He poured three whiskeys and shoved two of them across the bar. Siegler picked his up and held it out, ready for a toast. Joe didn't move.

"I better wait 'til later," Joe said.

"You won't drink with me? That what you're sayin', Mundy?" Jarvis said. He held Joe's gaze for a moment, then looked at Siegler.

"Joe, we should toast this man and wish his new business well." Siegler looked anxiously at Joe and then to the glass in front of him.

Joe hesitated for a moment and looked at Jarvis. He picked up the shot and held it up. "To success."

"To success!" The other two joined in and downed their whiskey.

"S'pose I should thank you, Mundy, for cuttin' down on the competition for me," Jarvis said.

"Smiley didn't have anything to do with you," Joe said.

"All the same, he's closed for the next sixty days at least."

"You gonna give Lucy a job, Mister Jarvis?" Joe asked.

"She's respectable enough lookin'. I was considerin' it, but now, well you know," Jarvis said and shrugged.

"You could pay her for cleaning up the place at least."

"People here gotta' work, Mundy. Now I don't like what them animals did to her anymore than the next man, but I can't have her workin' here. Hell, I'd spend most of my time pickin' her up," Jarvis said.

Joe's face showed his distaste for Jarvis's statement.

Jarvis said, "I do want to ask you a question, Mundy. Would you be holdin' any objections to my sellin' the meat market to Dan Loman, if Judge Worden would see his way to go lenient with him, I mean?"

"That wouldn't be any of my concern," Joe said.

"What I mean to say is, if I approach the judge, you won't throw anything in the way?"

"Like I said, that wouldn't be any of my concern."

"Okay, then," Jarvis said. He refilled the glasses. "To the future."

Joe and Adam leaned against the front of the office while waiting for the defense attorney from Gracie Flats to talk privately with his two clients. After taking a short break, winter had set in again and brought the bitter temperatures back. Joe sipped steaming coffee and watched Main Street which was busier than usual. The trial of Ace Todd and Dan Loman would start at nine o'clock, while the grand opening of

Jarvis's saloon would be the following night. These two attractions brought more people to town than usual. Joe hoped the trial would be over before the saloon opened at six o'clock on Friday.

Adam was watching the attorney through the window. "I couldn't never figure out why lawyers stand up in a court of law and try to get outlaws free of their charges. Even ones whose crime was murderin'."

Joe smiled on the inside. "Adam, you might make a lawman yet."

"Well, it ain't right for 'em to help some a' them escape the penalty for what they done."

"Well, you're right. 'Cept our law system says everybody gets a proper defense when accused. Be the same for you or me," Joe said.

Adam looked at the gray sky thoughtfully. "I can see that. It's just when they *know* a man killed wrongfully, and a fancified lawyer does his job so well, the killer gets to go free . . . without no damned penalty at all, why that's wrong. All there is to it. It's just wrong. I've heard of that happenin' too."

"It has . . ." Joe coughed. "It has for a fact. Never said our law system is foolproof. Just the best we have for now."

"Bet that don't help the killed feller feel any better," Adam said after a few moments of silence.

Joe said, "You are most assuredly right about that."

Christmas Evans approached from across the street, wearing the long buffalo coat that Joe had first seen him in. As he stepped up onto the boardwalk he looked at Joe and then at Adam. "Little brisk to be lollygagging about outdoors, don't you think, gentlemen?"

"Mornin', Pastor," Adam said and nodded.

"Christmas, you're movin' about early."

"Well, Marshal, thought I'd enjoy a cup of that good coffee you serve before I head down to Doc's. I may even let you *spill* some rye into the cup to keep the coffee company."

"Be glad to, but we're waitin' for the lawyer from Gracie Flats to finish talkin' with his clients," Joe said.

"I shall, in that event, take my business elsewhere," Evans said. "Good day, gentlemen."

"Say, Christmas, before you go. How are things down at Doc's? When he sewed up my forehead, he seemed a little off his feed, if you know what I mean."

Evans looked down the street while he replied. "Frankly, just between us, I'm worried about our good doctor. His abilities are not of what concerns me, but how he's taken to drink since that young child's death. Right now, there are two children, both boys, under his care with the same ailment. One of them is not doing well. If he loses another . . ." His voice trailed off. "Has it not been a long winter?" He ambled his way down the boardwalk.

Adam looked at Joe and turned back to look at Evans. "Been a long winter, that's a fact. Gettin' tired a' my joints freezin' up on me."

"Afraid our boots are parked in the wrong location to be expectin' a surround of warmth," Joe said, as the office door opened.

"Marshal, I am finished. You may escort my clients down to the courtroom now," the lawyer said. "Trial will begin in ten minutes." He donned a clean, brown bowler and, with briefcase in hand, made his way down the walk.

"We *may* escort *our prisoners,* is what we *may* be escortin'," Adam said under his breath as they went into the office. Although Joe had to force back a smile, he was surprised at Adam's apparent dislike of lawyers.

Joe handed Adam the keys, and he unlocked the cell. "Todd first," Joe said and picked up handcuffs from the desk.

Todd stepped out, and Adam walked up to him. "You were sayin' something about me? Some kinda problem with me, Mister Todd?"

Joe stood by and watched.

"Don't be squarin' off on me, boy, you'll be wearin' your hat on your ass!" Todd said and looked at Adam. Joe's deputy was only slightly taller than Todd.

"I am squarin' off on you, Mister Todd. You gonna back me down?" Adam said. Todd became enraged, but his roundhouse swing was cut short when Adam's fist smashed into his stomach. Todd apparently had forgotten that with all that dungin' out of stalls came strong arms and shoulders. He wheezed and fell to his knees, holding himself with both arms. Todd made strange squeaking sounds, and his face turned blue. A few minutes went by before he could raise his head to speak, his voice raspy. "Your damned deputy hit me, Mundy, what are ya' gonna do about it?" Joe gave Adam the handcuffs and helped Todd back to his feet.

Joe said, "What I'm gonna do is give you some advice. Don't try swingin' at him. You ain't too good at it."

■ ■ ■ ■

"In closing, Your Honor, the state has proven that the receiving, slaughtering, and selling of stolen livestock occurred at the Jarvis Meat Market under the auspices of Mister Ace Todd, the manager. While the exact part played by Mister Loman in this illegal enterprise is difficult to pinpoint, he, Mister Loman, did carry out the butchering of said stolen livestock under direction and orders of Mister Todd, and therefore holds some accountability for his part. On that note, Mister Loman has, according to Marshal Mundy, been cooperative in furnishing information, and the state would not obviate a light sentence, if that pleases the court."

The prosecutor looked at Judge Worden and then at the jury as he continued, "In that light, Mister Jarvis, owner of the market, has indicated his willingness to sell the business to Mister Loman upon his recompense of legal entanglements. As for Mister Todd, it is clear that he orchestrated the illegal activities, which included issuing a call for stolen animals, in effect asking others to do the stealing on his behalf, to be delivered to him in the dead of night. And Mister

Todd himself transported by wagon the stolen goods to other parts for the purpose of selling those ill-gotten gains. He has refused to name any of those persons involved in furnishing him with the stock, even though the possibility of a lesser sentence for him, in doing so, exists. Your Honor, Mister Todd's guilt is absolute, and I'm afraid his repentance, absent. Thank you." The prosecutor then took his seat.

"Mister Hansen, do you care to close for the defense?" Judge Worden asked.

"I do indeed, Your Honor." Hansen stood and walked past the bench to the side of the room where Joe was sitting, the ten-gauge across his lap. He turned and started back, talking as he paced the floor.

"Your Honor, esteemed members of the jury, the defense has shown that Marshal Mundy broke into a closed business in the middle of the night, and charges of that burglary notwithstanding, has produced so-called evidence that he had no legal right to seize, let alone bring in and present to this court, as evidence. Mister Todd testified that he believed the purchases of the beeves in question were from the duly constituted representatives of said ranches involved, and holding this belief, which he felt was supported by the sellers' remarks, did not feel compelled to ask for a bill of sale. We feel he is guilty of no more than careless management of the business to which he was entrusted, and that, as the court knows, is not a crime at all."

"Do not portend as to what this court knows or doesn't know, Mister Hansen. Now get on with it!" Worden directed. Hansen was momentarily stunned. His face turned ashen.

"Of course, Your Honor. In addition, ah, Mister Todd has learned his lesson well, and if the court sees fit to realize the noncriminal error of his ways, he has offered his assurance that he will prove to be an asset to the community from this day forward."

The trial had lasted most of the day, excluding an hour break for lunch. It was four ten. Worden said, "The jury will retire to the back room for deliberations. Court adjourned."

Once the prisoners were housed back in the cell, Adam sat down with a cup of coffee. Joe stepped out to the privy, and when he returned, Christmas Evans was in the office, slumped into the extra chair.

"Coffee or that whiskey you were here for earlier?" Joe said cautiously. He could see a strained sadness on the pastor's face.

"Whiskey. Please, Marshal."

"Is somethin' wrong, Pastor?" Adam said.

"I just came from Doc Sullivan's. It seems that he's down to one patient now." He downed the shot in one gulp and set it down for a refill. Joe poured and kept silent.

"Ike Raymond's boy, Grant, just passed. The influenza, you know." Evans voice was soft and without vigor. "He was nine years old." Joe exchanged glances with Adam.

"Don't know Mister Raymond, I guess," Joe said.

Evans cleared his throat. "He farms a few miles east of here near the river. Lost his wife two summers ago. The boy was all the family he had still living."

"There anything we can do, Christmas?" Joe said. Evans shook his head. "We will need to keep an eye on Doc. Sarah is still there to help out. Poor man has refused sleep for three days."

"Pastor, do you believe that things like this, the boy dyin' with the inflenza, was God's doin'?" Adam asked. "You know, some say, 'Well that was God's plan, he had a reason to call him back home.' "

"What I think is, the boy caught hold of a bad sickness, and it took life from him. But, rest assured, Adam, our Lord will care for him now, in a better place than this will ever be. And that's all that we can hope, isn't it?" Evans got up without another word and walked out.

"How did the trial come out?" Sarah asked.

Joe finished chewing a mouthful of potato before he answered. He had reluctantly accepted a supper invitation from Sarah, knowing how little sleep she had been getting while helping Doc Sullivan. She had prepared a simple meal of boiled potatoes and sausage.

"Jury found them both guilty. Worden gave Loman sixty days in the county jail and Todd five years hard labor at Lincoln."

"Todd deserved it. Why such a light sentence for Dan Loman?"

"Jarvis talked to Worden and told him he felt Todd was the responsible one, that he'd be willing to sell Loman the meat market. I happen to agree. Guess the judge felt that since Jarvis, being a victim, felt this way, that it was okay with him."

"Do you have to take Todd to Lincoln?"

"No. Canfield's deputy will be here tomorrow for the saloon opening. When he goes back to Gracie Flats Saturday, he'll take them. Move Todd to the prison on their schedule, I s'pose." Joe coughed several times.

"Your head looks terrible. Does it still pain

you?" Sarah looked concerned.

"Not so much anymore."

"There's something I want to tell you," Sarah said. She refilled their coffee cups and returned the pot to the stove. "Budd Jarvis stopped over to Doc's when I was there. He asked me to work at his new saloon." Joe put down his fork, still loaded with sausage.

"What did you tell him?"

Sarah said, "Told him I would."

"Thought you were going to try to work here, with mendin' and sewing and stuff?"

"Just ain't enough work to live on, as I explained before. And I won't live on hand-outs from you!"

"They ain't handouts. I eat your food and drink your coffee —"

"I don't ask you to pay to eat with me, and besides, a meal don't cost five bucks. It's not the bed you think you're payin' for, is it? 'Cuz we already had that discussion."

Joe shook his head, knowing when to quit, and picked up his fork. "How's Doc doin', losin' another patient?"

Sarah stared at him for a moment before answering. "It didn't do him any good. He's taken to drinking a bit, which I hope doesn't run away with him. Mister Raymond took his boy back home with him. Bury him there. Not another damned child's funeral to go through at least."

"That's good, I guess," Joe said. Sarah nodded and finished her food.

"I visited Lucy. She's a mess."

"I was glad to get my coat back," Joe said.

"It's strange, her knocking around by herself in the Palace." Sarah picked up the dishes and set them in the dry sink.

"She gettin' any callers?"

"She's had four transactions since she got beat," Sarah said. "And the cowboys know the Palace is closed, so they don't bother goin' by anymore."

Sarah stopped behind Joe and draped her arms around him. "Are you my caller?"

"You look tired, I should be gettin' back," Joe said.

"I am tired, but not too tired." She leaned over and kissed him on the ear.

# CHAPTER TWENTY-FOUR

By noon on Friday, the streets of Taylorsville were getting busy. Cowhands from nearby ranches were coming in at regular intervals and tying up wherever they could find a place. Budd Jarvis had replaced Todd with a man from his ranch to run the livery, which was already full up. People arrived in farm wagons and buckboards, parking them willy-nilly up and down Main Street. Dogs ran around the streets barking and chasing each other, children following in high spirits.

Jarvis opened the doors of the new saloon at eleven o'clock and still planned for the celebration to kick off at six. That would be the time for the cooking to begin and when the saloon's new name would be unveiled.

Joe stood inside the front door of the vacated North Star with Gib Hadley watching Main Street. Both were drinking coffee from tin cups in the deserted saloon.

"How you feelin' about havin' more competition, Gib?" Joe said.

Gib turned around and feigned a look around his business. "As you might imagine, at this particular juncture, I ain't all a twitter."

"Jarvis is gettin' a piano," Joe said.

"Shoulda' bought one of them," Hadley said, "but didn't have nobody who could play the damned thing. Budd's okay. All in all, I guess I wish him luck, just not too much."

Joe watched a farmer hoist his wife down from the seat of their wagon. "I didn't thank you for your willingness to step in on my behalf with Smiley."

"That clodplate had no call to blindside you that way. I do enjoy that he'll be sittin' in that jail up at the Flats for the next two months." Hadley smiled slightly as he said it, looking out to the street. "I do enjoy that a great deal."

They watched Thord Sanderson and a helper unload two iron gratings from a wagon. After Sanderson left in his wagon, another pulled up with a second load of firewood. Other men lined up buckets of water in case the fires got out of hand. The two holes in front of Jarvis's new saloon had already been packed tightly with firewood and set ablaze. As was intended, some folks were content to warm themselves by the fires and occasionally tip a bottle while others had drinks inside.

"Looks like you got help for tonight," Hadley said and nodded west toward the side window. Joe looked out across the street and saw Canfield's deputy stepping down from his horse. He tied up at the rail beside another horse and headed up the street. Joe noticed the butt of the short shotgun still protruding from his saddle scabbard. The deputy climbed onto the boardwalk by the North Star and walked by toward Jarvis's place.

Joe said, "What's his story?"

"Clyde Davey. Came from Lincoln. 'Bout all anybody knows about him."

"Looks like a schoolteacher."

"That's what everybody says," Hadley said and smiled.

"Thanks for the coffee. Think I'll go down and see how Doc's doin." Joe placed the tin cup on the bar and picked up the ten-gauge.

"Freight wagon's due in about an hour. Gonna come and see the new piano?"

"Gib, that's an event I wouldn't miss," Joe said and walked out.

Joe could smell the whiskey as soon as he walked in. Doc Sullivan wasn't drunk, but he'd had a few. One drink was still on the table where he'd been sitting when Joe knocked. Sullivan returned to a rocking chair that was positioned so he could see into the room with his remaining patient.

"Care for coffee, or a drink?" Sullivan asked. The dark circles around his eyes were still there, perhaps no worse, and he had two days' growth on his face.

"No, thanks, just had coffee with Gib," Joe said. He sat down at the table. Sullivan was quiet.

"Sorry to hear about Mister Raymond's boy."

Sullivan turned to look at Joe and downed the whiskey. "Sorrys all around. But sorrys don't save anyone, do they? And neither, apparently, do I."

"Doc, you do what you can. That's all folks expect of you," Joe said.

"They *expect* . . . what they expect is, that I'll not let their families die!" Sullivan refilled the glass.

"No one can work miracles, Doc. Not even you, or Pastor Evans. That's the plain cold fact of it." Joe coughed.

"A professor of mine in Boston once told me that I wasn't cut from the cloth of physicians. He was right. But I didn't listen to him. I decided to move out here and have a nice quiet practice delivering babies."

"How's he doin'?" Joe said and nodded toward the patient room.

"He'll live, through no assistance of mine," Sullivan said.

Joe coughed and cleared his throat. "Everyone here respects you and what you do for 'em, knowin' that you can't do magic or the like. They depend on you to *be here* for 'em."

Sullivan looked at Joe. "I'll do *my best* to remain sober. *Happy?*"

"Plum stirred."

"How long you been coughing?" Sullivan asked. He walked over to the cabinet and took out a small aqua-colored bottle.

"Not long. Takin' on a cold in the head, I guess."

Sullivan approached him with the bottle. "Take a sample of this."

"Doc, thanks, but I have to retain all my functions right now," Joe said.

Sullivan returned to the cabinet and brought back another small bottle and poured some into a spoon. "You'll taste mint. It won't slow you down any."

Joe took it and was surprised that it didn't taste as bad as most medicines he'd had before.

"Mister Jarvis's new piano will be here

within the hour. Comin' to take a look?"

Sullivan shook his head. "I'll see it later."

Joe dropped a coin on the table and stopped at the front door. "Thanks for the potion. You can't help but help folks, can you?"

"Good day, Marshal Mundy."

The freight wagon was just rolling to a stop in front of Jarvis's saloon when Joe crossed Main Street. It was heavily loaded as usual, with three extra passengers that Joe took special care to note. Folks gathered around to gawk at the newcomers. At the rear of the wagon Joe helped the first passenger, a woman dressed in a silver and black taffeta dress and a tall hat. She was golden-haired and had a pretty face with a hardness that seemed to linger in the background. A younger, auburn-haired woman with a handsome slender face and big round eyes was next. Her dress was dark blue with a white lace collar. Joe helped the women onto the boardwalk and turned around to watch the third passenger, a small man, who looked his way as if expecting assistance in jumping down from the crates and trunks that were tightly packed beside the piano. One of the teamsters picked up the little man and carried him over to the walk and dropped him. The man, all of five feet tall and a hundred pounds wet, gave the teamster a disgusted glance and straightened his vest and coat. Jarvis met the three and directed them inside the saloon.

The teamsters unloaded the trunks belonging to the passengers onto the boardwalk. They enlisted the help of men who were standing nearby and slid the canvas-wrapped piano out of the wagon. Six men strained as they bore the full weight and carried it uneasily to the boardwalk, where they carefully placed it. Progress in rolling the piano into the saloon was hindered by the uneven boards of the walk, so it was necessary to pick it up and move it along until they finally got it inside. Mismatched notes could be heard as it was knocked about.

Inside, Joe noticed Deputy Sheriff Davey leaning against the full bar drinking coffee. Joe walked over and wedged into a spot beside him.

"Deputy," Joe said. "Are we expecting Sheriff Canfield's company as well?"

Davey looked over at Joe with his bulging eyes. "Guess not." He took another sip from his cup. A couple of shots were fired outside, so Joe made his way to the door. Davey stayed put. A farmer holding a bottle and an old Walker Colt was capering drunkenly, near one of the fires. He managed to cock the pistol again, raised it up, and fired.

Joe yanked it from his hand. "Don't need any shootin' guns off in town! You can pick it up at the bar when you leave." The farmer looked at Joe and hoisted the bottle again. "Okay . . . 'arshal."

As Joe gave the bartender the pistol, he saw that the piano had been uncovered and was being wiped off by the little man. It was positioned against the middle of the wall opposite the bar. Before heading to his office, Joe glanced up to the balcony where the new *lady* employees had been lodged. No activity there yet.

The little man started playing short chords on the piano. It added immensely to the festive atmosphere, and Joe thought it a worthwhile addition to the town.

"Did the piano come in, Marshal?" Adam said.

"Yep, it's a beauty. Came in with a man to play it and a couple other beauties."

"Since I'm still wearing this badge," Adam stopped to double-check his question. "What I mean to ask is, would I be able to make rounds with you tonight?"

"Sure. Our guests aren't going anywhere.

But if anybody goes to celebratin' too much and fires off a gun, I'll handle it." Adam nodded his agreement.

Joe stretched his arms out and rotated his shoulders to loosen them up. Muscles all over his body were starting to ache, and his brow was moist. He sat down at his desk and poured a whiskey, holding it in the back of his mouth momentarily before swallowing. It burned much more than usual and brought on a coughing fit. He quickly downed a second.

Adam said, "You feelin' okay, Marshal? You look a little peaked."

"I'm fine, let's go."

"Marshal, how about bringin' us a couple them steaks Budd's gonna cook up?" Dan Loman said. He was looking through an opening in the strap iron.

"Don't see why not. You want one, Todd?" Joe said.

Todd raised his head from the upper bunk. "Yeah."

Joe and Adam did a regular walk of the town and, after a few short visits, ended up in front of the new saloon. Joe stood with the ten-gauge under his arm. It was nearing six o'clock and the unveiling of the saloon sign. Two poles with torches on the ends were stuck almost in the middle of street, which added to the light from the lanterns on the front of the building. Families gathered outside, while men who came alone filled the saloon. Four short stumps were positioned around each fire pit and served as legs to rest the iron grating on.

Budd Jarvis stepped out front and waved his big hat. "Attention! Can I have everyone's attention?" He stepped up onto a chair that had been positioned for him. "I want to thank everyone for comin' and hope you enjoy the festivities. Now it's time to commence. Pastor."

Christmas Evans stepped forward from the crowd. "We bless this new establishment and everyone who enters her doors. Amen." Everyone seemed somewhat surprised by Evans' brevity and assumed he must have been told to keep it short. Jarvis yanked the canvas from the sign revealing the name, which didn't much surprise anyone: TEXAN SALOON. The crowd cheered and drank from whatever they had with them.

Jarvis spoke again. "Those who know me, know where I come from, and I just couldn't think of another damned name for the saloon!" The crowd laughed. "The boys are throwin' the beef on so it won't be long. One to each person, though, so everybody wants one, gets one!" He swept the crowd with an index finger.

The wood-hauling wagon sat empty nearby, and a young lady and older man climbed aboard. The man began playing an Irish jig on his fiddle, and the girl danced to it. The crowd clapped and stomped their feet to the beat. Some children formed daisy chains and danced to the music in ever-growing circles. One of Jarvis's hands was juggling three tin plates in the middle of the street.

"Ain't this a regular wing-ding, Marshal?" Adam said.

"It is." Joe walked over to one of the cooks and asked for two steaks for his prisoners. The cook loaded two thin wood shingles, on hand for that purpose, and gave them to Joe. Adam carried them off to the jail.

Joe stood inside the saloon for a while and looked for Deputy Davey but didn't see him. *Be fine if he stays out of my way.* His thoughts drifted off to Luther and Cookie in the shack and what must have happened when Canfield and Davey came to visit. They must have got the drop on them and shot them in the back of the head.

*Sure wish I could prove it.*

Joe listened to the little man hammer out tunes on the new piano in a near-professional manner. He expected nothing less of Jarvis. He was sure he could enjoy it more if his head didn't pound with every note. Joe thought that the costs of the new saloon might have been reason for Jarvis to sell off the meat market. Seemed like the man ought to be a little overextended. The two *ladies* were milling around the tables, dressed differently than when they'd been traveling. Their new dresses were revealing, in a more tasteful way than the old dress Lucy wore at the Palace. That thought reminded him of her.

Back out front Joe asked for another steak, telling the cowhand who it was for: Lucy.

"Glad to, Marshal," the hand said. Joe carried it to the front door of the Palace and knocked hard. It was dark inside, and after a few minutes of pounding, Lucy stumbled into view and unlocked it. She stood, wavering back and forth, and stared at Joe.

"Evenin', Lucy," Joe let loose with a cough. "Thought you'd like one of Budd Jarvis's steaks."

She was inebriated again.

"I want you to eat that, Lucy," Joe said.

"I will, thank you ever so much, Joe. You wanna come in?" She pulled her dress partly open.

"Why don't you eat and get dressed. Come over and enjoy the festivities?"

She closed the door and stumbled to the bar where she picked up the steak with both hands and bit into it.

In front of the Texan, Joe watched the people dancing and singing. He felt a tapping on his shoulder and turned to see Booth, the farmer he'd arrested for being drunk and foolish.

"Marshal, good to see you again." The big man wore an old coat, but it appeared to be freshly brushed.

"Hello, Booth, how ya' been?"

"Real good. Ain't been gamblin' and not drinkin', much. Brought my family in for this." He pointed across the street to a farm wagon and his wife and children sitting in it. Joe waved, and they waved back. "Ain't the music jus' somethin'?"

Joe said, "Tell you what, Booth, if I had a pretty wife like that, I'd have her out in the street a dancin' up a storm!"

"I believe you're right, Marshal! Good to see you." Booth shook hands with Joe and started toward his wagon. Joe noticed Adam coming across the street. At the same time, he heard two powerful gunshots.

The shots sounded like they came from the alley behind the North Star so Joe trotted to the corner and turned north. Gib Hadley was locking the front door of his saloon, and Joe almost ran into him. Adam ran toward the alley, and Joe tried to catch up to him.

"Adam, hold. Hold it!"

Adam stepped into the alley just ahead of Joe, and the gun roared again. Adam stumbled and fell. Thinking he'd just lost his footing, Joe reached down to pull him up and saw the blood. Adam looked at him with wide eyes, saying nothing. Joe turned around and saw Gib coming down the sidewalk.

"Get Adam to Doc's right now!"

Gib turned and ran back to the crowd on the main street.

"You'll be fine. Help's comin' for you," Joe said. He wasn't sure how bad Adam had been hit and wasn't sure he'd be okay. He couldn't help and wasn't about to let the shooter get away. He ran into the darkness, the ten-gauge at the ready, and stopped to let his eyes adjust. He heard someone crash through a pile of refuse.

Joe continued further down the alley, trying not to expose himself. Just as he wondered where the shooter had gone, he saw the silhouette of a head stick up from behind a wagon box. He barely ducked in time, as the blast of a shotgun tore through the wood siding next to him. Wood splinters peppered his face. Joe fired one barrel at the wagon box, and while the shooter ducked, he ran out away from the buildings and used a privy for cover. Joe now had a view out of the line of fire. Again, the shooter blasted the spot where Joe had been. He stepped slowly and quietly out beyond the wagon box until he could see the shooter, who at the last minute saw him. The ten-gauge rocked against Joe's shoulder lighting the area between them. He heard the shooter thump to the ground. Joe laid the empty shotgun down, pulled his Colt, cocked it, and waited.

"Joe! It's Gib. Budd and I have guns, where are you?" Hadley yelled from the rear corner of the North Star.

Joe remained silent while he eased up to where the shooter was on the ground. Two loud snaps told Joe that the man tried shooting again, but the shotgun was empty. He pulled it from his hands and laid it aside. He felt around the man's waist, pulled out a revolver, and stuck it in his belt. It was too dark to see well, but Joe could hear gurgling with each labored breath the man took.

Joe said, "Gib, down here, almost to Mac-Nab's, bring a lantern!"

Joe watched the lantern dancing around

as it drew nearer. He looked at the shooter as the light crossed his face.

"Damned if it isn't Clyde Davey!" Jarvis said.

"You okay, Joe?" Hadley asked.

"Fine," Joe coughed and cleared his throat. He looked at the deputy, whose bulging eyes seemed to have gotten bigger. The deputy was still breathing, but his chest and neck were covered in blood. The shiny star pinned to his shirt was more red than silver.

"Why'd you shoot Adam?" Joe said.

"I'll . . . I'll tell it all," he coughed, and blood ran from the corners of his mouth toward his ears. He coughed again to clear it. "Promise, first . . . tell my mother . . . I died doin' my job good . . . proudly."

"Who's your mother, and where?" Joe talked fast. He knew he wouldn't have long to get anything out of Davey.

"Missus Nellie . . . Nellie . . . Tillmer . . . Falls City," Davey coughed and started breathing with a rasp. "My name —"

Joe interrupted, "We know, Clyde Davey!"

"No! No, name's Herm . . . Tillmer . . . tell her? Your word?" His chest squeaked as he tried to suck in more air.

"My word on it. I will notify her," Joe said. "Now, why did you shoot Adam? Did you kill Luther and Cookie? Tell me damnit!"

Tillmer coughed again. His eyes were becoming glassy. "It wasn't Adam . . ."

Little bloody bubbles emerged from his lips and popped, quickly at first, and then slowly, until one last bubble formed and held. His head rolled slightly to the left. His bulging eyes stared without seeing.

The repeated gunshots had quieted the celebrants on the main street. An uneasy crowd watched men rushing around the corner of the North Star. The music had stopped, and people whispered to each other. The shots had sobered the crowd inside the saloon as well. The piano was silent.

"Look. Look there. Someone's being carried to Doc's place!" one man shouted.

"Was it the marshal?" another asked.

A young boy ran to the crowd and issued his report. "Adam Carr got shot. They're takin' him to Doc's!" As people do, rumors were started by those who had no knowledge of what had taken place.

Budd Jarvis returned and mounted the chair again to restart the party. "Folks, there was a little trouble. Everything's all right now. Please enjoy yourselves. Start that damned fiddle again, Sam!" Jarvis walked inside and motioned to the little man to get the piano going. He went behind the bar and poured himself a whiskey. The merriment commenced again and nearly regained its previous level.

"What was all the shootin'?" The voice held no excitement considering the subject of the question.

Jarvis looked up at the customer. He didn't know the man. He would have remembered those dark eyes.

"Just a little shootin' scrape. Everything's fine now," Jarvis said. "New in town?"

"Just rode in, in the midst of all the shots."

"Hellava' way to welcome you to our town. Buy you a drink?"

"That'd be real nice," the stranger said.

Jarvis was off-put, slightly, by the way the man replied, by his stiff face, and the way only his lips moved when he talked, but shucked it off to a bad night. He refilled the man's whiskey and picked up his own. He noticed the butts of two pistols protruding from under the man's long coat as he turned around to watch the piano player.

Byron Siegler signaled for Jarvis from the other end of the bar. When he joined him, he noticed Siegler's worried look.

"Budd, what the hell was all the shooting? I'd taken a steak home for Fern when we

305

heard it." Jarvis motioned him to step outside away from the crowd.

"Mundy and Adam Carr ran back to the alley where the shots came from. Adam got shot, and Mundy killed the man who shot 'im. It was . . ." Jarvis looked down shaking his head.

"Who? Who in the hell was it?"

"Clyde Davey," Jarvis replied.

"What? Canfield's deputy? Why —"

"But that ain't his name, either," Jarvis said. "Said it was Herm Tillmer. Wanted his mother in Falls City told he was dead."

"Why? Why'd Davey, Tillmer, or whoever he was, do that?" Siegler said.

"I think he was tryin' for Mundy." Budd looked at Siegler.

"Don't like all this. Don't like it at all," Siegler said shaking his head. His eyes darted around the street.

Jarvis looked back at the saloon. "What is it?" Siegler said.

"Ah, some stranger I jus' talked to. Just something off-center about 'im."

Siegler nodded. "Doc working on Adam now at — Wait! What'd this stranger look like?"

Jarvis said, "It's nothing Byron, just —"

"What'd he look like!"

Jarvis frowned at Siegler. "I don't know,

had real dark eyes, though."

"Was he wearing two pistols, butt for-ward?" Siegler asked.

"Yeah, he was. How'd you —"

"Oh, God."

"What is it?" Jarvis said.

"He's from Kansas. He's come to kill Joe —"

"Christ! Mundy sure is popular. What the hell for?"

"Can't tell you now. Where's Joe?" Siegler said with a renewed urgency.

"Think he's down at Doc's," Jarvis said. "That hombre is still in my saloon. I'll just go throw a rope on 'im, drag 'im out of town, by God!"

"Budd, you'll do no such thing! You leave him alone! You have no idea what that man's capable of," Siegler said and looked toward the Texan. "I'll explain later. Your word on it? Leave him alone, and don't say anything 'til I talk to Joe?"

"All right, all right, Byron. Jesus, take it easy, 'fore you have a spell."

Siegler started to say something and then walked off a few steps. He stopped and turned around. "Nothing, do nothing, say nothing to anyone!" He pointed a finger at Jarvis.

# Chapter Twenty-Five

"Hold him still, damnit!" With his hands covered in blood, Doc Sullivan worked the probe into Adam's shoulder. Two of Jarvis's cowhands were trying to keep Adam still as he worked.

"Ahhh. Ahhhh!" Adam screamed and twisted back and forth. Sullivan exchanged the probe for forceps and went in again.

"Hold him still!"

"Ahhh!" The piece of buckshot made a "tink" sound when Sullivan dropped it into a small tin pan to join the first two.

"Okay, Adam, okay, I'll give you a break. Take another drink," Sullivan said. Doc lifted Adam's head slightly and put the whiskey bottle to his mouth.

Adam was panting, trying to catch his breath. Sweat ran down his face, and his hair was soaked. He choked a little on the whiskey, and some leaked out of his mouth and ran down his cheek.

Sullivan took a draw on the bottle himself and wiped the sweat from his own eyes.

"Let's finish this up, Adam. Now hold on. You hear me, son? You're doing fine, just fine," Sullivan said, easing the probe into another hole.

"Ahhh!" Adam swung his head from side to side.

"Hold him still, goddamnit!"

Joe walked in and leaned the ten-gauge against the wall. He threw off his coat and moved in to take the place of one of the cowhands at the examining table. "How's he doin', Doc?" Joe looked at the blood pool at Adam's side. He could count five distinct holes in the upper right side of Adam's bare chest. Blood ran freely from the hole Doc Sullivan was working in, and slowly oozed from the others.

Joe could see the stark terror in Adam's eyes when they met his.

"I know it's painful, but you'll be okay. Do you understand me? You won't die," Joe said. "You'll be okay." Adam blinked his eyes and tried to mouth words that wouldn't come.

Joe felt dizzy, and his stomach was turning again. "I'll be right back." He motioned for the spare cowhand to return to the table. Joe stumbled outside and fell to his knees and wretched. He heard footsteps in the snow but couldn't stop.

"Joe, what happened? Are you all right?" Sarah said and knelt down by him. "Oh my God, you're wringing wet!"

"It's Adam. Go help Doc. I'm okay," he said and wretched again. The sight of blood wasn't what bothered him. Joe knew he was getting sick.

"There, there, Adam. We're all done. Got them all out. Now you try to rest." Doc Sullivan carried his instruments and metal pan to a kitchen table. He thanked the two hands for their help before they left.

Sarah finished cleaning the blood from Adam's chest and the table under him. He was slowly catching his breath when Sullivan returned to bandage him. "His right arm's broken. We'll need to wrap this tightly around these splints." Sarah helped support his arm while Doc wrapped it.

Joe sat across the room leaning on the muzzle of the ten-gauge, watching. Pastor Evans finished checking on the young boy in the patient room and came out and sat down at the table. "Is that safe, Marshal?"

Joe swiveled his head at Evans. "It's unloaded."

"Doc needs to look at you."

"When he's finished with Adam."

The door opened, and Byron Siegler stepped inside. He surveyed the room before proceeding over to Joe. "Need to talk to you outside — it's *very* important."

Joe looked up without lifting his chin. "Afraid you'll have to sit down here and tell me, Mister Siegler. Not feelin' like any walks."

Siegler said, "You're all sweaty, Joe. You don't look so good."

"We've already established that, Mister Siegler. What the hell is it?"

"I think he's here."

"Who's here?" Joe's impatience showed more quickly than when he felt well. Evans was looking at Siegler now.

"The *gentleman* from Kansas," Siegler said. "At Budd's saloon."

Joe slowly raised his head from the shotgun. "You seen him?"

Siegler shook his head. "Budd did. The way he described him, just like you said, dark eyes, two pistols butt forward. Budd thought he was a little strange."

"Shit. Not now . . ." Joe said. He rested his chin back on the shotgun.

"Pardon my eavesdropping, but is this man from Kansas a problem?" Evans asked with concern.

"Likely," Joe said.

"He's intent on killing Joe!" Siegler said. His outburst was easily heard by Doc Sullivan and Sarah.

"Who wants to kill Joe?" Sullivan said.

Sarah looked up from her work. "Is *he* here?"

Joe looked at Siegler.

"I'm sorry, but they need to know what's going on, too," Siegler said.

"None of their business, Mister Siegler. Only my business, just like I said before."

"I can gather up Budd, Gib, the Martins, couple of Budd's hands and —"

"You'll *do nothing!*" Joe said. "Yeah, you might get 'im, after three or four of you are dead. I won't have it!" He got up and staggered over to a slop bucket in the patient room, dropped to his knees, and wretched. He fell over on his side and let the shotgun lay.

"Oh, dear God, he can't even defend himself!" Sarah said.

Siegler and Evans took hold of Joe's arms and sat him up. "Leave me alone. Just need to rest before I . . ."

Doc Sullivan finished with Adam's arm and knelt next to Joe. He felt his forehead. "He's got a fever."

The four of them stood him up. Sarah

pulled the cavalry Colt from his belt and unbuckled the gun belt before they walked him to the bed across from the young boy. Sarah placed the gun belt and extra gun in a drawer next to Joe's bed.

"I just need to rest a bit . . ." Joe said.

Doc Sullivan slipped a thermometer into his mouth. "One hundred two," he said to no one in particular. "I'll check it again later and see if it's still rising."

"It's the influenza, isn't it, Doctor?" Evans asked. Sullivan nodded.

"He . . . he hasn't felt right . . . couple days," Adam's voice was weak and slurred, but they could all hear him.

"Okay, Adam, you stay quiet and rest," Sullivan said.

"Doc, I'll sleep a little while, then you wake me up. I mean it," Joe said.

Sullivan said, "Okay, Joe, just get some sleep." Sarah looked at Doc and started to say something, but he shook his head. They all stepped out of the room.

"You're not going to get him up later, are you?" Sarah said.

"No, of course not. If the fever gets worse, he won't be able to anyway," Sullivan said. "But I would like you and Pastor Evans to stay if you would."

They both nodded.

# CHAPTER TWENTY-SIX

"Got your message, Byron," Jarvis said. "What's going on?" He stepped into Siegler's tiny office at the rear of the store and closed the door. It was midafternoon on Saturday. Harold and Harvey Martin were already present.

"I need to explain to you what has transpired and what may," Siegler said. He related to them Joe's shooting in Baxter Springs and the reason the dark-eyed stranger was in town. When he finished, there was silence and looks of disbelief on the faces of Jarvis and the Martins.

"What's Kinney wanted for?" Harold Martin said.

"He killed a family in cold blood. The father, mother, and a baby in the mother's arms," Siegler said.

"Good God!"

"Why don't Mundy arrest him before any trouble starts, if he's a wanted man?" Jarvis said. "That *is* his job as I recall, why you two hired him."

"He can't," Siegler said. "Not right now, anyway. He's sick as a dog, in bed at Doc's. Doc thinks it's the influenza."

"Jesus, and Adam is shot. That means we're without a lawman again," Harold Martin said. His searching eyes darted to the other men. "We have to send for Sheriff Canfield right away!"

"A man was sent this morning to notify him of his deputy's death. I'd expect him anytime, but . . ." Siegler let the words hang while he thought about how to proceed. "I think I need to tell you that Joe was informed by Luther Brennan and Cookie Jones that it was Canfield and his deputy they rustled cattle for."

"The men killed behind MacNab's?" Harold Martin said.

"What?" Jarvis said.

"The same."

"You believe Mundy?" Jarvis said.

"*We* have no reason to doubt him, Budd!" Siegler said.

"Before being killed, they also told Joe that Deputy Sheriff Davey killed that Carlson fellow, on Canfield's order, right in front of them. That's why they came in to tell their story. They were afraid Canfield would kill them eventually. And the good sheriff has made it known that he suspects Joe of killing Carlson."

"So, you're saying we can't trust the sheriff to do his job, like arrest this Lute Kinney?" Jarvis said. He rubbed his chin whiskers as he talked.

"Wouldn't you say that the attempted assassination of our marshal and Adam, by Canfield's man, casts an even larger shadow on him?"

"I'm a little confused, Byron," Martin said. "Why would the sheriff want Marshal Mundy dead?"

"Joe thinks the sheriff suspects those two men talked before they were killed."

"Hell, looks like the sheriff will have to wait in line," Jarvis said.

"I fail to see the humor in that, Budd," Siegler said.

"It wasn't meant to be funny. Just seems like this town's gone to hell in a handcart since Mundy came."

"These outlaws were here. Joe rooted them out, doing his job!" Siegler said.

Jarvis nodded and held up his hands as if fending off an attack.

"I guess we . . ." Light tapping on the office door interrupted Siegler. "What is it?"

"Byron, Sheriff Canfield is here to see

you," Earl said.

"Tell him we'll be with him in a minute." They listened to Earl's footsteps as he walked away.

"What I was going to say is, I guess we tell Canfield about Kinney while he's here, and see if he'll arrest him. I gave Joe my word that none of us would try to take Kinney. Did Kinney get a room at the hotel?"

Harold looked at Harvey, and they both shook their head. "We're full up, but no one like you described, Byron," Harvey Martin said.

"You'd have remembered him," Jarvis said.

"All right. Let's go out and see the sheriff. It's too close in here," Siegler said.

# Chapter Twenty-Seven

*Standing on the top of a tall ledge, he could see all the way across the mighty river and the land on the other side. The water raced by, tossing huge walls of brown water that tore viciously into the bank, cutting away the earth inches at a time. He soon had to step back as the water splashed ever closer. He wondered what made the water move so violently, there being no wind. Panic filled him as he saw two heads bobbing up and down between the waves. Even though the eyes were wide with terror, he saw no hands or arms flailing at the water. They raced by, petrified, though seemingly resigned to their fate. He knew that he must help them, but could only stand on the ledge watching, his body immovable. He felt his stomach ulcerating, bile leaking from his mouth, as punishment for his inaction.*

*A legion of riderless horses coming across the river from the other side drew his eyes away from the heads. They magically vaulted*

318

*into and out of the deep water, their shimmering forms mesmerizing. With each leap, golden streams flowed from their backs. Brown fluid gushed from their noses and ears. As they approached his side of the river, the horses' heads transformed into those of hideous disfigured dragons, ragged fins protruded from their backs. The golden water that streamed down their bodies changed into blood and turned the river red. Instead of flames shooting from their mouths, blood spewed forth. Their eyes turned narrow, green, and evil. He turned to run, but his feet wouldn't move. He pulled, feeling muscles tear as the horse-dragons came closer . . .*

"What is it now?" Sarah said. It was difficult to wipe the sweat from Joe's face with his head swinging back and forth. He arched his back and then sat upright. His eyes were mostly closed, and he mumbled things neither she nor Sullivan could understand.

Sullivan eased Joe back down on the bed. "It's still a hundred and three."

"Has it leveled out? Will it start going down now?"

"Maybe," Sullivan said. "If it doesn't . . ."

"Isn't there nothing more we can do?" Her eyes were moist. She held one of Joe's hands and wiped at his face with the other.

"Keep wiping him with cool water. Time will tell."

"Pray to yourselves, if not out loud," Pastor Evans said.

They didn't hear the front door open and close. The stranger was standing in the patient room doorway when they first noticed him.

"Can I do something for you?" Sullivan said.

"You the doc?"

"I am. Doctor Thomas Sullivan. And you are?"

"Passin' through. Thought I'd stop and say hello to Joe, an old friend." He stepped up to the bed and looked down.

Sarah was instantly frightened by the man. She didn't know why, but his black eyes were part of it. She realized that this could be Lute Kinney. Would he try to kill Joe right there? She prepared to jump at him if he pulled one of his pistols. Sullivan glanced at Sarah and Evans.

"You're a friend of Joe's?" Sullivan said.

"Somethin' like that," the stranger said. "He gonna die?"

"He could."

After a long moment, the stranger spoke again in a slightly different tone. "You give your life for that man?"

"Well, ah, I do whatever I can to help him . . ." Sullivan said.

"Good answer for a question I didn't ask. Would you give your life for him if you had to?"

"Ah, sure . . . sure I would," Sullivan said, his commitment growing stronger as he talked.

"Good. He dies, you might have to." The stranger turned around and walked out.

"Evil incarnate, if I've ever seen it," Evans said. He gripped his Bible with both hands.

"Sheriff," Siegler said.

Harvey Martin walked out of the store to return to the hotel, leaving his brother, Jarvis, and Siegler.

"Gentlemen," Canfield said, and took off his hat. "It is with a heavy heart I come today. I'm told that Clyde shot someone. And that's why he was killed. Would you tell me what happened?"

The town board members looked at each other, trying to digest the sheriff's contrite disposition and wondered how to respond.

"I was there when he drew his last breath, Wick," Jarvis said. "He ambushed Adam Carr in a dark alley. Why do you think he done that?"

"Budd, that's what I'd like to know."

Jarvis said, "His name wasn't Clyde Davey, either. It was Herm Tillmer. Said so just before dyin'."

"The hell you say?"

"It's true, Sheriff. He asked Marshal Mundy to notify his mother in Falls City of his passing," Siegler said.

"I'm afraid I didn't know Clyde, or Herm, like I thought I did." Canfield looked at the floor and slowly shook his head.

"That said, Sheriff, why do you think he shot Adam, in what we can reasonably assume was also an attempt on Marshal Mundy's life?" Siegler said.

"I haven't the faintest idea, Byron. I was aware of no bad blood between them. In fact, I was hoping someone here could enlighten me."

"Well, that's not likely," Harold said.

"I went to Clyde's room, before coming here, to try and find a name of a relative I could notify. I found a gun and pair of spurs and some other things that I know belonged to Bob Carlson, the fellow that was found dead here," Canfield said. "With what you've told me, it appears that he may have been the one who killed Carlson. Why he would do it, I just don't know."

"Carlson, being the one you accused

Mundy of killin', that the one?" Jarvis said. Canfield met Jarvis's cold stare for a moment, slowly shook his head, and looked at the floor. "All I can figure."

"Well, it's pointless to continue this speculation," Siegler said. "We have another matter that requires your immediate attention, Sheriff. There's a man in town who's come from Kansas aiming to kill Marshal Mundy. He's a wanted man. Name's Lute Kinney. Joe has the flyer in his office."

For a fraction of a second, a spark of glee seemed to arise in Canfield's eyes. A flash and it was gone.

"Why's he want to kill the marshal?"

"He was hired to kill him for a vendetta, resulting from Mundy's job in Kansas," Jarvis said. "Will you arrest him?"

"Yeah . . . sure. Of course. Judge expects me to move these two prisoners now that they're sentenced. But I'll check around before I take them back with me," Canfield said. "What's he look like?"

Jarvis described Kinney, and Sheriff Canfield left to start his search.

# Chapter Twenty-Eight

Sarah and Doc Sullivan sat at the table and drank coffee. They could hear Pastor Evans reading softly to Joe from his Bible.

"And the Lord will take away from thee all sickness . . ."

Sullivan got up and walked over to the examination table and gently slid Adam back toward the middle. Adam looked up at Doc, his eyes hazy. "How's Joe?"

"His temperature has started to fall. It's still high, but better than it was. As soon as the Thorbergs come for their son, we'll move you to his bed. You'll be in with Joe." Adam nodded slowly.

Sullivan returned to the table, opened a whiskey bottle, and added some to his coffee.

". . . forget not all his benefits, who healeth all thy diseases."

Sullivan glanced at Pastor Evans in the patient room.

"Think it helps?" Sarah asked.

"Certainly can't hurt," Sullivan said. "So that was the man who wants to kill Joe."

Sarah nodded. "What are we going to do if he comes back? He threatened you. Joe's guns are in the drawer."

"Are you a gunman, Sarah?" Sullivan said.

"I can shoot, a little."

"Neither am I." Sullivan drank down the last of his coffee.

"What do you suggest?"

"I guess we'll pray along with Pastor Evans that Joe gets well . . . soon." Sullivan said. He poured whiskey into his empty cup.

"Have any left?" Pastor Evans sat down at the table. Sullivan shoved a glass to him and filled it halfway.

"Did any of that take, Pastor?" Sarah asked.

"We won't know until He wants us to." Evans sipped the whiskey.

# Chapter Twenty-Nine

"Is there a problem, Mister Hotelman?" Kinney asked. "Maybe you have a problem with me, is that it?"

Harold Martin tried not to shake, but he couldn't help it. It wasn't just his hands either — it was his whole body. His eyes danced around uncontrollably. He felt glad only that he'd relieved himself before Kinney arrived. There were no other customers. In fact the streets were oddly quiet, especially after the previous night's celebration.

"Ah, no. No, sir. No problem, no problem at all." He tried to look away from the man's black eyes and expressionless face, but he couldn't.

"Why do ya' keep lookin' out the window then?" Kinney said slowly. He pointed with his fork to emphasize his point. "Expectin' someone?"

"No, no, sir." Martin started to get up.

"Sit down! I invited you to sit with me.

Not polite to get up like that, is it?"

"No, sir." Martin felt like he might faint. Beads of perspiration appeared on his forehead, but he was too scared to wipe them off. Although he tried not to, his mind wouldn't stop wondering if Kinney would kill him after finishing his apple pie. *The man was after Joe, not me. That's right, I have nothing to worry about.* He felt strangely peaceful when he remembered that Joe was Kinney's target, not him. At the same time, he felt ashamed for being relieved about it. He thought he might vomit.

"So if you don't mind, I'll finish my pie," Kinney said.

"No, not at all. I hope your meal was satisfactory?" Martin could think of nothing else to say. He didn't want to beg for his life, on the off chance that Kinney hadn't thought of killing him in the first place. *Where was that damned Canfield anyway? And why wasn't Harvey back yet?* He was beginning to feel abandoned. Alone in the world.

The waitress returned to the table with a coffeepot. "Would you like anything else, sir?"

Kinney held out his cup for more coffee. "Think that'll do it. Thank you, ma'am."

She blushed slightly and picked up his

dinner plate. Martin tried sending her frantic messages with his eyes, but she didn't notice. What would she think he wanted, if she had seen him? She didn't know anything of the danger the man he was seated with represented. It was futile. She went back to the kitchen with the dirty dishes. In a quick glance out of the window, Martin saw Canfield across the street, heading toward the marshal's office.

"I should probably get back to work, if you need any —"

"Shut up! You *can* do that, can't you? I'll tell you when I'm through with your company," Kinney said. He took a sip from his cup.

Jarvis poured Gib Hadley and Byron Siegler each a tumbler of whiskey and refilled his own. The Texan was empty save for three cowhands from out of town and the piano player. The two working girls had given up and gone to their rooms alone.

"When I saw 'im, he said he couldn't find hide nor hair of Kinney," Jarvis said shaking his head. "In a town this size, how damned hard is it to find a man. Especially *that one!*"

"Maybe the fearless sheriff holds the notion of a rendezvous with Mister Kinney in a position somewhere less than a priority,"

Hadley said.

"That would be my bet," Siegler added.

Jarvis glanced out to the street. "It's like folks can sense there's somethin' wrong. Hardly anyone movin' about. It's been dead in here all day."

"Same at my place," Hadley said. He pushed his tumbler around in small circles on the bar.

"Any news on Joe?" Jarvis asked. Siegler didn't remember Budd calling him Joe before, only Mundy.

"Doc says his fever has declined a little. He's hopeful." Siegler looked at his friends. Instead of friendliness, orneriness, and levity, he saw uncertainty in their solemn faces. So much of life was uncertain in this part of the world, but this was something that was out of their control. They knew that if they did try to act on it, they would probably lose their lives. That's why they hired a marshal, wasn't it? To protect them from the evil in the world . . . and paid him fifty dollars a month to do it. That made Siegler slightly nauseous, and he downed his whiskey in one gulp.

"If Kinney finds out Joe's sick in bed, he may decide it's opportunity knockin'. We should arm ourselves and go down to Doc's!" Hadley said.

"Kinney knows he's there," Siegler said. He moved his empty tumbler toward Jarvis who refilled it. "Doc says he appeared in the room with them and Joe. Made no sound whatsoever comin' in or when he left, he said. Like some damn evil spirit or something." The others stared at Siegler. If he'd looked up from the bar, he would have seen their pale faces. "I guess if he meant to do it there, he would have."

"Now, come on, Byron. You're making 'im sound like some goddamned ghost or something," Jarvis said. "I seen 'im with my own two eyes."

"You're the only one in this flock *has* seen him!" Hadley's eyes were wide. "Why ain't anybody seen him ramblin' about town? Answer me that!"

"Doc and Sarah and Pastor Evans saw him too, Gib." Siegler's statement was somewhat less than comforting to them. It quickly became obvious that their next visitor wouldn't make them feel much better.

"Where the hell have all you been?" Harold Martin nearly screamed when he crashed through the front doors, causing all three men leaning on the bar to flinch. "You been hiding in here all this time?"

"Jesus, Harold settle down before ya' throw a shoe," Jarvis said. He grabbed a tumbler from a neat pyramid on the bar and filled it for him, while Hadley closed the front doors.

As Siegler started to tell Jarvis, "He doesn't drink . . ." Martin downed the entire glass. Coughing and choking, he offered it to Jarvis for a refill.

"Better let that one settle, Harold. What in hell's gotten into you?" Hadley said.

Martin's hands were shaking so badly, they were amazed he didn't spill any of his whiskey.

"He held me against my will." His eyes jumped to each of the men as he tried to catch his breath. He glanced back at the doors as if someone might be chasing him. "I was in fear for my life!"

"Harold, slow down and tell us what happened," Siegler said calmly. "Better give him a little more, Budd."

Jarvis nodded and refilled his glass.

Martin sipped the whiskey this time. "He was there."

"Who, Harold?" Hadley asked.

"That hired killer! Who do you think!" He took a bigger sip this time. "I was at the desk, relieving Harvey . . . and there he was standing right next to me. Like he appeared out of thin air."

"You just didn't notice him come in,

Harold. Then what happened?" Siegler asked.

"He didn't come in through the door. That's what I'm trying to tell you. One minute I was alone, and the next I wasn't!" They looked at each other and tried to act untroubled.

"Well, then, he must have come in through the back door," Jarvis said.

"He invited me, firmly, to sit down with him while he had a meal. And then a piece of pie, and then another cup of coffee!" Martin produced a handkerchief and mopped his face. "After he finished, he said I could go. Before I reached the hallway, I looked back, and he was gone."

"He's not a ghost, Harold, just a bad man," Siegler said. "Did you tell the sheriff?"

"When I composed myself a little, I went down to the jail. He was getting the prisoners ready to go. I told him about Kinney being at the hotel. He said, 'He there now?' I told him, 'No, he just left.' He said he had to get the prisoners to Gracie Flats while he still had some daylight left."

"You come here straight from talking to him?" Siegler said.

"I certainly did. Ran all the way!"

"That yellow cur. He had only about

twenty minutes of daylight left anyway," Jarvis said.

"Like I said before, findin' Kinney wasn't a priority for 'im," Hadley said with disgust. "Now we're all alone with that animal roaming the streets."

Kinney stood by the front door and watched Canfield ride by, leading two other horses with handcuffed men aboard. "Looks like the sheriff's leavin' town with some prisoners." He double-checked the front doors to make sure they were locked and walked back to the table where Lucy was sitting. Little light was left in the Palace as the sun went down.

"I'll fire a lamp if you want," Lucy said.

"If I want, I'll tell you."

"Who are you? My name's Lucy." She could tell he was staring at her. After a few moments of silence, she continued. "What is it ya' want here anyway?" she asked.

The punch rebroke her nose before she saw it coming. "Ahh!" She screamed and grabbed her face. She could feel the warm blood running into her mouth. She reached for a cleaning rag and held it against her nose.

"Didn't have to do that," she mumbled.

"Why ain't this place open?"

Lucy gagged and coughed on swallowed blood before answering. "Smiley, he runs the place, he's in jail."

"What'd he do?" Kinney asked.

"I heard he hit Marshal Mundy with a chair rung."

"You know Joe Mundy?" Kinney asked after several minutes of silence.

"Sure. Most everybody does. He's the marshal." She continued wiping the blood from her nose.

"For how long?"

"Maybe two months," Lucy said. She squinted her eyes, trying to tell which way he was looking.

"He kill anyone here?"

"Sure did. Right upstairs here."

"Why?" Kinney asked.

"Why'd he kill 'im? Ah, 'cuz a fella was tryin' to beat me to death, that's why."

"Knight in shining armor, is he?"

"Sure is in my eyes," Lucy said.

"The way you stumble around, you're not an idiot?"

"I am not!" Lucy said with disgust. "Was that animal that beat me."

"Mundy have any deputies?"

"Adam Carr helps him out with the jail, but he got shot up last night," Lucy said. "I hope he's okay."

"Must have been the other one I saw at the Doc's," Kinney said. "Your knight in shining armor is down with a sickness."

"I didn't know," Lucy said. "Hope he gets better."

"Believe he'll be around town in the morning." Lucy didn't like the way that sounded.

"Beds upstairs?" Kinney asked.

"Yeah."

He grabbed her arm and pulled her toward the stairs. "Let's go. Gotta' be up early."

# CHAPTER THIRTY

It was seven o'clock Sunday morning. The regular morning coffee gathering at the North Star was complete when Harold Martin walked in. Small flakes of snow fell, and wind pushed at the windows.

"About time, Harold, we almost give up on ya'," Hadley said. Martin sat down at the table and nodded when Hadley served his coffee.

"You don't look so good, Harold," Jarvis said.

"I feel dizzy, and somewhat sick to my stomach, and my head hurts." Martin's hands still shook, his eyes still busy.

The others chuckled. "A little hair of the dog?" Hadley held up a whiskey bottle.

Harold put his hand against his mouth, closed his eyes, and swallowed. He waved Hadley off with the other hand.

"We were asking if anyone has seen Kinney since we talked last night," Siegler said.

Harold shook his head and sipped his coffee, trying not to look at Hadley.

"Maybe he became tedious with all the waitin' 'round and went home," Hadley said hopefully.

Jarvis shook his head slowly. "Don't think, after he took this long to get here, clear from southern Kansas, that he got bored and went home."

Siegler said, "Budd's right. He's around, still bent on doing what he came to do. And be five hundred dollars richer afterwards."

"Damn cold in here, Gib," Martin said.

Hadley glanced over at the heating stove. "It's stoked as much as it'll hold. Hell, I feel the heat from here."

A front door rattled open, and all four men flinched. Martin spilled some of his coffee on the table. The first two paying customers of the day walked in. They were strangers, cowhands from out of town.

"Got any hot coffee?" the older one said. The two sat down at the table next to theirs.

"Sure do. Welcome, gentlemen," Hadley said. He sat two cups down and filled them up. "Where you boys from?"

"Over near Ericson, the XO-Bar ranch. Been trackin' some strays but come up empty-handed," the old cowboy said. His dark-colored chaps had many holes and tears. "We see you got a telegraph wire headin' this way from Willow Springs and Burwell."

"Yes, we hope to have it operating by the first of summer," Siegler said.

"Damned near a waste of time now," the younger cowboy said. His accent plainly indicated a southern upbringing. The coffee club looked at him.

"Why would that be?" Hadley asked.

"Oh, Lord, here we go. Twenty years of life, they apparently ain't much this young'un can't tell ya', and volunteers what he thinks he knows freely to all who'll listen, and some *who don't,*" the old cowboy said and shook his head.

"You're just jealous 'cuz of a lack of serious knowledge," the young one said and grinned at his partner. "Fact has it, there's this Mister Bell, up in Boston. He just invented the telee-phone. Won't be no more need for the dots and dashes of a telegraph." The young cowboy slid his wide-brimmed hat back on his head and leaned back, proud of his announcement.

"What'n hell's a telee-phone?" Hadley asked. The group's interest was piqued, and very much relieved to have something other than Lute Kinney to think about, if only temporarily.

The young cowboy's face grew serious as he tried to explain the new invention. "Well, fellas, this Mister Bell took his voice and plum shoved it into a telegraph wire, and it came out the other end, in his cellar, as plain as if he was standin' there talkin'." The little group's laughter was instantaneous.

When it died down, the old cowboy spoke. "These here yarns are what I have to put up with, night and day, every day. Yap, yap, yap, all day long, like a coyote. And as luck would have it, he can't sing a note."

"It's a fact. Ain't no yarn at all, I swear," he said. "Read all about it in the Chicago newspaper. Why you didn't know about it 'cuz ya' can't read." He gave the old man a frown.

"I ain't got no idea where he got a Chicago newspaper, neither," the old man said, as he rolled a cigarette.

"Well, tell us. Who was this Mister Bell talkin' to . . . in his cellar?" Jarvis asked, grinning at the others.

"Why, it was his assistant, Mister Watson, but that ain't all. After they done that, they took and strung a telegraph wire between two towns up in Canada that were ten miles apart, and did it again. Mister Bell talked to Mister Watson, and he talked back to Mister

Bell." The laughter broke out again.

"Just how in the hell'd he do that?" Jarvis asked, trying to control himself. The exuberant laughter that the coffee club exhibited was due, no doubt, to their nervous energy.

"I don't know the exactedness of it, but when he spoke, his assistant heard 'im plain as day. They say it'll replace the telegraph. Why send dots and dashes someone has to figger out, when they can talk through the wire?" The men laughed again.

"Take no offense from our level of enthusiasm, but that's quite a story," Hadley said. "You read all that in the newspaper?"

"Yeah," he said. "Hell, everybody knowed Mister Bell's invention was at the Centennial Exhibition at Philadelphia last year." The men raised their eyebrows and nodded to each other in jest of the cowboy's statement.

The young man started to say something when the front door opened again, and the coffee club's jocularity evaporated.

"Mornin', gents." Lute Kinney walked in and faced the group. His ankle-length black overcoat was open, and they saw the butts of his two Smith & Wesson pistols sticking out.

"Now with a show of hands, who in here's heeled?" Kinney asked.

"Well, hell, you can see we both got pistols," the young cowboy said, "whatever business it is of yours." The old man gripped the young man's arm to say shut up, without actually saying it.

Kinney held his eyes on the young cowboy, who tried in vain to return the stare.

"What about you?" He turned his head to look at the coffee club.

"None of us are armed," Siegler said. Kinney nodded upward once. The men stood slowly and pulled their coats open.

"Okay, sit."

"I, I better be getting back," Martin stood again.

"I said sit, Mister Hotelman. Is everybody in this town hard a' hearin'?" Kinney said. "I'll kill the next person stands up without bein' told." His words were deliberate.

"Harold, sit down," Jarvis said, and nodded.

Kinney walked over to the two cowboys, picked up the younger one's coffee, and carried it back to the bar.

"I'm, ah, Gib Hadley, owner of the North Star. Be glad to get your coffee for ya'."

"Got some, but I'll keep that in mind, Mister Hadley," Kinney said while staring at the young cowboy.

Siegler looked at Jarvis and then at Hadley. Harold Martin held his eyes on the tabletop. He was shaking again.

"Boy, I got a errand for you," Kinney said. "Walk over here and slowly lay that pistol on the bar. Then go down to the Doc's and bring the marshal back here."

"Who the hell ya' think . . ."

"Shut up, Drew! God's sake, just do what the man said." The old cowboy gave a stern look to the younger man. He still held his partner's arm.

Siegler said, "Ah, sir, these men aren't from around here. Ah, they don't know where to find Doc. One of us would be happy to go."

"Boy, go straight south from here. First house you come to past the hotel," Kinney said, his eyes were still fixed on the young man.

"Marshal's sick in bed. He couldn't come if the place was on fire," Jarvis said.

The shot rang out before they noticed the gun in Kinney's hand. The young cowboy fell over sideways out of his chair. Kinney held the Smith & Wesson on the old man, and calmly cocked it again. "How about now?"

"Goddamn you!" the old man screamed. The dark hole at the end of Kinney's gun barrel silenced him.

"Guess the chore falls to you, old-timer. Carry the boy down to the Doc's, and while you're there, send the marshal back. Leave them shooters on the table first."

The old man did as he was told and struggled to pull the young man up and over his shoulder. Kinney walked over to the door and opened it for him.

"Then that son-of-a-bitch shot Drew. Tol' me to bring 'im here and send the marshal back."

Doc Sullivan tore Drew's shirt open. Blood trickled from the hole in the middle of his chest. He gently inserted the probe as far as he could and slowly moved it around. A few minutes later, he said, "I can't find it. I'm sorry, mister, I'm afraid he's gone."

"He killed Drew? Why? Why'd he do that?" the old cowboy was shocked. "He's plum the meanest I've seen, that one. Kill a boy for no reason." He stood beside his friend and stared down at him.

Sullivan heard Evans say, "You shouldn't be out of bed!" They turned to see Joe leaning against the door frame. He finished buttoning his trousers and started to slowly tuck in his shirt. He struggled to strap on his gun belt and hesitated for a moment until the dizziness subsided. His face and hair glistened with sweat. When he pulled on his black vest, the old cowboy saw the badge.

"Christ a'mighty! He's the marshal?"

"He is," Doc said.

"He can't go up there. That man will kill 'im sure!" He looked from Doc to Joe again. "Ain't ya' got anybody else?"

"Afraid not," Doc said. He walked over to Joe. "Joe, you still have a fever. You can't do this."

"Who can, Doc? I don't go up there, he'll come here," Joe coughed and hesitated a moment before continuing. "Maybe after he shoots those still in the North Star."

Sarah put her arms around Joe. "Isn't there any other way? What if we went up with you?"

"No need in givin' 'im more targets," Joe said. "This is my show." He pushed off from the door sill and waited to steady himself. He picked up the cavalry Colt, checked its load, and slid it into the left side of his belt.

Sarah turned to the old man. "What about you? You could go with him!" She was crying now.

"I'm sorry, ma'am, I ain't no gun hand. I'm jus' a worn-out cowpuncher." He looked down shaking his head.

"Hand me that scattergun, Christmas,"

Joe said.

Evans handed Joe the ten-gauge, and he popped open the action. It was still empty, and he left it that way.

"Joe, it's not loaded."

"I know, Christmas. Need it to steady me. Don't want to shoot my hand off." Joe rested the butt on the floor and gripped the muzzle. "Now if you'll hand me my coat and hat."

Doc handed them over. "How are you feeling?"

"Real cold. A little dizzy and a headache like I've never known before. Might puke on 'im. What do ya' s'pose he'd think of that?"

Doc looked at Joe, shook his head and opened his mouth but was unable to reply.

Evans began mumbling verses from the twenty-third Psalm as Joe weaved his way to the door, stopped, and looked down at the dead cowboy. He opened the door and walked out without looking back. Sarah and Pastor Evans stood in the open doorway.

Evans watched Joe as he made his way toward the main street. "But if thou do that which is evil, be afraid, for he beareth not the sword in vain."

The silence in the North Star was deafening. Jarvis looked over at the table where the two cowboys had been sitting and saw the two pistols. He then noticed Kinney watching him in the mirror above the back-bar. He looked down at his coffee cup until he heard Kinney chuckle. All four saw that he was looking out the front windows.

"Boys, here comes your knight in shining armor," and chuckled again.

They turned to look and saw Joe walking drunkenly across the main street toward the saloon, using his shotgun for a crutch.

Joe tried to figure out a strategy, a way to handle Kinney. However he would do it, he would give him no chance and expected the same in return. He shook almost uncontrollably from the cold wind pushing against him from the north. With each step, he re-stuck the shotgun butt in the snow, leaned on it as he walked by, and repeated the process. Halfway across the main street, the wind caught his hat and sent it flying. He made no attempt to stop it.

Once at the steps that led up to the boardwalk, he moved even slower, trying not to fall down. Making it onto the walk, he moved to the wall between the windows and the doors and pulled the cavalry Colt with his left hand. He cocked it and held it behind his left leg in the folds of his open overcoat.

At the door, he saw Kinney leaning over the bar like drunks do, with his head turned toward him. Joe couldn't see Kinney's right hand. After kicking the door shut behind him, Joe made it to the end of the bar, which gave half his body cover. He leaned unsteadily on the shotgun and met Kinney's eyes.

Kinney glanced at the shotgun before speaking. "I'd been real disappointed if you died before I got to see you. Oh, Missus Ranswood sends her regards."

Joe let go of the shotgun and grabbed the bar to steady himself, hoping Kinney would glance at the gun. When it clattered to the floor, Kinney's eyes flashed down to it. As soon as they did, Joe raised the muzzle of the Colt just above the edge of the bar with his left hand. He hoped for a solid chest hit to end it quickly, but was disappointed. Joe's bullet caught him in the jaw line, plowing out teeth and cutting through his ear. The heating stove sizzled from the blood and teeth sprayed against it. Kinney's pistol fired before he was knocked backward, which told Joe he'd been ready to shoot. Kinney's shot cut through the top of Joe's left forearm and smashed a window behind him.

Joe transferred the Colt to his right hand

in time to be shot through the left shoulder. He thumbed the Colt twice, the first shot glancing off the stove and the second hitting Kinney in the hip, which brought the outlaw to a knee. Kinney's third shot cut through Joe's coat and smashed the door glass. Joe's fourth shot missed, and he thumbed the hammer again. He slowed down to aim, when Kinney fired again, hitting Joe in the upper right leg. From his knees, he aimed and hit Kinney in the lower chest, knocking him down. Kinney had trouble cocking the pistol again, and when he did, he fired one bullet into the bar and another into the ceiling. He pulled out his second pistol as Joe aimed at his head. Shaking badly now, Joe pulled the trigger. His last shot hit Kinney in the right arm, which prevented him from raising his gun. Kinney reached for it with his left hand, while Joe dropped the empty pistol on the floor and pulled the other Colt from his holster. He cocked and fired, and the bullet tore through Kinney's chest. The killer stopped moving.

The gunsmoke in the saloon was thick and made it hard to breath. Joe held onto the bar with his left hand and looked around. Harold Martin lay on the floor shaking. Jarvis, Siegler, and Hadley were all still seated, their eyes and mouths wide. A blood pool grew from under Kinney. Joe could feel the cold air coming in through the broken windows behind him. A glass shard let go and smashed to the floor. Joe collapsed onto his back. The strength he had left was draining away. He saw faces above him and heard distorted voices. Then his world went dark.

# CHAPTER THIRTY-ONE

"What day is it?" Joe asked. Clearing his eyes was a struggle but worth it. The first face he saw was Sarah's.

"It's Tuesday," Sarah said.

"I've been sleeping for two days?"

"Doc got some laudanum. Been making you rest," she said. "You been in and out for a little over two weeks. We weren't so sure you'd pull through this." Her eyes filled.

"How's Adam doin'?"

Sarah said, "Ask him yourself," and nodded at the other bed.

Joe slowly turned his head to look and saw Adam sitting on the other bed with his back against the wall. His arm was in a sling, and his face was a bit pale.

"Sure glad to see you, Marshal," Adam said. "Doc's lettin' me go today."

"Good. I'm sure the office needs some cleaning." He offered Adam a slight grin.

"I'll keep an eye on things for you, and come visit regular," Adam said. "In fact, I'll bring my book of con-nun-drums and read to you, to wile away the hours."

Joe's eye twitched a bit. "That, ah, that would be real good of you, Adam."

Sarah noticed Joe's glance at the doorway. "The town board decided to protect you two bums 'til you're on your feet again." She struggled to talk without breaking down.

"That's why Jarvis is here? He's guardin' us?" Joe asked.

"They're all supposed to be taking turns. But Budd has been here most of the time. Byron asked him to be temporary marshal, 'til you're able to go back to work."

"He did?" Joe asked.

"Know what he said?"

Joe shook his head.

"Budd said 'No.' Said he'd only be a temporary deputy. Said, 'We already got a marshal.'"

# ABOUT THE AUTHOR

**Monty McCord** is a retired police lieutenant and a graduate of the FBI National Academy at Quantico, Virginia. He writes fiction and nonfiction books relating to crime and law enforcement from the Old West period to the mid-twentieth century. He lives in Nebraska with his wife, Ann.

www.montymccord.com

The employees of Thorndike Press hope you have enjoyed this Large Print book. All our Thorndike, Wheeler, and Kennebec Large Print titles are designed for easy reading, and all our books are made to last. Other Thorndike Press Large Print books are available at your library, through selected bookstores, or directly from us.

For information about titles, please call:
(800) 223-1244

or visit our Web site at:
http://gale.cengage.com/thorndike

To share your comments, please write:
Publisher
Thorndike Press
10 Water St., Suite 310
Waterville, ME 04901